Penguin Books
Ancient Sorceries and Other Stories

Algernon Blackwood was born in 1869,
educated at the Moravian School in the Black
Forest, at Wellington College, and Edinburgh
University. His early life was adventurous and
varied, and included farming in Canada,
prospecting for gold, and conducting a hotel.
Finally he drifted into journalism, becoming a
reporter on the staff of the New York *Sun*, and
subsequently of the New York *Times*.
It was not until 1906, at the age of thirty-seven,
that he published his first book, *The Empty
House*, a collection of short stories. The rest of
his life he devoted entirely to writing, and
amongst his many titles were *John Silence*
(1908), *The Centaur* (1911), *Incredible
Adventures* (1914), and, perhaps the best-known,
Tales of the Uncanny and Supernatural (1949).
Another selection of his stories, *The Insanity of
Jones and Other Tales*, is already in Penguins.

Algernon Blackwood spent much of his time
abroad but was well known to listeners on the
radio, where he had a considerable public. He
died in 1951.

Algernon Blackwood

Ancient Sorceries
and Other Stories

Penguin Books

Penguin Books Ltd, Harmondsworth, Middlesex, England
Penguin Books Australia Ltd, Ringwood, Victoria, Australia
Penguin Books Canada Ltd, 41 Steelcase Road West, Markham,
Ontario, Canada

'The Empty House' first published 1906
'A Haunted Island' first published 1906
'A Case of Eavesdropping' first published 1906
'Keeping His Promise' first published 1906
'Ancient Sorceries' first published 1908
'The Nemesis of Fire' first published 1908
Published in one volume in Penguin Books 1968
Reprinted 1974

Made and printed in Great Britain
by C. Nicholls & Company Ltd
Set in Intertype Times

Contents

The Empty House

Certain houses, like certain persons, manage somehow to proclaim at once their character for evil. In the case of the latter, no particular feature need betray them; they may boast an open countenance and an ingenuous smile; and yet a little of their company leaves the unalterable conviction that there is something radically amiss with their being: that they are evil. Willy nilly, they seem to communicate an atmosphere of secret and wicked thoughts which makes those in their immediate neighbourhood shrink from them as from a thing diseased.

And, perhaps, with houses the same principle is operative, and it is the aroma of evil deeds committed under a particular roof, long after the actual doers have passed away, that makes the gooseflesh come and the hair rise. Something of the original passion of the evil-doer, and of the horror felt by his victim, enters the heart of the innocent watcher, and he becomes suddenly conscious of tingling nerves, creeping skin, and a chilling of the blood. He is terror-stricken without apparent cause.

There was manifestly nothing in the external appearance of this particular house to bear out the tales of the horror that was said to reign within. It was neither lonely nor unkempt. It stood, crowded into a corner of the square, and looked exactly like the houses on either side of it. It had the same number of windows as its neighbours; the same balcony overlooking the gardens; the same white steps leading up to the heavy black front door; and, in the rear, there was the same narrow strip of green, with neat box borders, running up to the wall that divided it from the backs of the adjoining houses. Apparently, too, the number of chimney pots on the roof was the same; the breadth and angle of the eaves; and even the height of the dirty area railings.

And yet this house in the square, that seemed precisely similar to its fifty ugly neighbours, was as a matter of fact entirely different – horribly different.

Wherein lay this marked, invisible difference is impossible to say. It cannot be ascribed wholly to the imagination, because persons who had spent some time in the house, knowing nothing of the facts, had declared postively that certain rooms were so disagreeable they would rather die than enter them again, and that the atmosphere of the whole house produced in them symptoms of a genuine terror; while the series of innocent tenants who had tried to live in it and been forced to decamp at the shortest possible notice, was indeed little less than a scandal in the town.

When Shorthouse arrived to pay a 'week-end' visit to his Aunt Julia in her little house on the sea-front at the other end of the town, he found her charged to the brim with mystery and excitement. He had only received her telegram that morning, and he had come anticipating boredom; but the moment he touched her hand and kissed her apple-skin wrinkled cheek, he caught the first wave of her electrical condition. The impression deepened when he learned that there were to be no other visitors, and that he had been telegraphed for with a very special object.

Something was in the wind, and the 'something' would doubtless bear fruit; for this elderly spinster aunt, with a mania for psychical research, had brains as well as will power, and by hook or by crook she usually managed to accomplish her ends. The revelation was made soon after tea, when she sidled close up to him as they paced slowly along the sea-front in the dusk.

'I've got the keys,' she announced in a delighted, yet half awesome voice. 'Got them till Monday!'

'The keys of the bathing-machine, or – ?' he asked innocently, looking from the sea to the town. Nothing brought her so quickly to the point as feigning stupidity.

'Neither,' she whispered. 'I've got the keys of the haunted house in the square – and I'm going there tonight.'

Shorthouse was conscious of the slightest possible tremor down his back. He dropped his teasing tone. Something in her voice and manner thrilled him. She was in earnest.

'But you can't go alone –' he began.

'That's why I wired for you,' she said with decision.

He turned to look at her. The ugly, lined, enigmatical face was alive with excitement. There was the glow of genuine enthusiasm round it like a halo. The eyes shone. He caught another wave of her excitement, and a second tremor, more marked than the first, accompanied it.

'Thanks, Aunt Julia,' he said politely; 'thanks awfully.'

'I should not dare to go quite alone,' she went on, raising her voice; 'but with you I should enjoy it immensely. You're afraid of nothing, I know.'

'Thanks *so* much,' he said again. 'Er – is anything likely to happen?'

'A great deal *has* happened,' she whispered, 'though it's been most cleverly hushed up. Three tenants have come and gone in the last few months, and the house is said to be empty for good now.'

In spite of himself Shorthouse became interested. His aunt was so very much in earnest.

'The house is very old indeed,' she went on, 'and the story – an unpleasant one – dates a long way back. It has to do with a murder committed by a jealous stableman who had some affair with a servant in the house. One night he managed to secrete himself in the cellar, and when everyone was asleep, he crept upstairs to the servants' quarters, chased the girl down to the next landing, and before anyone could come to the rescue threw her bodily over the banisters into the hall below.'

'And the stableman –?'

'Was caught, I believe, and hanged for murder; but it all happened a century ago, and I've not been able to get more details of the story.'

Shorthouse now felt his interest thoroughly aroused; but, though he was not particularly nervous for himself, he hesitated a little on his aunt's account.

'On one condition,' he said at length.

'Nothing will prevent my going,' she said firmly; 'but I may as well hear your condition.'

'That you guarantee your power of self-control if anything really horrible happens. I mean – that you are sure you won't get too frightened.'

'Jim,' she said scornfully, 'I'm not young, I know, nor are my nerves; but *with you* I should be afraid of nothing in the world!'

This, of course, settled it, for Shorthouse had no pretensions to being other than a very ordinary young man, and an appeal to his vanity was irresistible. He agreed to go.

Instinctively, by a sort of sub-conscious preparation, he kept himself and his forces well in hand the whole evening, compelling an accumulative reserve of control by that nameless inward process of gradually putting all the emotions away and turning the key upon them – a process difficult to describe, but wonderfully effective, as all men who have lived through severe trials of the inner man well understand. Later, it stood him in good stead.

But it was not until half-past ten, when they stood in the hall, well in the glare of friendly lamps and still surrounded by comforting human influences, that he had to make the first call upon this store of collected strength. For, once the door was closed, and he saw the deserted silent street stretching away white in the moonlight before them, it came to him clearly that the real test that night would be in dealing with *two fears* instead of one. He would have to carry his aunt's fear as well as his own. And, as he glanced down at her sphinx-like countenance and realized that it might assume no pleasant aspect in a rush of a real terror, he felt satisfied with only one thing in the whole adventure – that he had confidence in his own will and power to stand against any shock that might come.

Slowly they walked along the empty streets of the town; a bright autumn moon silvered the roofs, casting deep shadows; there was no breath of wind; and the trees in the formal gardens by the sea-front watched them silently as they passed along. To his aunt's occasional remarks Shorthouse made no reply, realizing that she was simply surrounding herself with mental buffers – saying ordinary things to prevent herself thinking of extra-ordinary things. Few windows showed lights, and from scarcely a single chimney came smoke or sparks. Shorthouse had already begun to notice everything, even the smallest details. Presently they stopped at the street corner and looked up at the name on the side of the house full in the moonlight, and with one accord, but without remark, turned into the square and crossed over to the side of it that lay in shadow.

'The number of the house is thirteen,' whispered a voice at his side; and neither of them made the obvious reference, but passed across the broad sheet of moonlight and began to march up the pavement in silence.

It was about half-way up the square that Shorthouse felt an arm slipped quietly but significantly into his·own, and knew then that their adventure had begun in earnest, and that his companion was already yielding imperceptibly to the influences against them. She needed support.

A few minutes later they stopped before a tall, narrow house that rose before them into the night, ugly in shape and painted a dingy white. Shutterless windows, without blinds, stared down upon them, shining here and there in the moonlight. There were weather streaks in the wall and cracks in the paint, and the balcony bulged out from the first floor a little unnaturally. But, beyond this generally forlorn appearance of an unoccupied house, there was nothing at first sight to single out this particular mansion for the evil character it had most certainly acquired.

Taking a look over their shoulders to make sure they had not been followed, they went boldly up the steps and stood against the huge black door that fronted them forbiddingly.

But the first wave of nervousness was now upon them, and Shorthouse fumbled a long time with the key before he could fit it into the lock at all. For a moment, if truth were told, they both hoped it would not open, for they were a prey to various unpleasant emotions as they stood there on the threshold of their ghostly adventure. Shorthouse, shuffling with the key and hampered by the steady weight on his arm, certainly felt the solemnity of the moment. It was as if the whole world – for all experience seemed at that instant concentrated in his own consciousness – were listening to the grating noise of that key. A stray puff of wind wandering down the empty street woke a momentary rustling in the trees behind them, but otherwise this rattling of the key was the only sound audible; and at last it turned in the lock and the heavy door swung open and revealed a yawning gulf of darkness beyond.

With a last glance at the moonlit square, they passed quickly in, and the door slammed behind them with a roar that echoed prodigiously through empty halls and passages. But, instantly, with the echoes, another sound made itself heard, and Aunt Julia leaned suddenly so heavily upon him that he had to take a step backwards to save himself from falling.

A man had coughed close beside them – so close that it seemed they must have been actually by his side in the darkness.

With the possibility of practical jokes in his mind, Shorthouse at once swung his heavy stick in the direction of the sound; but it met nothing more solid than air. He heard his aunt give a little gasp beside him.

'There's someone here,' she whispered; 'I heard him.'

'Be quiet!' he said sternly. 'It was nothing but the noise of the front door.'

'Oh! get a light – quick!' she added, as her nephew, fumbling with a box of matches, opened it upside down and let them all fall with a rattle on to the stone floor.

The sound, however, was not repeated; and there was no evidence of retreating footsteps. In another minute they had a candle burning, using an empty end of a cigar case as a holder;

and when the first flare had died down he held the impromptu lamp aloft and surveyed the scene. And it was dreary enough in all conscience, for there is nothing more desolate in all the abodes of men than an unfurnished house dimly lit, silent, and forsaken, and yet tenanted by rumour with the memories of evil and violent histories.

They were standing in a wide hall-way; on their left was the open door of a spacious dining-room, and in front the hall ran, ever narrowing, into a long, dark passage that led apparently to the top of the kitchen stairs. The broad uncarpeted stair-case rose in a sweep before them, everywhere draped in shadows, except for a single spot about half-way up where the moonlight came in through the window and fell on a bright patch on the boards. This shaft of light shed a faint radiance above and below it, lending to the objects within its reach a misty outline that was infinitely more suggestive and ghostly than complete darkness. Filtered moonlight always seems to paint faces on the surrounding gloom, and as Shorthouse peered up into the well of darkness and thought of the count-less empty rooms and passages in the upper part of the old house, he caught himself longing again for the safety of the moonlit square, or the cosy, bright drawing-room they had left an hour before. Then realizing that these thoughts were dangerous, he thrust them away again and summoned all his energy for concentration on the present.

'Aunt Julia,' he said aloud, severely, 'we must now go through the house from top to bottom and make a thorough search.'

The echoes of his voice died away slowly all over the build-ing, and in the intense silence that followed he turned to look at her. In the candle-light he saw that her face was already ghastly pale; but she dropped his arm for a moment and said in a whisper, stepping close in front of him –

'I agree. We must be sure there's no one hiding. That's the first thing.'

She spoke with evident effort, and he looked at her with admiration.

'You feel quite sure of yourself? It's not too late –'

'I think so,' she whispered, her eyes shifting nervously towards the shadows behind. 'Quite sure, only one thing –'

'What's that?'

'You must never leave me alone for an instant.'

'As long as you understand that any sound or appearance must be investigated at once, for to hesitate means to admit fear. That is fatal.'

'Agreed,' she said, a little shakily, after a moment's hesitation. 'I'll try –'

Arm in arm, Shorthouse holding the dripping candle and the stick, while his aunt carried the cloak over her shoulders, figures of utter comedy to all but themselves, they began a systematic search.

Stealthily, walking on tip-toe and shading the candle lest it should betray their presence through the shutterless windows, they went first into the big dining-room. There was not a stick of furniture to be seen. Bare walls, ugly mantel-pieces and empty grates stared at them. Everything, they felt, resented their intrusion, watching them, as it were, with veiled eyes; whispers followed them; shadows flitted noiselessly to right and left; something seemed ever at their back, watching, waiting an opportunity to do them injury. There was the inevitable sense that operations which went on when the room was empty had been temporarily suspended till they were well out of the way again. The whole dark interior of the old building seemed to become a malignant Presence that rose up, warning them to desist and mind their own business; every moment the strain on the nerves increased.

Out of the gloomy dining-room they passed through large folding doors into a sort of library or smoking-room, wrapt equally in silence, darkness, and dust; and from this they regained the hall near the top of the back stairs.

Here a pitch black tunnel opened before them into the lower regions, and – it must be confessed – they hesitated. But only for a minute. With the worst of the night still to come it was essential to turn from nothing. Aunt Julia stumbled at the top step of the dark descent, ill lit by the flickering candle, and even Shorthouse felt at least half the decision go out of his legs.

'Come on!' he said peremptorily, and his voice ran on and lost itself in the dark, empty spaces below.

'I'm coming,' she faltered, catching his arm with unnecessary violence.

They went a little unsteadily down the stone steps, a cold, damp air meeting them in the face, close and mal-odorous. The kitchen, into which the stairs led along a narrow passage, was large, with a lofty ceiling. Several doors opened out of it – some into cupboards with empty jars still standing on the shelves, and others into horrible little ghostly back offices, each colder and less inviting than the last. Black beetles scurried over the floor, and once, when they knocked against a deal table standing in a corner, something about the size of a cat jumped down with a rush and fled, scampering across the stone floor into the darkness. Everywhere there was a sense of recent occupation, an impression of sadness and gloom.

Leaving the main kitchen, they next went towards the scullery. The door was standing ajar, and as they pushed it open to its full extent Aunt Julia uttered a piercing scream, which she instantly tried to stifle by placing her hand over her mouth. For a second Shorthouse stood stock-still, catching his breath. He felt as if his spine had suddenly become hollow and someone had filled it with particles of ice.

Facing them, directly in their way between the doorposts, stood the figure of a woman. She had dishevelled hair and wildly staring eyes, and her face was terrified and white as death.

She stood there motionless for the space of a single second. Then the candle flickered and she was gone – gone utterly – and the door framed nothing but empty darkness.

'Only the beastly jumping candle-light,' he said quickly, in a voice that sounded like someone else's and was only half under control. 'Come on, aunt. There's nothing there.'

He dragged her forward. With a clattering of feet and a

great appearance of boldness they went on, but over his body the skin moved as if crawling ants covered it, and he knew by the weight on his arm that he was supplying the force of loco-motion for two. The scullery was cold, bare, and empty; more like a large prison cell than anything else. They went round it, tried the door into the yard, and the windows, but found them all fastened securely. His aunt moved beside him like a person in a dream. Her eyes were tightly shut, and she seemed merely to follow the pressure of his arm. Her courage filled him with amazement. At the same time he noticed that a cer-tain odd change had come over her face, a change which somehow evaded his power of analysis.

'There's nothing here, aunty,' he repeated aloud quickly. 'Let's go upstairs and see the rest of the house. Then we'll choose a room to wait up in.'

She followed him obediently, keeping close to his side, and they locked the kitchen door behind them. It was a relief to get up again. In the hall there was more light than before, for the moon had travelled a little further down the stairs. Cau-tiously they began to go up into the dark vault of the upper house, the boards creaking under their weight.

On the first floor they found the large double drawing-rooms, a search of which revealed nothing. Here also was no sign of furniture or recent occupancy; nothing but dust and neglect and shadows. They opened the big folding doors be-tween front and back drawing-rooms and then came out again to the landing and went on upstairs.

They had not gone up more than a dozen steps when they both simultaneously stopped to listen, looking into each other's eyes with a new apprehension across the flickering candle flame. From the room they had left hardly ten seconds before came the sound of doors quietly closing. It was beyond all question; they heard the booming noise that accompanies the shutting of heavy doors, followed by the sharp catching of the latch.

'We must go back and see,' said Shorthouse briefly, in a low tone, and turning to go downstairs again.

Somehow she managed to drag after him, her feet catching in her dress, her face livid.

When they entered the front drawing-room it was plain that the folding doors had been closed – half a minute before. Without hesitation Shorthouse opened them. He almost expected to see someone facing him in the back room; but only darkness and cold air met him. They went through both rooms, finding nothing unusual. They tried in every way to make the doors close of themselves, but there was not wind enough even to set the candle flame flickering. The doors would not move without strong pressure. All was silent as the grave. Undeniably the rooms were utterly empty, and the house utterly still.

'It's beginning,' whispered a voice at his elbow which he hardly recognized as his aunt's.

He nodded acquiescence, taking out his watch to note the time. It was fifteen minutes before midnight; he made the entry of exactly what had occurred in his notebook, setting the candle in its case upon the floor in order to do so. It took a moment or two to balance it safely against the wall.

Aunt Julia always declared that at this moment she was not actually watching him, but had turned her head towards the inner room, where she fancied she heard something moving; but, at any rate, both positively agreed that there came a sound of rushing feet, heavy and very swift – and the next instant the candle was out!

But to Shorthouse himself had come more than this, and he has always thanked his fortunate stars that it came to him alone and not to his aunt too. For, as he rose from the stooping position of balancing the candle, and before it was actually extinguished, a face thrust itself forward so close to his own that he could almost have touched it with his lips. It was a face working with passion; a man's face, dark, with thick features, and angry, savage eyes. It belonged to a common man, and it was evil in its ordinary normal expression, no doubt, but as he saw it, alive with intense, aggressive emotion it was a malignant and terrible human countenance.

There was no movement of the air; nothing but the sound of rushing feet – stockinged or muffled feet; the apparition of the face; and the almost simultaneous extinguishing of the candle.

In spite of himself, Shorthouse uttered a little cry, nearly losing his balance as his aunt clung to him with her whole weight in one moment of real, uncontrollable terror. She made no sound, but simply seized him bodily. Fortunately, however, she had seen nothing, but had only heard the rushing feet, for her control returned almost at once, and he was able to disentangle himself and strike a match.

The shadows ran away on all sides before the glare, and his aunt stooped down and groped for the cigar case with the precious candle. Then they discovered that the candle had not been *blown* out at all; it had been *crushed* out. The wick was pressed down into the wax, which was flattened as if by some smooth, heavy instrument.

How his companion so quickly overcame her terror, Shorthouse never properly understood; but his admiration for her self-control increased tenfold, and at the same time served to feed his own dying flame – for which he was undeniably grateful. Equally inexplicable to him was the evidence of physical force they had just witnessed. He at once suppressed the memory of stories he had heard of 'physical mediums' and their dangerous phenomena; for if these were true, and either his aunt or himself was unwittingly a physical medium, it meant that they were simply aiding to focus the forces of a haunted house already charged to the brim. It was like walking with unprotected lamps among uncovered stores of gunpowder.

So, with as little reflection as possible, he simply relit the candle and went up to the next floor. The arm in his trembled, it is true, and his own tread was often uncertain, but they went on with thoroughness, and after a search revealing nothing they climbed the last flight of stairs to the top floor of all.

Here they found a perfect nest of small servants' rooms, with broken pieces of furniture, dirty cane-bottomed chairs, chests of drawers, cracked mirrors, and decrepit bedsteads. The rooms had low sloping ceilings already hung here and there with cobwebs, small windows, and badly plastered walls – a depressing and dismal region which they were glad to leave behind.

It was on the stroke of midnight when they entered a small room on the third floor, close to the top of the stairs, and arranged to make themselves comfortable for the remainder of their adventure. It was absolutely bare, and was said to be the room – then used as a clothes closet – into which the infuriated groom had chased his victim and finally caught her. Outside, across the narrow landing, began the stairs leading up to the floor above, and the servants' quarters where they had just searched.

In spite of the chilliness of the night there was something in the air of this room that cried for an open window. But there was more than this. Shorthouse could only describe it by saying that he felt less master of himself here than in any other part of the house. There was something that acted directly on the nerves, tiring the resolution, enfeebling the will. He was conscious of this result before he had been in the room five minutes, and it was in the short time they stayed there that he suffered the wholesale depletion of his vital forces, which was, for himself, the chief horror of the whole experience.

They put the candle on the floor of the cupboard, leaving the door a few inches ajar, so that there was no glare to confuse the eyes, and no shadow to shift about on walls and ceiling. Then they spread the cloak on the floor and sat down to wait, with their backs against the wall.

Shorthouse was within two feet of the door on to the landing; his position commanded a good view of the main staircase leading down into the darkness, and also of the beginning of the servants' stairs going to the floor above; the heavy stick lay beside him within easy reach.

The moon was now high above the house. Through the open window they could see the comforting stars like friendly eyes watching in the sky. One by one the clocks of the town struck midnight, and when the sounds died away the deep silence of a windless night fell again over everything. Only the boom of the sea, far away and lugubrious, filled the air with hollow murmurs.

Inside the house the silence became awful; awful, he thought, because any minute now it might be broken by sounds portending terror. The strain of waiting told more and more severely on the nerves; they talked in whispers when they talked at all, for their voices aloud sounded queer and unnatural. A chilliness, not altogether due to the night air, invaded the room, and made them cold. The influences against them, whatever these might be, were slowly robbing them of self-confidence, and the power of decisive action; their forces were on the wane, and the possibility of real fear took on a new and terrible meaning. He began to tremble for the elderly woman by his side, whose pluck could hardly save her beyond a certain extent.

He heard the blood singing in his veins. It sometimes seemed so loud that he fancied it prevented his hearing properly certain other sounds that were beginning very faintly to make themselves audible in the depths of the house. Every time he fastened his attention on these sounds, they instantly ceased. They certainly came no nearer. Yet he could not rid himself of the idea that movement was going on somewhere in the lower regions of the house. The drawing-room floor, where the doors had been so strangely closed, seemed too near; the sounds were further off than that. He thought of the great kitchen, with the scurrying black-beetles, and of the dismal little scullery; but, somehow or other, they did not seem to come from there either. Surely they were not *outside* the house!

Then, suddenly, the truth flashed into his mind, and for the space of a minute he felt as if his blood had stopped flowing and turned to ice.

The sounds were not downstairs at all; they were *upstairs* – upstairs, somewhere among those horrid gloomy little servants' rooms with their bits of broken furniture, low ceilings, and cramped windows – upstairs where the victim had first been disturbed and stalked to her death.

And the moment he discovered where the sounds were, he began to hear them more clearly. It was the sound of feet, moving stealthily along the passage overhead, in and out among the rooms, and past the furniture.

He turned quickly to steal a glance at the motionless figure seated beside him, to note whether she had shared his discovery. The faint candle-light coming through the crack in the cupboard door, threw her strongly-marked face into vivid relief against the white of the wall. But it was something else that made him catch his breath and stare again. An extraordinary something had come into her face and seemed to spread over her features like a mask; it smoothed out the deep lines and drew the skin everywhere a little tighter so that the wrinkles disappeared; it brought into the face – with the sole exception of the old eyes – an appearance of youth and almost of childhood.

He stared in speechless amazement – amazement that was dangerously near to horror. It was his aunt's face indeed, but it was her face of forty years ago, the vacant innocent face of a girl. He had heard stories of that strange effect of terror which could wipe a human countenance clean of other emotions, obliterating all previous expressions; but he had never realized that it could be literally true, or could mean anything so simply horrible as what he now saw. For the dreadful signature of overmastering fear was written plainly in that utter vacancy of the girlish face beside him; and when, feeling his intense gaze, she turned to look at him, he instinctively closed his eyes tightly to shut out the sight.

Yet, when he turned a minute later, his feelings well in hand, he saw to his intense relief another expression; his aunt was smiling, and though the face was deathly white, the awful veil had lifted and the normal look was returning.

'Anything wrong?' was all he could think of to say at the moment. And the answer was eloquent, coming from such a woman.

'I feel cold – and a little frightened,' she whispered.

He offered to close the window, but she seized hold of him and begged him not to leave her side even for an instant.

'It's upstairs, I know,' she whispered, with an odd half laugh; 'but I can't possibly go up.'

But Shorthouse thought otherwise, knowing that in action lay their best hope of self-control.

He took the brandy flask and poured out a glass of neat spirit, stiff enough to help anybody over anything. She swallowed it, with a little shiver. His only idea now was to get out of the house before her collapse became inevitable; but this could not safely be done by turning tail and running from the enemy. Inaction was no longer possible; every minute he was growing less master of himself, and desperate, aggressive measures were imperative without further delay. Moreover, the action must be taken *towards* the enemy, not away from it; the climax, if necessary and unavoidable, would have to be faced boldly. He could do it now; but in ten minutes he might not have the force left to act for himself, much less for both!

Upstairs, the sounds were meanwhile becoming louder and closer, accompanied by occasional creaking of the boards. Someone was moving stealthily about, stumbling now and then awkwardly against the furniture.

Waiting a few moments to allow the tremendous dose of spirits to produce its effect, and knowing this would last but a short time under the circumstances, Shorthouse then quietly got on his feet, saying in a determined voice –

'Now, Aunt Julia, we'll go upstairs and find out what all this noise is about. You must come too. It's what we agreed.'

He picked up his stick and went to the cupboard for the candle. A limp form rose shakily beside him breathing hard, and he heard a voice say very faintly something about being 'ready to come'. The woman's courage amazed him; it was so much greater than his own; and, as they advanced, holding aloft the dripping candle, some subtle force exhaled from this trembling, white-faced old woman at his side that was the true source of his inspiration. It held something really great that shamed him and gave him the support without which he would have proved far less equal to the occasion.

They crossed the dark landing, avoiding with their eyes the deep black space over the banisters. Then they began to mount the narrow staircase to meet the sounds which, minute by minute, grew louder and nearer. About half-way up the stairs Aunt Julia stumbled and Shorthouse turned to catch her by the arm, and just at that moment there came a terrific crash in the servants' corridor overhead. It was instantly followed by a shrill, agonized scream that was a cry of terror and a cry for help melted into one.

Before they could move aside, or go down a single step, someone came rushing along the passage overhead, blundering horribly, racing madly, at full speed, three steps at a time, down the very staircase where they stood. The steps were light and uncertain; but close behind them sounded the heavier tread of another person, and the staircase seemed to shake.

Shorthouse and his companion just had time to flatten themselves against the wall when the jumble of flying steps was upon them, and two persons, with the slightest possible interval between them, dashed past at full speed. It was a perfect whirlwind of sound breaking in upon the midnight silence of the empty building.

The two runners, pursuer and pursued, had passed clean through them where they stood, and already with a thud the boards below had received first one, then the other. Yet they had seen absolutely nothing – not a hand, or arm, or face, or even a shred of flying clothing.

There came a second's pause. Then the first one, the lighter of the two, obviously the pursued one, ran with uncertain footsteps into the little room which Shorthouse and his aunt had just left. The heavier one followed. There was a sound of scuffling, gasping, and smothered screaming; and then out on to the landing came the step – of a single person *treading weightily*.

A dead silence followed for the space of half a minute, and then was heard a rushing sound through the air. It was

23

followed by a dull, crashing thud in the depths of the house below – on the stone floor of the hall.

Utter silence reigned after. Nothing moved. The flame of the candle was steady. It had been steady the whole time, and the air had been undisturbed by any movement whatsoever. Palsied with terror, Aunt Julia, without waiting for her companion, began fumbling her way downstairs; she was crying gently to herself, and when Shorthouse put his arm round her and half carried her he felt that she was trembling like a leaf. He went into the little room and picked up the cloak from the floor, and, arm in arm, walking very slowly, without speaking a word or looking once behind them, they marched down the three flights into the hall.

In the hall they saw nothing, but the whole way down the stairs they were conscious that someone followed them; step by step; when they went faster IT was left behind, and when they went more slowly IT caught them up. But never once did they look behind to see; and at each turning of the staircase they lowered their eyes for fear of the following horror they might see upon the stairs above.

With trembling hands Shorthouse opened the front door, and they walked out into the moonlight and drew a deep breath of the cool night air blowing in from the sea.

A Haunted Island

The following events occurred on a small island of isolated position in a large Canadian lake, to whose cool waters the inhabitants of Montreal and Toronto flee for rest and recreation in the hot months. It is only to be regretted that events of such peculiar interest to the genuine student of the psychical should be entirely uncorroborated. Such unfortunately, however, is the case.

Our own party of nearly twenty had returned to Montreal that very day, and I was left in solitary possession for a week or two longer, in order to accomplish some important 'reading' for the law which I had foolishly neglected during the summer.

It was late in September, and the big trout and maskinonge were stirring themselves in the depths of the lake, and beginning slowly to move up to the surface waters as the north winds and early frosts lowered their temperature. Already the maples were crimson and gold, and the wild laughter of the loons echoed in sheltered bays that never knew their strange cry in the summer.

With a whole island to oneself, a two-storey cottage, a canoe, and only the chipmunks, and the farmer's weekly visit with eggs and bread, to disturb one, the opportunities for hard reading might be very great. It all depends!

The rest of the party had gone off with many warnings to beware of Indians, and not to stay late enough to be the victim of a frost that thinks nothing of forty below zero. After they had gone, the loneliness of the situation made itself unpleasantly felt. There were no other islands within six or seven miles, and though the mainland forests lay a couple of miles behind me, they stretched for a very great distance unbroken by any signs of human habitation. But, though the island was completely deserted and silent, the rocks and trees that had echoed human laughter and voices almost every hour of the day for two months could not fail to retain some memories of it all; and I was not surprised to fancy I heard a shout or a cry as I passed from rock to rock, and more than once to imagine that I heard my own name called aloud.

In the cottage there were six tiny little bedrooms divided from one another by plain unvarnished partitions of pine. A wooden bedstead, a mattress, and a chair, stood in each room, but I only found two mirrors, and one of these was broken.

The boards creaked a good deal as I moved about, and the signs of occupation were so recent that I could hardly believe I was alone. I half expected to find someone left behind, still trying to crowd into a box more than it would hold. The door of one room was stiff, and refused for a moment to open, and it required very little persuasion to imagine someone was holding the handle on the inside, and that when it opened I should meet a pair of human eyes.

A thorough search of the floor led me to select as my own sleeping quarters a little room with a diminutive balcony over the verandah roof. The room was very small, but the bed was large, and had the best mattress of them all. It was situated directly over the sitting-room where I should live and do my 'reading', and the miniature window looked out to the rising sun. With the exception of a narrow path which led from the front door and verandah through the trees to the boat-landing, the island was densely covered with maples, hemlocks, and cedars. The trees gathered in round the cottage so closely that the slightest wind made the branches scrape the roof and tap the wooden walls. A few moments after sunset the darkness became impenetrable, and ten yards beyond the glare of the lamps that shone through the sitting-room windows – of which there were four – you could not see an inch before your nose, nor move a step without running up against a tree.

The rest of that day I spent moving my belongings from my tent to the sitting-room, taking stock of the contents of the larder, and chopping enough wood for the stove to last me for a week. After that, just before sunset, I went round the island a couple of times in my canoe for precaution's sake. I had never dreamed of doing this before, but when a man is alone he does things that never occur to him when he is one of a large party.

How lonely the island seemed when I landed again! The sun was down, and twilight is unknown in these northern regions. The darkness comes up at once. The canoe safely pulled up and turned over on her face, I groped my way up the little narrow pathway to the verandah. The six lamps were soon burning merrily in the front room; but in the kitchen, where I 'dined', the shadows were so gloomy, and the lamp-light was so inadequate, that the stars could be seen peeping through the cracks between the rafters.

I turned in early that night. Though it was calm and there was no wind, the creaking of my bedstead and the musical gurgle of the water over the rocks below were not the only sounds that reached my ears. As I lay awake, the appalling emptiness of the house grew upon me. The corridors and vacant rooms seemed to echo innumerable footsteps, shuf-flings, the rustle of skirts, and a constant undertone of whis-pering. When sleep at length overtook me, the breathings and noises, however, passed gently to mingle with the voices of my dreams.

A week passed by, and the 'reading' progressed favourably. On the tenth day of my solitude, a strange thing happened. I awoke after a good night's sleep to find myself possessed with a marked repugnance for my room. The air seemed to stifle me. The more I tried to define the cause of this dislike, the more unreasonable it appeared. There was something about the room that made me afraid. Absurd as it seems, this feeling clung to me obstinately while dressing, and more than once I caught myself shivering, and conscious of an inclination to get out of the room as quickly as possible. The more I tried to laugh it away, the more real it became; and when at last I was dressed, and went out into the passage, and downstairs into the kitchen, it was with feelings of relief, such as I might imagine would accompany one's escape from the presence of a dangerous contagious disease.

While cooking my breakfast, I carefully recalled every night spent in the room, in the hope that I might in some way connect the dislike I now felt with some disagreeable incident that had occurred in it. But the only thing I could recall was one stormy night when I suddenly awoke and heard the boards creaking so loudly in the corridor that I was convinced there were people in the house. So certain was I of this, that I had descended the stairs, gun in hand, only to find the doors and windows securely fastened, and the mice and black-beetles in sole possession of the floor. This was certainly not sufficient to account for the strength of my feelings.

The morning hours I spent in steady reading; and when I broke off in the middle of the day for a swim and luncheon, I was very much surprised, if not a little alarmed, to find that my dislike for the room had, if anything, grown stronger. Going upstairs to get a book, I experienced the most marked aversion to entering the room, and while within I was conscious all the time of an uncomfortable feeling that was half uneasiness and half apprehension. The result of it was that, instead of reading, I spent the afternoon on the water paddling and fishing, and when I got home about sundown, brought with me half a dozen delicious black bass for the supper-table and the larder.

As sleep was an important matter to me at this time, I had decided that if my aversion to the room was so strongly marked on my return as it had been before, I would move my bed down into the sitting-room, and sleep there. This was, I argued, in no sense a concession to an absurd and fanciful fear, but simply a precaution to ensure a good night's sleep. A bad night involved the loss of the next day's reading, – a loss I was not prepared to incur.

I accordingly moved my bed downstairs into a corner of the sitting-room facing the door, and was moreover uncommonly glad when the operation was completed, and the door of the bedroom closed finally upon the shadows, the silence, and the strange *fear* that shared the room with them.

The croaking stroke of the kitchen clock sounded the hour of eight as I finished washing up my few dishes, and closing the kitchen door behind me, passed into the front room. All the lamps were lit, and their reflectors, which I had polished up during the day, threw a blaze of light into the room.

Outside the night was still and warm. Not a breath of air was stirring; the waves were silent, the trees motionless, and heavy clouds hung like an oppressive curtain over the heavens. The darkness seemed to have rolled up with unusual swiftness, and not the faintest glow of colour remained to show where the sun had set. There was present in the atmosphere that ominous and overwhelming silence which so often precedes the most violent storms.

I sat down to my books with my brain unusually clear, and in my heart the pleasant satisfaction of knowing that five black bass were lying in the ice-house, and that tomorrow morning the old farmer would arrive with fresh bread and eggs. I was soon absorbed in my books.

As the night wore on the silence deepened. Even the chipmunks were still; and the boards of the floors and walls ceased creaking. I read on steadily till, from the gloomy shadows of the kitchen, came the hoarse sound of the clock striking nine. How loud the strokes sounded! They were like blows of a big hammer. I closed one book and opened another, feeling that I was just warming up to my work.

This, however, did not last long. I presently found that I was reading the same paragraphs over twice, simple paragraphs that did not require such effort. Then I noticed that my mind began to wander to other things, and the effort to recall my thoughts became harder with each digression. Concentration was growing momentarily more difficult. Presently I discovered that I had turned over two pages instead of one, and had not noticed my mistake until I was well down the page. This was becoming serious. What was the disturbing influence? It could not be physical fatigue. On the contrary, my mind was unusually alert, and in a more receptive condition than usual. I made a new and determined effort to read, and for a short time succeeded in giving my whole attention to my subject. But in a very few moments again I found myself leaning back in my chair, staring vacantly into space.

Something was evidently at work in my subconsciousness. There was something I had neglected to do. Perhaps the kitchen door and windows were not fastened. I accordingly went to see, and found that they were! The fire perhaps needed attention. I went to see, and found that it was all right! I looked at the lamps, went upstairs into every bedroom in turn, and then went round the house, and even into the ice-house. Nothing was wrong; everything was in its place. Yet something *was* wrong! The conviction grew stronger and stronger within me.

When I at length settled down to my books again and tried to read, I became aware, for the first time, that the room seemed growing cold. Yet the day had been oppressively warm, and evening had brought no relief. The six big lamps, moreover, gave out heat enough to warm the room pleasantly. But a chilliness, that perhaps crept up from the lake, made itself felt in the room, and caused me to get up to close the glass door opening on to the verandah.

For a brief moment I stood looking out at the shaft of light that fell from the windows and shone some little distance down the pathway, and out for a few feet into the lake.

As I looked, I saw a canoe glide into the pathway of light, and immediately crossing it, pass out of sight again into the darkness. It was perhaps a hundred feet from the shore, and it moved swiftly.

I was surprised that a canoe should pass the island at that time of night, for all the summer visitors from the other side of the lake had gone home weeks before, and the island was a long way out of any line of water traffic.

My reading from this moment did not make very good progress, for somehow the picture of that canoe, gliding so dimly

and swiftly across the narrow track of light on the black
waters, silhouetted itself against the background of my mind
with singular vividness. It kept coming between my eyes and
the printed page. The more I thought about it the more surprised I became. It was of larger build than any I had seen
during the past summer months, and was more like the old
Indian war canoes with the high curving bows and stern and
wide beam. The more I tried to read, the less success attended
my efforts; and finally I closed my books and went out on the
verandah to walk up and down a bit, and shake the chilliness
out of my bones.

The night was perfectly still, and as dark as imaginable. I
stumbled down the path to the little landing wharf, where the
water made the very faintest of gurgling under the timbers.
The sound of a big tree falling in the mainland forest, far
across the lake, stirred echoes in the heavy air, like the first
guns of a distant night attack. No other sound disturbed the
stillness that reigned supreme.

As I stood upon the wharf in the broad splash of light that
followed me from the sitting-room windows, I saw another
canoe cross the pathway of uncertain light upon the water, and
disappear at once into the impenetrable gloom that lay beyond. This time I saw more distinctly than before. It was like
the former canoe, a big birch-bark, with high-crested bows
and stern and broad beam. It was paddled by two Indians, of
whom the one in the stern – the steerer – appeared to be a very
large man. I could see this very plainly; and though the second
canoe was much nearer the island than the first, I judged that
they were both on their way home to the Government Reser-
vation, which was situated some fifteen miles away upon the
mainland.

I was wondering in my mind what could possibly bring any
Indians down to this part of the lake at such an hour of the
night, when a third canoe, of precisely similar build, and also
occupied by two Indians, passed silently round the end of the
wharf. This time the canoe was very much nearer shore, and it
suddenly flashed into my mind that the three canoes were in

reality one and the same, and that only one canoe was circling the island!

This was by no means a pleasant reflection, because, if it were the correct solution of the unusual appearance of the three canoes in this lonely part of the lake at so late an hour, the purpose of the two men could only reasonably be considered to be in some way connected with myself. I had never known of the Indians attempting any violence upon the settlers who shared the wild, inhospitable country with them; at the same time, it was not beyond the region of possibility to suppose ... But then I did not care even to think of such hideous possibilities, and my imagination immediately sought relief in all manner of other solutions to the problem, which indeed came readily enough to my mind, but did not succeed in recommending themselves to my reason.

Meanwhile, by a sort of instinct, I stepped back out of the bright light in which I had hitherto been standing, and waited in the deep shadow of a rock to see if the canoe would again make its appearance. Here I could see, without being seen, and the precaution seemed a wise one.

After less than five minutes the canoe, as I had anticipated, made its fourth appearance. This time it was not twenty yards from the wharf, and I saw that the Indians meant to land. I recognized the two men as those who had passed before, and the steerer was certainly an immense fellow. It was unquestionably the same canoe. There could be no longer any doubt that for some purpose of their own the men had been going round and round the island for some time, waiting for an opportunity to land. I strained my eyes to follow them in the darkness, but the night had completely swallowed them up, and not even the faintest swish of the paddles reached my ears as the Indians plied their long and powerful strokes. The canoe would be round again in a few moments, and this time it was possible that the men might land. It was well to be prepared. I knew nothing of their intentions, and two to one (when the two are big Indians!) late at night on a lonely island was not exactly my idea of pleasant intercourse.

In a corner of the sitting-room, leaning up against the back wall, stood my Marlin rifle, with ten cartridges in the magazine and one lying snugly in the greased breech. There was just time to get up to the house and take up a position of defence in that corner. Without an instant's hesitation I ran up to the verandah, carefully picking my way among the trees, so as to avoid being seen in the light. Entering the room, I shut the door leading to the verandah, and as quickly as possible turned out every one of the six lamps. To be in a room so brilliantly lighted, where my every movement could be observed from outside, while I could see nothing but impenetrable darkness at every window, was by all laws of warfare an unnecessary concession to the enemy. And this enemy, if enemy it was to be, was far too wily and dangerous to be granted any such advantages.

I stood in the corner of the room with my back against the wall, and my hand on the cold rifle-barrel. The table, covered with my books, lay between me and the door, but for the first few minutes after the lights were out the darkness was so intense that nothing could be discerned at all. Then, very gradually, the outline of the room became visible, and the framework of the windows began to shape itself dimly before my eyes.

After a few minutes the door (its upper half of glass), and the two windows that looked out upon the front verandah, became specially distinct; and I was glad that this was so, because if the Indians came up to the house I should be able to see their approach, and gather something of their plans. Nor was I mistaken, for there presently came to my ears the peculiar hollow sound of a canoe landing and being carefully dragged up over the rocks. The paddles I distinctly heard being placed underneath, and the silence that ensued thereupon I rightly interpreted to mean that the Indians were stealthily approaching the house. . . .

While it would be absurd to claim that I was not alarmed – even frightened – at the gravity of the situation and its possible outcome, I speak the whole truth when I say that I was not overwhelmingly afraid for myself. I was conscious that even at this stage of the night I was passing into a psychical condition in which my sensations seemed no longer normal. Physical fear at no time entered into the nature of my feelings; and though I kept my hand upon my rifle the greater part of the night, I was all the time conscious that its assistance could be of little avail against the terrors that I had to face. More than once I seemed to feel most curiously that I was in no real sense a part of the proceedings, nor actually involved in them, but that I was playing the part of a spectator – a spectator, moreover, on a psychic rather than on a material plane. Many of my sensations that night were too vague for definite description and analysis, but the main feeling that will stay with me to the end of my days is the awful horror of it all, and the miserable sensation that if the strain had lasted a little longer than was actually the case my mind must inevitably have given way.

Meanwhile I stood still in my corner, and waited patiently for what was to come. The house was as still as the grave, but the inarticulate voices of the night sang in my ears, and I seemed to hear the blood running in my veins and dancing in my pulses.

If the Indians came to the back of the house, they would find the kitchen door and window securely fastened. They could not get in there without making considerable noise, which I was bound to hear. The only mode of getting in was by means of the door that faced me, and I kept my eyes glued on that door without taking them off for the smallest fraction of a second.

My sight adapted itself every minute better to the darkness. I saw the table that nearly filled the room, and left only a narrow passage on each side. I could also make out the straight backs of the wooden chairs pressed up against it, and could even distinguish my papers and inkstand lying on the white oilcloth covering. I thought of the gay faces that had gathered round that table during the summer, and I longed for the sunlight as I had never longed for it before.

Less than three feet to my left the passage-way led to the kitchen, and the stairs leading to the bedrooms above commenced in this passage-way, but almost in the sitting-room itself. Through the windows I could see the dim motionless outlines of the trees: not a leaf stirred, not a branch moved.

A few moments of this awful silence, and then I was aware of a soft tread on the boards of the verandah, so stealthy that it seemed an impression directly on my brain rather than upon the nerves of hearing. Immediately afterwards a black figure darkened the glass door, and I perceived that a face was pressed against the upper panes. A shiver ran down my back, and my hair was conscious of a tendency to rise and stand at right angles to my head.

It was the figure of an Indian, broad-shouldered and immense; indeed, the largest figure of a man I have ever seen outside of a circus hall. By some power of light that seemed to generate itself in the brain, I saw the strong dark face with the aquiline nose and high cheek-bones flattened against the glass. The direction of the gaze I could not determine; but faint gleams of light as the big eyes rolled round and showed their whites, told me plainly that no corner of the room escaped their searching.

For what seemed fully five minutes the dark figure stood there, with the huge shoulders bent forward so as to bring the head down to the level of the glass; while behind him, though not nearly so large, the shadowy form of the other Indian swayed to and fro like a bent tree. While I waited in an agony of suspense and agitation for their next movement little currents of icy sensation ran up and down my spine and my heart seemed alternately to stop beating and then start off again with terrifying rapidity. They must have heard its thumping and the singing of the blood in my head! Moreover, I was conscious, as I felt a cold stream of perspiration trickle down my face, of a desire to scream, to shout, to bang the walls like a child, to make a noise, or do anything that would relieve the suspense and bring things to a speedy climax.

It was probably this inclination that led me to another discovery, for when I tried to bring my rifle from behind my back to raise it and have it pointed at the door ready to fire, I found that I was powerless to move. The muscles, paralysed by this strange fear, refused to obey the will. Here indeed was a terrifying complication!

*

There was a faint sound of rattling at the brass knob, and the door was pushed open a couple of inches. A pause of a few seconds, and it was pushed open still further. Without a sound of footsteps that was appreciable to my ears, the two figures glided into the room, and the man behind gently closed the door after him.

They were alone with me between the four walls. Could they see me standing there, so still and straight in my corner? Had they, perhaps, already seen me? My blood surged and sang like the roll of drums in an orchestra; and though I did my best to suppress my breathing, it sounded like the rushing of wind through a pneumatic tube.

My suspense as to the next move was soon at an end – only, however, to give place to a new and keener alarm. The men had hitherto exchanged no words and no signs, but there were general indications of a movement across the room, and whichever way they went they would have to pass round the table. If they came my way they would have to pass within six inches of my person. While I was considering this very disagreeable possibility, I perceived that the smaller Indian (smaller by comparison) suddenly raised his arm and pointed to the ceiling. The other fellow raised his head and followed the direction of his companion's arm. I began to understand at last. They were going upstairs, and the room directly overhead to which they pointed had been until this night my bedroom. It was the room in which I had experienced that very morning so strange a sensation of fear, and but for which I should then have been lying asleep in the narrow bed against the window.

The Indians then began to move silently around the room;

they were going upstairs, and they were coming round my side of the table. So stealthy were their movements that, but for the abnormally sensitive state of the nerves, I should never have heard them. As it was, their cat-like tread was distinctly audible. Like two monstrous black cats they came round the table toward me, and for the first time I perceived that the smaller of the two dragged something along the floor behind him. As it trailed along over the floor with a soft, sweeping sound, I somehow got the impression that it was a large dead thing with outstretched wings, or a large, spreading cedar branch. Whatever it was, I was unable to see it even in outline, and I was too terrified, even had I possessed the power over my muscles, to move my neck forward in the effort to determine its nature.

Nearer and nearer they came. The leader rested a giant hand upon the table as he moved. My lips were glued together, and the air seemed to burn in my nostrils. I tried to close my eyes, so that I might not see as they passed me; but my eyelids had stiffened, and refused to obey. Would they never get by me? Sensation seemed also to have left my legs, and it was as if I were standing on mere supports of wood or stone. Worse still, I was conscious that I was losing the power of balance, the power to stand upright, or even to lean backwards against the wall. Some force was drawing me forward, and a dizzy terror seized me that I should lose my balance, and topple forward against the Indians just as they were in the act of passing me.

Even moments drawn out into hours must come to an end some time, and almost before I knew it the figures had passed me and had their feet upon the lower step of the stairs leading to the upper bedrooms. There could not have been six inches between us, and yet I was conscious only of a current of cold air that followed them. They had not touched me, and I was convinced that they had not seen me. Even the trailing thing on the floor behind them had not touched my feet, as I had dreaded it would, and on such an occasion as this I was grateful even for the smallest mercies.

The absence of the Indians from my immediate neighbourhood brought little sense of relief. I stood shivering and shuddering in my corner, and, beyond being able to breathe more freely, I felt no whit less uncomfortable. Also, I was aware that a certain light, which, without apparent source or rays, had enabled me to follow their every gesture and movement, had gone out of the room with their departure. An unnatural darkness now filled the room, and pervaded its every corner so that I could barely make out the positions of the windows and the glass doors.

As I said before, my condition was evidently an abnormal one. The capacity for feeling surprise seemed, as in dreams, to be wholly absent. My senses recorded with unusual accuracy every smallest occurrence, but I was able to draw only the simplest deductions.

The Indians soon reached the top of the stairs, and there they halted for a moment. I had not the faintest clue as to their next movement. They appeared to hesitate. They were listening attentively. Then I heard one of them, who by the weight of his soft tread must have been the giant, cross the narrow corridor and enter the room directly overhead – my own little bedroom. But for the insistence of that unaccountable dread I had experienced there in the morning, I should at that very moment have been lying in the bed with the big Indian in the room standing beside me.

For the space of a hundred seconds there was silence, such as might have existed before the birth of sound. It was followed by a long quivering shriek of terror, which rang out into the night, and ended in a short gulp before it had run its full course. At the same moment the other Indian left his place at the head of the stairs, and joined his companion in the bedroom. I heard the 'thing' trailing behind him along the floor. A thud followed, as of something heavy falling, and then all became as still and silent as before.

It was at this point that the atmosphere, surcharged all day with the electricity of a fierce storm, found relief in a dancing flash of brilliant lightning simultaneously with a crash of loudest thunder. For five seconds every article in the room was visible to me with amazing distinctness, and through the windows I saw the tree trunks standing in solemn rows. The thunder pealed and echoed across the lake and among the distant islands, and the flood-gates of heaven then opened and let out their rain in streaming torrents.

The drops fell with a swift rushing sound upon the still waters of the lake, which leaped up to meet them, and pattered with the rattle of shot on the leaves of the maples and the roof of the cottage. A moment later, and another flash, even more brilliant and of longer duration than the first, lit up the sky from zenith to horizon, and bathed the room momentarily in dazzling whiteness. I could see the rain glistening on the leaves and branches outside. The wind rose suddenly, and in less than a minute the storm that had been gathering all day burst forth in its full fury.

Above all the noisy voices of the elements, the slightest sounds in the room overhead made themselves heard, and in the few seconds of deep silence that followed the shriek of terror and pain I was aware that the movements had commenced again. The men were leaving the room and approaching the top of the stairs. A short pause, and they began to descend. Behind them, tumbling from step to step, I could hear that trailing 'thing' being dragged along. It had become ponderous!

I awaited their approach with a degree of calmness, almost of apathy, which was only explicable on the ground that after a certain point Nature applies her own anaesthetic, and a merciful condition of numbness supervenes. On they came, step by step, nearer and nearer, with the shuffling sound of the burden behind growing louder as they approached.

They were already half-way down the stairs when I was galvanized afresh into a condition of terror by the consideration of a new and horrible possibility. It was the reflection that if another vivid flash of lightning were to come when the shadowy procession was in the room, perhaps when it was actually passing in front of me, I should see everything in detail, and worse, be seen myself! I could only hold my breath and wait – wait while the minutes lengthened into hours, and the procession made its slow progress round the room.

The Indians had reached the foot of the staircase. The form of the huge leader loomed in the doorway of the passage, and the burden with an ominous thud had dropped from the last step to the floor. There was a moment's pause while I saw the Indian turn and stoop to assist his companion. Then the procession moved forward again, entered the room close on my left, and began to move slowly round my side of the table. The leader was already beyond me, and his companion, dragging on the floor behind him the burden, whose confused outline I could dimly make out, was exactly in front of me, when the cavalcade came to a dead halt. At the same moment, with the strange suddenness of thunderstorms, the splash of the rain ceased altogether, and the wind died away into utter silence.

For the space of five seconds my heart seemed to stop beating, and then the worst came. A double flash of lightning lit up the room and its contents with merciless vividness.

The huge Indian leader stood a few feet past me on my right. One leg was stretched forward in the act of taking a step. His immense shoulders were turned towards his companion, and in all their magnificent fierceness I saw the outline of his features. His gaze was directed upon the burden his companion was dragging along the floor; but his profile, with the big aquiline nose, high cheek-bone, straight black hair and bold chin, burnt itself in that brief instant into my brain, never again to fade.

Dwarfish, compared with this gigantic figure, appeared the proportions of the other Indian, who, within twelve inches of my face, was stooping over the thing he was dragging in a position that lent to his person the additional horror of deformity. And the burden, lying upon a sweeping cedar branch which he held and dragged by a long stem, was the body of a white man. The scalp had been neatly lifted, and blood lay in a broad smear upon the cheeks and forehead.

Then, for the first time that night, the terror that had paralysed my muscles and my will lifted its unholy spell from my soul. With a loud cry I stretched out my arms to seize the big Indian by the throat, and, grasping only air, tumbled forward unconscious upon the ground.

I had recognized the body, and *the face was my own!* ...

It was bright daylight when a man's voice recalled me to consciousness. I was lying where I had fallen, and the farmer was standing in the room with the loaves of bread in his hands. The horror of the night was still in my heart, and as the bluff settler helped me to my feet and picked up the rifle which had fallen with me, with many questions and expressions of condolence, I imagined my brief replies were neither self-explanatory nor even intelligible.

That day, after a thorough and fruitless search of the house, I left the island, and went over to spend my last ten days with the farmer; and when the time came for me to leave, the necessary reading had been accomplished, and my nerves had completely recovered their balance.

On the day of my departure the farmer started early in his big boat with my belongings to row to the point, twelve miles distant, where a little steamer ran twice a week for the accommodation of hunters. Late in the afternoon I went off in another direction in my canoe, wishing to see the island once again, where I had been the victim of so strange an experience.

In due course I arrived there, and made a tour of the island. I also made a search of the little house, and it was not without a curious sensation in my heart that I entered the little upstairs bedroom. There seemed nothing unusual.

Just after I re-embarked, I saw a canoe gliding ahead of me around the curve of the island. A canoe was an unusual sight at this time of the year, and this one seemed to have sprung from nowhere. Altering my course a little, I watched it disappear around the next projecting point of rock. It had high curving bows, and there were two Indians in it. I lingered with some excitement, to see if it would appear again round the other side of the island; and in less than five minutes it came into view. There were less than two hundred yards between us, and the Indians, sitting on their haunches, were paddling swiftly in my direction.

I never paddled faster in my life than I did in those next few minutes. When I turned to look again, the Indians had altered their course, and were again circling the island.

The sun was sinking behind the forests on the mainland, and the crimson-coloured clouds of sunset were reflected in the waters of the lake, when I looked round for the last time, and saw the big bark canoe and its two dusky occupants still going round the island. Then the shadows deepened rapidly; the lake grew black, and the night wind blew its first breath in my face as I turned a corner, and a projecting bluff of rock hid from my view both island and canoe.

Keeping His Promise

It was eleven o'clock at night, and young Marriott was locked into his room, cramming as hard as he could cram. He was a 'Fourth Year Man' at Edinburgh University and he had been ploughed for this particular examination so often that his parents had positively declared they could no longer supply the funds to keep him there.

His rooms were cheap and dingy, but it was the lecture fees that took the money. So Marriott pulled himself together at last and definitely made up his mind that he would pass or die in the attempt, and for some weeks now he had been reading as hard as mortal man can read. He was trying to make up for lost time and money in a way that showed conclusively he did not understand the value of either. For no ordinary man – and Marriott was in every sense an ordinary man – can afford to drive the mind as he had lately been driving his, without sooner or later paying the cost.

Among the students he had few friends or acquaintances, and these few had promised not to disturb him at night, knowing he was at last reading in earnest. It was, therefore, with feelings a good deal stronger than mere surprise that he heard his door-bell ring on this particular night and realized that he was to have a visitor. Some men would simply have muffled the bell and gone on quietly with their work. But Marriott was not this sort. He was nervous. It would have bothered and pecked at his mind all night long not to know who the visitor was and what he wanted. The only thing to do, therefore, was to let him in – and out again – as quickly as possible.

The landlady went to bed at ten o'clock punctually, after which hour nothing would induce her to pretend she heard the bell, so Marriott jumped up from his books with an exclamation that augured ill for the reception of his caller, and prepared to let him in with his own hand.

The streets of Edinburgh were very still at this late hour – it was late for Edinburgh – and in the quiet neighbourhood of F— Street, where Marriott lived on the third floor, scarcely a sound broke the silence. As he crossed the floor, the bell rang a second time, with unnecessary clamour, and he unlocked the door and passed into the little hallway with considerable wrath and annoyance in his heart at the insolence of the double interruption.

'The fellows all know I'm reading for this exam. Why in the world do they come to bother me at such an unearthly hour?'

The inhabitants of the building, with himself, were medical students, general students, poor Writers to the Signet, and some others whose vocations were perhaps not so obvious. The stone staircase, dimly lighted at each floor by a gas-jet that would not turn above a certain height, wound down to the level of the street with no pretence at carpet or railing. At some levels it was cleaner than at others. It depended on the landlady of the particular level.

The acoustic properties of a spiral staircase seem to be peculiar. Marriott, standing by the open door, book in hand, thought every moment the owner of the footsteps would come into view. The sound of the boots was so close and so loud that they seemed to travel disproportionately in advance of their cause. Wondering who it could be, he stood ready with all manner of sharp greetings for the man who dared thus to disturb his work. But the man did not appear. The steps sounded almost under his nose, yet no one was visible.

A sudden queer sensation of fear passed over him – a faintness and a shiver down the back. It went, however, almost as soon as it came, and he was just debating whether he would call aloud to his invisible visitor, or slam the door and return to his books, when the cause of the disturbance turned the corner very slowly and came into view.

It was a stranger. He saw a youngish man short of figure and very broad. His face was the colour of a piece of chalk and the eyes, which were very bright, had heavy lines underneath them. Though the cheeks and chin were unshaven and the general appearance unkempt, the man was evidently a gentleman, for he was well dressed and bore himself with a certain air. But, strangest of all, he wore no hat, and carried none in his hand; and although rain had been falling steadily all the evening, he appeared to have neither overcoat nor umbrella.

A hundred questions sprang up in Marriott's mind and rushed to his lips, chief among which was something like 'Who in the world are you?' and 'What in the name of heaven do you come to me for?' But none of these questions found time to express themselves in words, for almost at once the caller turned his head a little so that the gas light in the hall fell upon his features from a new angle. Then in a flash Marriott recognized him.

'Field! Man alive! Is it you?' he gasped.

The Fourth Year Man was not lacking in intuition, and he perceived at once that here was a case for delicate treatment. He divined, without any actual process of thought, that the catastrophe often predicted had come at last, and that this man's father had turned him out of the house. They had been at a private school together years before, and though they had hardly met once since, the news had not failed to reach him from time to time with considerable detail, for the family lived near his own and between certain of the sisters there was great intimacy. Young Field had gone wild later, he remembered hearing about it all – drink, a woman, opium, or something of the sort – he could not exactly call to mind.

'Come in,' he said at once, his anger vanishing. 'There's been something wrong, I can see. Come in, and tell me all about it and perhaps I can help –' He hardly knew what to say, and stammered a lot more besides. The dark side of life, and the horror of it, belonged to a world that lay remote from his own select little atmosphere of books and dreamings. But he had a man's heart for all that.

He led the way across the hall, shutting the front door carefully behind him, and noticed as he did so that the other, though certainly sober, was unsteady on his legs, and evidently much exhausted. Marriott might not be able to pass his examinations, but he at least knew the symptoms of starvation – acute starvation, unless he was much mistaken – when they stared him in the face.

'Come along,' he said cheerfully, and with genuine sympathy in his voice. 'I'm glad to see you. I was going to have a bite of something to eat, and you're just in time to join me.'

The other made no audible reply, and shuffled so feebly with his feet that Marriot took his arm by way of support. He noticed for the first time that the clothes hung on him with pitiful looseness. The broad frame was literally hardly more than a frame. He was as thin as a skeleton. But, as he touched him, the sensation of faintness and dread returned. It only lasted a moment, and then passed off, and he ascribed it not unnaturally to the distress and shock of seeing a former friend in such a pitiful plight.

'Better let me guide you. It's shamefully dark – this hall. I'm always complaining,' he said lightly, recognizing by the weight upon his arm that the guidance was sorely needed, 'but the old cat never does anything except promise.' He led him to the sofa, wondering all the time where he had come from and how he had found out the address. It must be at least seven years since those days at the private school when they used to be such close friends.

'Now, if you'll forgive me for a minute,' he said, 'I'll get supper ready – such as it is. And don't bother to talk. Just take it easy on the sofa. I see you're dead tired. You can tell me about it afterwards, and we'll make plans.'

The other sat down on the edge of the sofa and stared in silence, while Marriott got out the brown loaf, scones, and huge pot of marmalade that Edinburgh students always keep in their cupboards. His eyes shone with a brightness that suggested drugs, Marriott thought, stealing a glance at him from behind the cupboard door. He did not like yet to take a full square look. The fellow was in a bad way, and it would have been so like an examination to stare and wait for explanations. Besides, he was evidently almost too exhausted to speak. So, for reasons of delicacy – and for another reason as well which he could not exactly formulate to himself – he let his visitor rest apparently unnoticed, while he busied himself with the supper. He lit the spirit lamp to make cocoa, and when the water was boiling he drew up the table with the good things to the sofa, so that Field need not have even the trouble of moving to a chair.

'Now, let's tuck in,' he said, 'and afterwards we'll have a pipe and a chat. I'm reading for an exam, you know, and I always have something about this time. It's jolly to have a companion.'

He looked up and caught his guest's eyes directed straight upon his own. An involuntary shudder ran through him from head to foot. The face opposite him was deadly white and wore a dreadful expression of pain and mental suffering.

'By Gad!' he said, jumping up, 'I quite forgot. I've got some whisky somewhere. What an ass I am. I never touch it myself when I'm working like this.'

He went to the cupboard and poured out a stiff glass which the other swallowed at a single gulp and without any water. Marriott watched him while he drank it, and at the same time noticed something else as well – Field's coat was all over dust, and on one shoulder was a bit of cobweb. It was perfectly dry; Field arrived on a soaking wet night without hat, umbrella, or overcoat, and yet perfectly dry, even dusty. Therefore he had been under cover. What did it all mean? Had he been hiding in the building . . . ?

It was very strange. Yet he volunteered nothing; and Marriott had pretty well made up his mind by this time that he would not ask any questions until he had eaten and slept. Food and sleep were obviously what the poor devil needed most and first – he was pleased with his powers of ready diagnosis – and it would not be fair to press him till he had recovered a bit.

They ate their supper together while the host carried on a running one-sided conversation, chiefly about himself and his exams and his 'old cat' of a landlady, so that the guest need not utter a single word unless he really wished to – which he evidently did not! But, while he toyed with his food, feeling no desire to eat, the other ate voraciously. To see a hungry man devour cold scones, stale oatcake, and brown bread laden with marmalade was a revelation to this inexperienced student who had never known what it was to be without at least three meals a day. He watched in spite of himself, wondering why the fellow did not choke in the process.

But Field seemed to be as sleepy as he was hungry. More than once his head dropped and he ceased to masticate the food in his mouth. Marriott had positively to shake him before he would go on with his meal. A stronger emotion will overcome a weaker, but this struggle between the sting of real hunger and the magical opiate of overpowering sleep was a curious sight to the student, who watched it with mingled astonishment and alarm. He had heard of the pleasure it was to feed hungry men, and watch them eat, but he had never actually witnessed it, and he had no idea it was like this. Field ate like an animal – gobbled, stuffed, gorged. Marriott forgot his reading, and began to feel something very much like a lump in his throat.

'Afraid there's been awfully little to offer you, old man,' he managed to blurt out when at length the last scone had disappeared, and the rapid, one-sided meal was at an end. Field still made no reply, for he was almost asleep in his seat. He merely looked up wearily and gratefully.

'Now you must have some sleep, you know,' he continued, 'or you'll go to pieces. I shall be up all night reading for this blessed exam. You're more than welcome to my bed. Tomorrow we'll have a late breakfast and – and see what can be done – and make plans – I'm awfully good at making plans, you know,' he added with an attempt at lightness.

Field maintained his 'dead sleepy' silence, but appeared to acquiesce, and the other led the way into the bedroom, apologizing as he did so to this half-starved son of a baronet – whose own home was almost a palace – for the size of the room. The weary guest, however, made no pretence of thanks or politeness. He merely steadied himself on his friend's arm as he staggered across the room, and then, with all his clothes on, dropped his exhausted body on the bed. In less than a minute he was to all appearances sound asleep.

For several minutes Marriott stood in the open door and watched him; praying devoutly that he might never find himself in a like predicament, and then fell to wondering what he would do with his unbidden guest on the morrow. But he did not stop long to think, for the call of his books was imperative, and happen what might, he must see to it that he passed that examination.

Having again locked the door into the hall, he sat down to his books and resumed his notes on *materia medica* where he had left off when the bell rang. But it was difficult for some time to concentrate his mind on the subject. His thoughts kept wandering to the picture of that white-faced, strange-eyed fellow, starved and dirty, lying in his clothes and boots on the bed. He recalled their schooldays together before they had drifted apart, and how they had vowed eternal friendship – and all the rest of it. And now! What horrible straits to be in. How could any man let the love of dissipation take such hold upon him?

But one of their vows together Marriott, it seemed, had completely forgotten. Just now, at any rate, it lay too far in the background of his memory to be recalled.

Through the half-open door – the bedroom led out of the sitting-room and had no other door – came the sound of deep, long-drawn breathing, the regular, steady breathing of a tired man, so tired that, even to listen to it made Marriott almost want to go to sleep himself.

'He needed it,' reflected the student, 'and perhaps it came only just in time!'

Perhaps so; for outside the bitter wind from across the Forth howled cruelly and drove the rain in cold streams against the window-panes, and down the deserted streets. Long before Marriott settled down again properly to his reading, he heard distantly, as it were, through the sentences of the book, the heavy, deep breathing of the sleeper in the next room.

A couple of hours later, when he yawned and changed his books, he still heard the breathing, and went cautiously up to the door to look round.

At first the darkness of the room must have deceived him, or else his eyes were confused and dazzled by the recent glare of the reading lamp. For a minute or two he could make out nothing at all but dark lumps of furniture, the mass of the chest of drawers by the wall, and the white patch where his bath stood in the centre of the floor.

Then the bed came slowly into view. And on it he saw the outline of the sleeping body gradually take shape before his eyes, growing up strangely into the darkness, till it stood out in marked relief – the long black form against the white counterpane.

He could hardly help smiling. Field had not moved an inch. He watched him a moment or two and then returned to his books. The night was full of the singing voices of the wind and rain. There was no sound of traffic; no hansoms clattered over the cobbles, and it was still too early for the milk carts. He worked on steadily and conscientiously, only stopping now and again to change a book, or to sip some of the poisonous stuff that kept him awake and made his brain so active, and on these occasions Field's breathing was always distinctly audible in the room. Outside, the storm continued to howl, but inside the house all was stillness. The shade of the reading lamp threw all the light upon the littered table, leaving the other end of the room in comparative darkness. The bedroom door was exactly opposite him where he sat. There was nothing to disturb the worker, nothing but an occasional rush of wind against the windows, and a slight pain in his arm.

This pain, however, which he was unable to account for, grew once or twice very acute. It bothered him; and he tried to remember how, and when, he could have bruised himself so severely – but without success.

At length the page before him turned from yellow to grey, and there were sounds of wheels in the street below. It was four o'clock. Marriott leaned back and yawned prodigiously. Then he drew back the curtains. The storm had subsided and the Castle Rock was shrouded in mist. With another yawn he turned away from the dreary outlook and prepared to sleep the remaining four hours till breakfast on the sofa. Field was still breathing heavily in the next room, and he first tip-toed across the floor to take another look at him.

Peering cautiously round the half-opened door his first glance fell upon the bed now plainly discernible in the grey light of morning. He stared hard. Then he rubbed his eyes. Then he rubbed his eyes again and thrust his head farther round the edge of the door. With fixed eyes he stared harder still, and harder.

But it made no difference at all. He was staring into an empty room.

The sensation of fear he had felt when Field first appeared upon the scene returned suddenly, but with much greater force. He became conscious, too, that his left arm was throbbing violently and causing him great pain. He stood wondering, and staring, and trying to collect his thoughts. He was trembling from head to foot.

By a great effort of the will he left the support of the door and walked forward boldly into the room.

There, upon the bed, was the impress of a body, where Field had lain and slept. There was the mark of the head on the pillow, and the slight indentation at the foot of the bed where the boots had rested on the counterpane. And there, plainer than ever – for he was closer to it – was *the breathing!*

Marriott tried to pull himself together. With a great effort he found his voice and called his friend aloud by name!

'Field! Is that you? Where are you?'

There was no reply; but the breathing continued without interruption, coming directly from the bed. His voice had such an unfamiliar sound that Marriott did not care to repeat his questions, but he went down on his knees and examined the bed above and below, pulling the mattress off finally, and taking the coverings away separately one by one. But though the sounds continued there were no visible sign of Field, nor was there any space in which a human being, however small, could have concealed itself. He pulled the bed out from the wall, but the sound *stayed where it was*. It did not move with the bed.

Marriott, finding self-control a little difficult in his weary condition, at once set about a thorough search of the room. He went through the cupboard, the chest of drawers, the little alcove where the clothes hung – everything. But there was no sign of anyone. The small window near the ceiling was closed; and, anyhow, was not large enough to let a cat pass. The sitting-room door was locked on the inside; he could not have got out that way. Curious thoughts began to trouble Marriott's mind, bringing in their train unwelcome sensations. He grew more and more excited; he searched the bed again till it resembled the scene of a pillow fight; he searched both rooms, knowing all the time it was useless – and then he searched again. A cold perspiration broke out all over his body; and the sound of heavy breathing, all this time, never ceased to come from the corner where Field had lain down to sleep.

Then he tried something else. He pushed the bed back exactly into its original position – and himself lay down upon it just where his guest had lain. But the same instant he sprang up again in a single bound. The breathing was close beside him, almost on his cheek, and between him and the wall! Not even a child could have squeezed into the space.

He went back into his sitting-room, opened the windows, welcoming all the light and air possible, and tried to think the whole matter over quietly and clearly. Men who read too hard, and slept too little, he knew were sometimes troubled with very vivid hallucinations. Again he calmly reviewed every incident of the night; his accurate sensations; the vivid details; the emotions stirred in him; the dreadful feast – no single hallucination could ever combine all these and cover so long a period of time. But with less satisfaction he thought of the recurring faintness, and curious sense of horror that had once or twice come over him, and then of the violent pains in his arm. These were quite unaccountable.

Moreover, now that he began to analyse and examine, there was one other thing that fell upon him like a sudden revelation: *During the whole time Field had not actually uttered a single word!* Yet, as though in mockery upon his reflections, there came ever from that inner room the sound of the breathing, long-drawn, deep, and regular. The thing was incredible. It was absurd.

Haunted by visions of brain fever and insanity, Marriott put on his cap and macintosh and left the house. The morning air on Arthur's Seat would blow the cobwebs from his brain; the scent of the heather, and above all, the sight of the sea. He roamed over the wet slopes above Holyrood for a couple of hours, and did not return until the exercise had shaken some of the horror out of his bones, and given him a ravening appetite into the bargain.

As he entered he saw that there was another man in the room, standing against the window with his back to the light. He recognized his fellow-student Greene, who was reading for the same examination.

'Read hard all night, Marriott,' he said, 'and thought I'd drop in here to compare notes and have some breakfast. You're out early?' he added, by way of a question. Marriott said he had a headache and a walk had helped it, and Greene nodded and said 'Ah!' But when the girl had set the steaming porridge on the table and gone out again, he went on with rather a forced tone, 'Didn't know you had any friends who drank, Marriott?'

This was obviously tentative, and Marriott replied drily that he did not know it either.

'Sounds just as if some chap were "sleeping it off" in there, doesn't it, though?' persisted the other, with a nod in the direction of the bedroom, and looking curiously at his friend.

The two men stared steadily at each other for several seconds, and then Marriott said earnestly –

'Then you hear it too, thank God!'

'Of course I hear it. The door's open. Sorry if I wasn't meant to.'

'Oh. I don't mean that,' said Marriott, lowering his voice. 'But I'm awfully relieved. Let me explain. Of course, if you hear it too, then it's all right; but really it frightened me more than I can tell you. I thought I was going to have brain fever, or something, and you know what a lot depends on this exam. It always begins with sounds, or visions, or some sort of beastly hallucination, and I –'

'Rot!' ejaculated the other impatiently. 'What *are* you talking about?'

'Now, listen to me, Greene,' said Marriott, as calmly as he could, for the breathing was still plainly audible, 'and I'll tell you what I mean, only don't interrupt.' And thereupon he related exactly what had happened during the night, telling everything, even down to the pain in his arm. When it was over he got up from the table and crossed the room.

'You hear the breathing now plainly, don't you?' he said. Greene said he did. 'Well, come with me, and we'll search the room together.' The other, however, did not move from his chair.

'I've been in already,' he said sheepishly; 'I heard the sounds and thought it was you. The door was ajar – so I went in.'

Marriott made no comment, but pushed the door open as wide as it would go. As it opened, the sound of breathing grew more and more distinct.

'*Someone* must be in there,' said Greene under his breath.

'*Someone* is in there, but *where*?' said Marriott. Again he urged his friend to go in with him. But Greene refused point-blank: said he had been in once and had searched the room and there was nothing there. He would not go in again for a good deal.

They shut the door and retired into the other room to talk

it all over with many pipes. Greene questioned his friend very closely, but without illuminating result, since questions cannot alter facts.

'The only thing that ought to have a proper, a logical, explanation is the pain in my arm,' said Marriott, rubbing that member with an attempt at a smile. 'It hurts so infernally and aches all the way up. I can't remember bruising it, though.'

'Let me examine it for you,' said Greene. 'I'm awfully good at bones in spite of the examiners' opinion to the contrary.' It was a relief to play the fool a bit, and Marriot took his coat off and rolled up his sleeve.

'By George, though, I'm bleeding!' he exclaimed. 'Look here! What on earth's this?'

On the forearm, quite close to the wrist, was a thin red line. There was a tiny drop of apparently fresh blood on it. Greene came over and looked closely at it for some minutes. Then he sat back in his chair, looking curiously at his friend's face.

'You've scratched yourself without knowing it,' he said presently.

'There's no sign of a bruise. It must be something else that made the arm ache.'

Marriott sat very still, staring silently at his arm as though the solution of the whole mystery lay there actually written upon the skin.

'What's the matter? I see nothing very strange about a scratch,' said Greene, in an unconvincing sort of voice. 'It was your cuff links probably. Last night in your excitement –'

But Marriott, white to the very lips, was trying to speak. The sweat stood in great beads on his forehead. At last he leaned forward close to his friend's face.

'Look,' he said, in a low voice that shook a little. 'Do you see that red mark? I mean *underneath* what you call the scratch?'

Greene admitted he saw something or other, and Marriott wiped the place clean with his handkerchief and told him to look again more closely.

'Yes, I see,' returned the other, lifting his head after a moment's careful inspection. 'It looks like an old scar.'

'It *is* an old scar,' whispered Marriott, his lips trembling. '*Now* it all comes back to me.'

'All what?' Greene fidgeted on his chair. He tried to laugh, but without success. His friend seemed bordering on collapse.

'Hush! Be quiet, and – I'll tell you,' he said. '*Field made that scar.*'

For a whole minute the two men looked each other full in the face without speaking.

'Field made that scar!' repeated Marriott at length in a louder voice.

'Field! You mean – last night?'

'No, not last night. Years ago – at school, with his knife. And I made a scar in his arm with mine.' Marriott was talking rapidly now.

'We exchanged drops of blood in each other's cuts. He put a drop into my arm and I put one into his –'

'In the name of heaven, what for?'

'It was a boys' compact. We made a sacred pledge, a bargain. I remember it all perfectly now. We had been reading some dreadful book and we swore to appear to one another – I mean, whoever died first swore to show himself to the other. And we sealed the compact with each other's blood. I remember it all so well – the hot summer afternoon in the playground, seven years ago – and one of the masters caught us and confiscated the knives – and I have never thought of it again to this day –'

'And you mean –' stammered Greene.

But Marriott made no answer. He got up and crossed the room and lay down wearily upon the sofa, hiding his face in his hands.

Greene himself was a bit nonplussed. He left his friend alone for a little while, thinking it all over again. Suddenly an idea seemed to strike him. He went over to where Marriott still lay motionless on the sofa and roused him. In any case it was better to face the matter, whether there was an explanation or not. Giving in was always the silly exit.

'I say, Marriott,' he began, as the other turned his white face up to him. 'There's no good being so upset about it. I mean – if it's all an hallucination we know what to do. And if it isn't – well, we know what to think, don't we?'

'I suppose so. But it frightens me horribly for some reason,' returned his friend in a hushed voice. 'And that poor devil –'

'But, after all, if the worst is true and – and that chap *has* kept his promise – well, he has, that's all, isn't it?'

Marriott nodded.

'There's only one thing that occurs to me,' Greene went on, 'and that is, are you quite sure that – that he really ate like that – I mean that he actually *ate anything at all*?' he finished, blurting out all his thought.

Marriott stared at him for a moment and then said he could easily make certain. He spoke quietly. After the main shock no lesser surprise could affect him.

'I put the things away myself,' he said, 'after we had finished. They are on the third shelf in that cupboard. No one's touched 'em since.'

He pointed without getting up, and Greene took the hint and went over to look.

'Exactly,' he said, after a brief examination; 'just as I thought. It was partly hallucination, at any rate. The things haven't been touched. Come and see for yourself.'

Together they examined the shelf. There was the brown loaf, the plate of stale scones, the oatcake, all untouched. Even the glass of whisky Marriott had poured out stood there with the whisky still in it.

'You were feeding – no one,' said Greene. 'Field ate and drank nothing. He was not there at all!'

'But the breathing?' urged the other in a low voice, staring with a dazed expression on his face.

Greene did not answer. He walked over to the bedroom, while Marriott followed him with his eyes. He opened the door, and listened. There was no need for words. The sound of deep, regular breathing came floating through the air. There was no hallucination about that, at any rate. Marriott could hear it where he stood on the other side of the room.

Greene closed the door and came back. 'There's only one thing to do,' he declared with decision. 'Write home and find out about him, and meanwhile come and finish your reading in my rooms. I've got an extra bed.'

'Agreed,' returned the Fourth Year Man; 'there's no hallucination about that exam; I must pass that whatever happens.'

And this was what they did.

It was about a week later when Marriott got the answer from his sister. Part of it he read out to Greene –

'It is curious,' she wrote, 'that in your letter you should have inquired after Field. It seems a terrible thing, but you know only a short while ago Sir John's patience became exhausted, and he turned him out of the house, they say without a penny. Well, what do you think? He has killed himself. At least, it looks like suicide. Instead of leaving the house, he went down into the cellar and simply starved himself to death. ... They're trying to suppress it, of course, but I heard it all from my maid, who got it from their footman. . . . They found the body on the 14th and the doctor said he had died about twelve hours before. . . . He was dreadfully thin. . . .'

'Then he died on the 13th,' said Greene.

Marriott nodded.

'That's the very night he came to see you.'

Marriott nodded again.

A Case of Eavesdropping

Jim Shorthouse was the sort of fellow who always made a mess of things. Everything with which his hands or mind came into contact issued from such contact in an unqualified and irremediable state of mess. His college days were a mess: he was twice rusticated. His schooldays were a mess: he went to half a dozen, each passing him on to the next with a worse character and in a more developed state of mess. His early boyhood was the sort of mess that copy-books and dictionaries spell with a big 'M', and his babyhood – ugh! was the embodiment of howling, yowling, screaming mess.

At the age of forty, however, there came a change in his troubled life, when he met a girl with half a million in her own right, who consented to marry him, and who very soon succeeded in reducing his most messy existence into a state of comparative order and system.

Certain incidents, important and otherwise, of Jim's life would never have come to be told here but for the fact that in getting into his 'messes' and out of them again he succeeded in drawing himself into the atmosphere of peculiar circumstances and strange happenings. He attracted to his path the curious adventures of life as unfailingly as meat attracts flies, and jam wasps. It is to the meat and jam of his life, so to speak, that he owes his experiences; his after-life was all pudding, which attracts nothing but greedy children. With marriage the interest of his life ceased for all but one person, and his path became regular as the sun's instead of erratic as a comet's.

The first experience in order of time that he related to me shows that somewhere latent behind his disarranged nervous system there lay psychic perceptions of an uncommon order.

About the age of twenty-two – I think after his second rusti-
cation – his father's purse and patience had equally given out,
and Jim found himself stranded high and dry in a large American city. High and dry! And the only clothes that had no
holes in them safely in the keeping of his uncle's wardrobe.

Careful reflection on a bench in one of the city parks led
him to the conclusion that the only thing to do was to persuade
the city editor of one of the daily journals that he possessed
an observant mind and a ready pen, and that he could 'do
good work for your paper, sir, as a reporter'. This, then, he
did, standing at a most unnatural angle between the editor
and the window to conceal the whereabouts of the holes.

'Guess we'll have to give you a week's trial,' said the editor,
who, ever on the lookout for good chance material, took on
shoals of men in that way and retained on the average one
man per shoal. Anyhow it gave Jim Shorthouse the where-
withal to sew up the holes and relieve his uncle's wardrobe of
its burden.

Then he went to find living quarters; and in this proceeding
his unique characteristics already referred to – what theoso-
phists would call his Karma – began unmistakably to assert
themselves, for it was in the house he eventually selected that
this sad tale took place.

There are no 'diggings' in American cities. The alternatives
for small incomes are grim enough – rooms in a boarding-
house where meals are served, or in a room-house where no
meals are served – not even breakfast. Rich people live in
palaces, of course, but Jim had nothing to do with 'sich-like'.
His horizon was bounded by boarding-houses and room-
houses; and, owing to the necessary irregularity of his meals
and hours, he took the latter.

It was a large, gaunt-looking place in a side street, with
dirty windows and a creaking iron gate, but the rooms were
large, and the one he selected and paid for in advance was on
the top floor. The landlady looked gaunt and dusty as the
house, and quite as old. Her eyes were green and faded, and
her features large.

'Waal,' she twanged, with her electrifying Western drawl, 'that's the room, if you like it, and that's the price I said. Now, if you want it, why, just say so; and if you don't, why, it don't hurt me any.'

Jim wanted to shake her, but he feared the clouds of long-accumulated dust in her clothes, and as the price and size of the room suited him, he decided to take it.

'Anyone else on this floor?' he asked.

She looked at him queerly out of her faded eyes before she answered.

'None of my guests ever put such questions to me before,' she said; 'but I guess you're different. Why, there's no one at all but an old gent that's stayed here every bit of five years. He's over thar,' pointing to the end of the passage.

'Ah! I see,' said Shorthouse feebly. 'So I'm alone up here?'

'Reckon you are, pretty near,' she twanged out, ending the conversation abruptly by turning her back on her new 'guest', and going slowly and deliberately downstairs.

The newspaper work kept Shorthouse out most of the night. Three times a week he got home at 1 a.m., and three times at 3 a.m. The room proved comfortable enough, and he paid for a second week. His unusual hours had so far prevented his meeting any inmates of the house, and not a sound had been heard from the 'old gent' who shared the floor with him. It seemed a very quiet house.

One night, about the middle of the second week, he came home tired after a long day's work. The lamp that usually stood all night in the hall had burned itself out, and he had to stumble upstairs in the dark. He made considerable noise in doing so, but nobody seemed to be disturbed. The whole house was utterly quiet, and probably everybody was asleep. There were no lights under any of the doors. All was in darkness. It was after two o'clock.

After reading some English letters that had come during the day, and dipping for a few minutes into a book, he became drowsy and got ready for bed. Just as he was about to get in between the sheets, he stopped for a moment and listened.

There rose in the night, as he did so, the sound of steps somewhere in the house below. Listening attentively, he heard that it was somebody coming upstairs – a heavy tread, and the owner taking no pains to step quietly. On it came up the stairs, tramp, tramp, tramp – evidently the tread of a big man, and one in something of a hurry.

At once thoughts connected somehow with fire and police flashed through Jim's brain, but there were no sounds of voices with the steps, and he reflected in the same moment that it could only be the old gentleman keeping late hours and tumbling upstairs in the darkness. He was in the act of turning out the gas and stepping into bed, when the house resumed its former stillness by the footsteps suddenly coming to a dead stop immediately outside his own room.

With his hand on the gas, Shorthouse paused a moment before turning it out to see if the steps would go on again, when he was startled by a loud knocking on his door. Instantly, in obedience to a curious and unexplained instinct, he turned out the light, leaving himself and the room in total darkness.

He had scarcely taken a step across the room to open the door, when a voice from the other side of the wall, so close it almost sounded in his ear, exclaimed in German, 'Is that you, father? Come in.'

The speaker was a man in the next room, and the knocking, after all, had not been on his own door, but on that of the adjoining chamber, which he had supposed to be vacant.

Almost before the man in the passage had time to answer in German, 'Let me in at once,' Jim heard someone cross the floor and unlock the door. Then it was slammed to with a bang, and there was audible the sound of footsteps about the room, and of chairs being drawn up to a table and knocking against furniture on the way. The men seemed wholly regardless of their neighbour's comfort, for they made noise enough to waken the dead.

'Serves me right for taking a room in such a cheap hole,' reflected Jim in the darkness. 'I wonder whom she's let the room to!'

The two rooms, the landlady had told him, were originally one. She had put up a thin partition – just a row of boards – to increase her income. The doors were adjacent, and only separated by the massive upright beam between them. When one was opened or shut the other rattled.

With utter indifference to the comfort of the other sleepers in the house, the two Germans had meanwhile commenced to talk both at once and at the top of their voices. They talked emphatically, even angrily. The words 'Father' and 'Otto' were freely used. Shorthouse understood German, but as he stood listening for the first minute or two, an eavesdropper in spite of himself, it was difficult to make head or tail of the talk, for neither would give way to the other, and the jumble of guttural sounds and unfinished sentences was wholly unintelligible. Then, very suddenly, both voices dropped together; and, after a moment's pause, the deep tones of one of them, who seemed to be the 'father', said, with the utmost distinctness –

'You mean, Otto, that you refuse to get it?'

There was a sound of someone shuffling in the chair before the answer came. 'I mean that I don't know how to get it. It is so much, father. It is *too* much. A part of it –'

'A part of it!' cried the other, with an angry oath, 'a part of it, when ruin and disgrace are already in the house, is worse than useless. If you can get half you can get all, you wretched fool. Half-measures only damn all concerned.'

'You told me last time –' began the other firmly, but was not allowed to finish. A succession of horrible oaths drowned his sentence, and the father went on, in a voice vibrating with anger –

'You know she will give you anything. You have only been married a few months. If you ask and give a plausible reason you can get all we want and more. You can ask it temporarily. All will be paid back. It will re-establish the firm, and she will never know what was done with it. With that amount, Otto, you know I can recoup all these terrible losses, and in less than a year all will be repaid. But without it. . . . You must get it,

Otto. Hear me, you must. Am I to be arrested for the misuse of trust moneys? Is our honoured name to be cursed and spat on?' The old man choked and stammered in his anger and desperation.

Shorthouse stood shivering in the darkness and listening in spite of himself. The conversation had carried him along with it, and he had been for some reason afraid to let his neighbourhood be known. But at this point he realized that he had listened too long and that he must inform the two men that they could be overheard to every single syllable. So he coughed loudly, and at the same time rattled the handle of his door. It seemed to have no effect, for the voices continued just as loudly as before, the son protesting and the father growing more and more angry. He coughed again persistently, and also contrived purposely in the darkness to tumble against the partition, feeling the thin boards yield easily under his weight, and making a considerable noise in so doing. But the voices went on unconcernedly, and louder than ever. Could it be possible they had not heard?

By this time Jim was more concerned about his own sleep than the morality of overhearing the private scandals of his neighbours, and he went out into the passage and knocked smartly at their door. Instantly, as if by magic, the sounds ceased. Everything dropped into utter silence. There was no light under the door and not a whisper could be heard within. He knocked again, but received no answer.

'Gentlemen,' he began at length, with his lips close to the keyhole and in German, 'please do not talk so loud. I can overhear all you say in the next room. Besides, it is very late, and I wish to sleep.'

He paused and listened, but no answer was forthcoming. He turned the handle and found the door was locked. Not a sound broke the stillness of the night except the faint swish of the wind over the skylight and the creaking of a board here and there in the house below. The cold air of a very early morning crept down the passage, and made him shiver. The silence of the house began to impress him disagreeably. He looked behind him and about him, hoping, and yet fearing, that something would break the stillness. The voices still seemed to ring on in his ears; but that sudden silence, when he knocked at the door, affected him far more unpleasantly than the voices, and put strange thoughts in his brain – thoughts he did not like or approve.

Moving stealthily from the door, he peered over the banisters into the space below. It was like a deep vault that might conceal in its shadows anything that was not good. It was not difficult to fancy he saw an indistinct moving to-and-fro below him. Was that a figure sitting on the stairs peering up obliquely at him out of hideous eyes? Was that a sound of whispering and shuffling down there in the dark halls and forsaken landings? Was it something more than the inarticulate murmur of the night?

The wind made an effort overhead, singing over the skylight, and the door behind him rattled and made him start. He turned to go back to his room, and the draught closed the door slowly in his face as if there were someone pressing against it from the other side. When he pushed it open and went in, a hundred shadowy forms seemed to dart swiftly and silently back to their corners and hiding-places. But in the adjoining room the sounds had entirely ceased, and Shorthouse soon crept into bed, and left the house with its inmates, waking or sleeping, to take care of themselves, while he entered the region of dreams and silence.

Next day, strong in the common sense that the sunlight brings, he determined to lodge a complaint against the noisy occupants of the next room and make the landlady request them to modify their voices at such late hours of the night and morning. But it so happened that she was not to be seen that day, and when he returned from the office at midnight it was, of course, too late.

Looking under the door as he came up to bed he noticed that there was no light, and concluded that the Germans were not in. So much the better. He went to sleep about one o'clock, fully decided that if they came up later and woke him with their horrible noises he would not rest till he had roused the landlady and made her reprove them with that authoritative twang, in which every word was like the lash of a metallic whip.

However, there proved to be no need for such drastic measures, for Shorthouse slumbered peacefully all night, and his dreams – chiefly of the fields of grain and flocks of sheep on the far-away farms of his father's estate – were permitted to run their fanciful course unbroken.

Two nights later, however, when he came home tired out, after a difficult day, and wet and blown about by one of the wickedest storms he had ever seen, his dreams – always of the fields and sheep – were not destined to be so undisturbed.

He had already dozed off in that delicious glow that follows the removal of wet clothes and the immediate snuggling under warm blankets, when his consciousness, hovering on the borderland between sleep and waking, was vaguely troubled by a sound that rose indistinctly from the depths of the house, and, between the gusts of wind and rain, reached his ears with an accompanying sense of uneasiness and discomfort. It rose on the night air with some pretence of regularity, dying away again in the roar of the wind to reassert itself distantly in the deep, brief hushes of the storm.

For a few minutes Jim's dreams were coloured only – tinged, as it were, by this impression of fear approaching from somewhere insensibly upon him. His consciousness, at first, refused to be drawn back from that enchanted region where it had wandered, and he did not immediately awaken. But the nature of his dreams changed unpleasantly. He saw the sheep suddenly run huddled together, as though frightened by the neighbourhood of an enemy, while the fields of waving corn became agitated as though some monster were moving uncouthly among the crowded stalks. The sky grew dark, and in his dream an awful sound came somewhere from the clouds. It was in reality the sound downstairs growing more distinct.

Shorthouse shifted uneasily across the bed with something like a groan of distress. The next minute he awoke, and found himself sitting straight up in bed – listening. Was it a nightmare? Had he been dreaming evil dreams, that his flesh crawled and the hair stirred on his head?

The room was dark and silent, but outside the wind howled dismally and drove the rain with repeated assaults against the rattling windows. How nice it would be – the thought flashed through his mind – if all winds, like the west wind, went down with the sun! They made such fiendish noises at night, like the crying of angry voices. In the daytime they had such a different sound. If only –

Hark! It was no dream after all, for the sound was momentarily growing louder, and its *cause* was coming up the stairs. He found himself speculating feebly what this cause might be, but the sound was still too indistinct to enable him to arrive at any definite conclusion.

The voice of a church clock striking two made itself heard above the wind. It was just about the hour when the Germans had commenced their performance three nights before. Shorthouse made up his mind that if they began it again he would not put up with it for very long. Yet he was already horribly conscious of the difficulty he would have of getting out of bed. The clothes were so warm and comforting against his back. The sound, still steadily coming nearer, had by this time become differentiated from the confused clamour of the elements, and had resolved itself into the footsteps of one or more persons.

'The Germans, hang 'em!' thought Jim. 'But what on earth is the matter with me? I never felt so queer in all my life.'

He was trembling all over, and felt as cold as though he were in a freezing atmosphere. His nerves were steady enough, and he felt no diminution of physical courage, but he was conscious of a curious sense of malaise and trepidation, such as even the most vigorous men have been known to experience when in the first grip of some horrible and deadly disease. As the footsteps approached this feeling of weakness increased. He felt a strange lassitude creeping over him, a sort of exhaustion, accompanied by a growing numbness in the extremities, and a sensation of dreaminess in the head, as if perhaps the consciousness were leaving its accustomed seat in the brain and preparing to act on another plane. Yet, strange to say, as the vitality was slowly withdrawn from his body, his senses seemed to grow more acute.

Meanwhile the steps were already on the landing at the top of the stairs, and Shorthouse, still sitting upright in bed, heard a heavy body brush past his door and along the wall outside, and almost immediately afterwards the loud knocking of someone's knuckles on the door of the adjoining room.

Instantly, though so far not a sound had proceeded from within, he heard, through the thin partition, a chair pushed back and a man quickly cross the floor and open the door.

'Ah! it's you,' he heard in the son's voice. Had the fellow, then, been sitting silently in there all this time, waiting for his father's arrival? To Shorthouse it came not as a pleasant reflection by any means.

There was no answer to this dubious greeting, but the door was closed, quickly, and then there was a sound as if a bag or parcel had been thrown on a wooden table and had slid some distance across it before stopping.

'What's that?' asked the son, with anxiety in his tone.

'You may know before I go,' returned the other gruffly. Indeed his voice was more than gruff: it betrayed ill-suppressed passion.

Shorthouse was conscious of a strong desire to stop the conversation before it proceeded any further, but somehow or other his will was not equal to the task, and he could not get out of bed. The conversation went on, every tone and inflexion distinctly audible above the noise of the storm.

In a low voice the father continued. Jim missed some of the words at the beginning of the sentence. It ended with: '... but now they've all left, and I've managed to get up to you. You know what I've come for.' There was distinct menace in his tone.

'Yes,' returned the other: 'I have been waiting.'

'And the money?' asked the father impatiently.

No answer.

'You've had three days to get it in, and I've contrived to stave off the worst so far – but tomorrow is the end.'

No answer.

'Speak, Otto! What have you got for me? Speak, my son; for God's sake, tell me.'

There was a moment's silence, during which the old man's vibrating accents seemed to echo through the rooms. Then came in a low voice the answer –

'I have nothing.'

'Otto!' cried the other with passion, 'nothing!'

'I can get nothing,' came almost in a whisper.

'You lie!' cried the other, in a half-stifled voice. 'I swear you lie. Give me the money.'

A chair was heard scraping along the floor. Evidently the men had been sitting over the table, and one of them had risen. Shorthouse heard the bag or parcel drawn across the table, and then a step as if one of the men was crossing to the door.

'Father, what's in that? I must know,' said Otto, with the first signs of determination in his voice. There must have been an effort on the son's part to gain possession of the parcel in question, and on the father's to retain it, for between them it fell to the ground. A curious rattle followed its contact with the floor. Instantly there were sounds of a scuffle. The men were struggling for the possession of the box. The elder man with oaths, and blasphemous imprecations, the other with short gasps that betokened the strength of his efforts. It was of short duration, and the younger man had evidently won, for a minute later was heard his angry exclamation.

'I knew it. Her jewels! You scoundrel, you shall never have them. It is a crime.'

The elder man uttered a short, guttural laugh, which froze Jim's blood and made his skin creep. No word was spoken, and for the space of ten seconds there was a living silence. Then the air trembled with the sound of a thud, followed immediately by a groan and the crash of a heavy body falling over on to the table. A second later there was a lurching from the table on to the floor and against the partition that separated the rooms. The bed quivered an instant at the shock, but the unholy spell was lifted from his soul and Jim Shorthouse sprang out of bed and across the floor in a single bound. He knew that ghastly murder had been done – the murder by a father of his son.

With shaking fingers but a determined heart he lit the gas, and the first thing in which his eyes corroborated the evidence of his ears was the horrifying detail that the lower portion of the partition bulged unnaturally into his own room. The glaring paper with which it was covered had cracked under the tension and the boards beneath it bent inwards towards him. What hideous load was behind them, he shuddered to think.

All this he saw in less than a second. Since the final lurch against the wall not a sound had proceeded from the room, not even a groan or a footstep. All was still but the howl of the wind, which to his ears had in it a note of triumphant horror.

Shorthouse was in the act of leaving the room to rouse the house and send for the police – in fact his hand was already on the door-knob – when something in the room arrested his attention. Out of the corner of his eyes he thought he caught sight of something moving. He was sure of it, and turning his eyes in the direction, he found he was not mistaken.

Something was creeping slowly towards him along the floor. It was something dark and serpentine in shape, and it came from the place where the partition bulged. He stooped down to examine it with feelings of intense horror and repugnance, and he discovered that it was moving towards him from the *other side* of the wall. His eyes were fascinated, and for the moment he was unable to move. Silently, slowly, from side to side like a thick worm, it crawled forward into the room beneath his frightened eyes, until at length he could stand it no longer and stretched out his arm to touch it. But at the instant of contact he withdrew his hand with a suppressed scream. It was sluggish – and it was warm! and he saw that his fingers were stained with living crimson.

A second more, and Shorthouse was out in the passage with his hand on the door of the next room. It was locked. He plunged forward with all his weight against it, and, the lock giving way, he fell headlong into a room that was pitch dark and very cold. In a moment he was on his feet again and trying to penetrate the blackness. Not a sound, not a movement. Not even the sense of a presence. It was empty, miserably empty!

Across the room he could trace the outline of a window with rain streaming down the outside, and the blurred lights of the city beyond. But the room was empty, appallingly empty; and so still. He stood there, cold as ice, staring, shivering, listening. Suddenly there was a step behind him and a light flashed into the room, and when he turned quickly with his arm up as if to ward off a terrific blow he found himself face to face with the landlady. Instantly the reaction began to set in.

It was nearly three o'clock in the morning, and he was standing there with bare feet and striped pyjamas in a small room, which in the merciful light he perceived to be absolutely empty, carpetless, and without a stick of furniture, or even a window-blind. There he stood staring at the disagreeable landlady. And there she stood too, staring and silent, in a black wrapper, her head almost bald, her face white as chalk, shading a sputtering candle with one bony hand and peering over it at him with her blinking green eyes. She looked positively hideous.

'Waal?' she drawled at length, 'I heard yer right enough. Guess you couldn't sleep! Or just prowlin' round a bit – is that it?'

The empty room, the absence of all traces of the recent tragedy, the silence, the hour, his striped pyjamas and bare feet – everything together combined to deprive him momentarily of speech. He stared at her blankly without a word.

'Waal?' clanked the awful voice.

'My dear woman,' he burst out finally, 'there's been something awful –' So far his desperation took him, but no farther. He positively stuck at the substantive.

'Oh! there hasn't been nothin',' she said slowly, still peering at him. 'I reckon you've only seen and heard what the others did. I never can keep folks on this floor long. Most of 'em catch on sooner or later – that is, the ones that's kind of quick and sensitive. Only you being an Englishman I thought you wouldn't mind. Nothin' really happens; it's only thinkin' like.'

Shorthouse was beside himself. He felt ready to pick her up and drop her over the banisters, candle and all.

'Look there,' he said, pointing at her within an inch of her blinking eyes with the fingers that had touched the oozing blood; 'look there, my good woman. Is that only thinking?'

She stared a minute, as if not knowing what he meant.

'I guess so,' she said at length.

He followed her eyes, and to his amazement saw that his fingers were as white as usual, and quite free from the awful stain that had been there ten minutes before. There was no sign of blood. No amount of staring could bring it back. Had he gone out of his mind? Had his eyes and ears played such tricks with him? Had his senses become false and perverted? He dashed past the landlady, out into the passage, and gained his own room in a couple of strides. Whew! ... the partition no longer bulged. The paper was not torn. There was no creeping, crawling thing on the faded old carpet.

'It's all over now,' drawled the metallic voice behind him. 'I'm going to bed again.'

He turned and saw the landlady slowly going downstairs again, still shading the candle with her hand and peering up at him from time to time as she moved. A black, ugly, unwholesome object, he thought, as she disappeared into the darkness below, and the last flicker of her candle threw a queer-shaped shadow along the wall and over the ceiling.

Without hesitating a moment, Shorthouse threw himself into his clothes and went out of the house. He preferred the

storm to the horrors of that top floor, and he walked the
streets till daylight. In the evening he told the landlady he
would leave next day, in spite of her assurances that nothing
more would happen.

'It never comes back,' she said – 'that is, not after he's
killed.'

Shorthouse gasped.

'You gave me a lot for my money,' he growled.

'Waal, it aren't my show,' she drawled. 'I'm no spirit
medium. You take chances. Some'll sleep right along and
never hear nothin'. Others, like yourself, are different and get
the whole thing.'

'Who's the old gentleman? – does he hear it?' asked Jim.

'There's no old gentleman at all,' she answered coolly. 'I
just told you that to make you feel easy like in case you did
hear anythin'. You were all alone on the floor.'

'Say now,' she went on, after a pause in which Shorthouse
could think of nothing to say but unpublishable things, 'say
now, do tell, did you feel sort of cold when the show was on,
sort of tired and weak, I mean, as if you might be going to
die?'

'How can I say?' he answered savagely; 'what I felt God
only knows.'

'Waal, but He won't tell,' she drawled out. 'Only I was
wonderin' how you really did feel, because the man who had
that room last was found one morning in bed –'

'In bed?'

'He was dead. He was the one before you. Oh! You don't
need to get rattled so. You're all right. And it all really happened, they do say. This house used to be a private residence
some twenty-five years ago, and a German family of the name
of Steinhardt lived here. They had a big business in Wall
Street, and stood 'way up in things.'

'Ah!' said her listener.

'Oh yes, they did, right at the top, till one fine day it all
burst and the old man skipped with the boodle –'

'Skipped with the boodle?'

'That's so,' she said; 'got clear away with all the money, and the son was found dead in his house, committed soocide it was thought. Though there was some as said he couldn't have stabbed himself and fallen in that position. They said he was murdered. The father died in prison. They tried to fasten the murder on him, but there was no motive, or no evidence, or no somethin'. I forget now.'

'Very pretty,' said Shorthouse.

'I'll show you somethin' mighty queer anyways,' she drawled, 'if you'll come upstairs a minute. I've heard the steps and voices lots of times; they don't pheaze me any. I'd just as lief hear so many dogs barkin'. You'll find the whole story in the newspapers if you look it up – not what goes on here, but the story of the Germans. My house would be ruined if they told all, and I'd sue for damages.'

They reached the bedroom, and the woman went in and pulled up the edge of the carpet where Shorthouse had seen the blood soaking in the previous night.

'Look thar, if you feel like it,' said the old hag. Stooping down, he saw a dark, dull stain in the boards that corresponded exactly to the shape and position of the blood as he had seen it.

That night he slept in a hotel, and the following day sought new quarters. In the newspapers on file in his office after a long search he found twenty years back the detailed story, substantially as the woman had said, of Steinhardt & Co.'s failure, the absconding and subsequent arrest of the senior partner, and the suicide, or murder, of his son Otto. The landlady's room-house had formerly been their private residence.

Ancient Sorceries

1

There are, it would appear, certain wholly unremarkable persons, with none of the characteristics that invite adventure, who yet once or twice in the course of their smooth lives undergo an experience so strange that the world catches its breath – and looks the other way! And it was cases of this kind, perhaps, more than any other, that fell into the widespread net of John Silence, the psychic doctor, and, appealing to his deep humanity, to his patience, and to his great qualities of spiritual sympathy, led often to the revelation of problems of the strangest complexity, and of the profoundest possible human interest.

Matters that seemed almost too curious and fantastic for belief he loved to trace to their hidden sources. To unravel a tangle in the very soul of things – and to release a suffering human soul in the process – was with him a veritable passion. And the knots he untied were, indeed, often passing strange.

The world, of course, asks for some plausible basis to which it can attach credence – something it can, at least, pretend to explain. The adventurous type it can understand: such people carry about with them an adequate explanation of their exciting lives, and their characters obviously drive them into the circumstances which produce the adventures. It expects nothing else from them, and is satisfied. But dull, ordinary folk have no right to out-of-the-way experiences, and the world having been led to expect otherwise, is disappointed with them, not to say shocked. Its complacent judgement has been rudely disturbed.

'Such a thing happen to *that* man!' it cries – 'a commonplace person like that! It is too absurd! There must be something wrong!'

Yet there could be no question that something did actually happen to little Arthur Vezin, something of the curious nature he described to Dr Silence. Outwardly, or inwardly, it happened beyond a doubt, and in spite of the jeers of his few friends who heard the tale, and observed wisely that 'such a thing might perhaps have come to Iszard, that crack-brained Iszard, or to that odd fish Minski, but it could never have happened to commonplace little Vezin, who was fore-ordained to live and die according to scale.'

But, whatever his method of death was, Vezin certainly did not 'live according to scale' so far as this particular event in his otherwise uneventful life was concerned; and to hear him recount it, and watch his pale delicate features change, and hear his voice grow softer and more hushed as he proceeded, was to know the conviction that his halting words perhaps failed sometimes to convey. He lived the thing over again each time he told it. His whole personality became muffled in the recital. It subdued him more than ever, so that the tale became a lengthy apology for an experience that he deprecated. He appeared to excuse himself and ask your pardon for having dared to take part in so fantastic an episode. For little Vezin was a timid, gentle, sensitive soul, rarely able to assert himself, tender to man and beast, and almost constitutionally unable to say No, or to claim many things that should rightly have been his. His whole scheme of life seemed utterly remote from anything more exciting than missing a train or losing an umbrella on an omnibus. And when this curious event came upon him he was already more years beyond forty than his friends suspected or he cared to admit.

John Silence, who heard him speak of his experience more than once, said that he sometimes left out certain details and put in others; yet they were all obviously true. The whole scene was unforgettably cinematographed on to his mind. None of the details were imagined or invented. And when he told the story with them all complete, the effect was undeniable. His appealing brown eyes shone, and much of the charming personality, usually so carefully repressed, came forward and revealed itself. His modesty was always there, of course, but in the telling he forgot the present and allowed himself to appear almost vividly as he lived again in the past of his adventure.

He was on the way home when it happened, crossing northern France from some mountain trip or other where he buried himself solitary-wise every summer. He had nothing but an unregistered bag in the rack, and the train was jammed to suffocation, most of the passengers being unredeemed holiday English. He disliked them, not because they were his fellow-countrymen, but because they were noisy and obtrusive, obliterating with their big limbs and tweed clothing all the quieter tints of the day that brought him satisfaction and enabled him to melt into insignificance and forget that he was anybody. These English clashed about him like a brass band, making him feel vaguely that he ought to be more self-assertive and obstreperous, and that he did not claim insistently enough all kinds of things that he didn't want and that were really valueless, such as corner seats, windows up or down, and so forth.

So that he felt uncomfortable in the train, and wished the journey were over and he was back again living with his unmarried sister in Surbiton.

And when the train stopped for ten panting minutes at the little station in northern France, and he got out to stretch his legs on the platform, and saw to his dismay a further batch of the British Isles debouching from another train, it suddenly seemed impossible to him to continue the journey. Even *his* flabby soul revolted, and the idea of staying a night in the little town and going on next day by a slower, emptier train, flashed into his mind. The guard was already shouting '*en voiture*' and the corridor of his compartment was already packed when the thought came to him. And, for once, he acted with decision and rushed to snatch his bag.

Finding the corridor and steps impassable, he tapped at the window (for he had a corner seat) and begged the Frenchman who sat opposite to hand his luggage out to him, explaining in his wretched French that he intended to break the journey there. And this elderly Frenchman, he declared, gave him a look, half of warning, half of reproach, that to his dying day he could never forget; handed the bag through the window of the moving train; and at the same time poured into his ears a long sentence, spoken rapidly and low, of which he was able to comprehend only the last few words: '*à cause du sommeil et à cause des chats.*'

In reply to Dr Silence, whose singular psychic acuteness at once seized upon this Frenchman as a vital point in the adventure, Vezin admitted that the man had impressed him favourably from the beginning, though without being able to explain why. They had sat facing one another during the four hours of the journey, and though no conversation had passed between them – Vezin was timid about his stuttering French – he confessed that his eyes were being continually drawn to his face, almost, he felt, to rudeness, and that each, by a dozen nameless little politenesses and attentions, had evinced the desire to be kind. The men liked each other and their personalities did not clash, or would not have clashed had they chanced to come to terms of acquaintance. The Frenchman, indeed, seemed to have exercised a silent protective influence over the insignificant little Englishman, and without words or gestures betrayed that he wished him well and would gladly have been of service to him.

'And this sentence that he hurled at you after the bag?' asked John Silence, smiling that peculiarly sympathetic smile that always melted the prejudices of his patient, 'were you unable to follow it exactly?'

'It was so quick and low and vehement,' explained Vezin, in his small voice, 'that I missed practically the whole of it. I only caught the few words at the very end, because he spoke them so clearly, and his face was bent down out of the carriage window so near to mine.'

'"*À cause du sommeil et à cause des chats*"' repeated Dr Silence, as though half speaking to himself.

'That's it exactly,' said Vezin; 'which, I take it, means something like "because of sleep and because of the cats", doesn't it?'

'Certainly, that's how I should translate it,' the doctor observed shortly, evidently not wishing to interrupt more than necessary.

'And the rest of the sentence – all the first part I couldn't understand, I mean – was a warning not to do something – not to stop in the town, or at some particular place in the town, perhaps. That was the impression it made on me.'

Then, of course, the train rushed off, and left Vezin standing on the platform alone and rather forlorn.

The little town climbed in straggling fashion up a sharp hill rising out of the plain at the back of the station, and was crowned by the twin towers of the ruined cathedral peeping over the summit. From the station itself it looked uninteresting and modern, but the fact was that the medieval position lay out of sight just beyond the crest. And once he reached the top and entered the old streets, he stepped clean out of modern life into a bygone century. The noise and bustle of the crowded train seemed days away. The spirit of this silent hill-town, remote from tourists and motor-cars, dreaming its own quiet life under the autumn sun, rose up and cast its spell upon him. Long before he recognized this spell he acted under it. He walked softly, almost on tiptoe down the winding narrow streets where the gables all but met over his head, and he entered the doorway of the solitary inn with a deprecating and modest demeanour that was in itself an apology for intruding upon the place and disturbing its dream.

At first, however, Vezin said, he noticed very little of all this. The attempt at analysis came much later. What struck him then was only the delightful contrast of the silence and peace after the dust and noisy rattle of the train. He felt soothed and stroked like a cat.

'Like a cat, you said?' interrupted John Silence, quickly catching him up.

'Yes. At the very start I felt that.' He laughed apologetically. 'I felt as though the warmth and the stillness and the comfort made me purr. It seemed to be the general mood of the whole place – then.'

The inn, a rambling ancient house, the atmosphere of the old coaching days still about it, apparently did not welcome him too warmly. He felt he was only tolerated, he said. But it was cheap and comfortable, and the delicious cup of afternoon tea he ordered at once made him feel really very pleased with himself for leaving the train in this bold, original way. For to him it had seemed bold and original. He felt something of a dog. His room, too, soothed him with its dark panelling and low irregular ceiling, and the long sloping passage that led to it seemed the natural pathway to a real Chamber of Sleep – a little dim cubby hole out of the world where noise could not enter. It looked upon the courtyard at the back. It was all very charming, and made him think of himself as dressed in very soft velvet somehow, and the floors seemed padded, the walls provided with cushions. The sounds of the streets could not penetrate there. It was an atmosphere of absolute rest that surrounded him.

On engaging the two-franc room he had interviewed the only person who seemed to be about that sleepy afternoon, an elderly waiter with Dundreary whiskers and a drowsy courtesy, who had ambled lazily towards him across the stone yard; but on coming downstairs again for a little promenade in the town before dinner he encountered the proprietress herself. She was a large woman whose hands, feet, and features seemed to swim towards him out of a sea of person. They emerged, so to speak. But she had great dark, vivacious eyes that counteracted the bulk of her body, and betrayed the fact that in reality she was both vigorous and alert. When he first caught sight of her she was knitting in a low chair against the sunlight of the wall, and something at once made him see her as a great tabby cat, dozing, yet awake, heavily sleepy, and yet at the same time prepared for instantaneous action. A great mouser on the watch occurred to him.

She took him in with a single comprehensive glance that was polite without being cordial. Her neck, he noticed, was extraordinarily supple in spite of its proportions, for it turned so easily to follow him, and the head it carried bowed so very flexibly.

'But when she looked at me, you know,' said Vezin, with that little apologetic smile in his brown eyes, and that faintly deprecating gesture of the shoulders that was characteristic of him, 'the odd notion came to me that really she had intended to make quite a different movement, and that with a single bound she could have leaped at me across the width of that stone yard and pounced upon me like some huge cat upon a mouse.'

He laughed a little soft laugh, and Dr Silence made a note in his book without interrupting, while Vezin proceeded in a tone as though he feared he had already told too much and more than we could believe.

'Very soft, yet very active she was, for all her size and mass, and I felt she knew what I was doing even after I had passed and was behind her back. She spoke to me, and her voice was smooth and running. She asked if I had my luggage, and was comfortable in my room, and then added that dinner was at seven o'clock, and that they were very early people in this little country town. Clearly, she intended to convey that late hours were not encouraged.'

Evidently, she contrived by voice and manner to give him the impression that here he would be 'managed', that everything would be arranged and planned for him, and that he had nothing to do but fall into the groove and obey. No decided action or sharp personal effort would be looked for from him. It was the very reverse of the train. He walked quietly out into the street feeling soothed and peaceful. He realized that he was in a *milieu* that suited him and stroked him the right way. It was so much easier to be obedient. He began to purr again, and to feel that all the town purred with him.

About the streets of that little town he meandered gently,
falling deeper and deeper into the spirit of repose that charac-
terized it. With no special aim he wandered up and down, and
to and fro. The September sunshine fell slantingly over the
roofs. Down winding alleyways, fringed with tumbling gables
and open casements, he caught fairylike glimpses of the great
plain below, and of the meadows and yellow copses lying like
a dream-map in the haze. The spell of the past held very po-
tently here, he felt.

The streets were full of picturesquely garbed men and
women, all busy enough, going their respective ways; but no
one took any notice of him or turned to stare at his obviously
English appearance. He was even able to forget that with his
tourist appearance he was a false note in a charming picture,
and he melted more and more into the scene, feeling delight-
fully insignificant and unimportant and unselfconscious. It
was like becoming part of a softly-coloured dream which he
did not even realize to be a dream.

On the eastern side the hill fell away more sharply, and the
plain below ran off rather suddenly into a sea of gathering
shadows in which the little patches of woodland looked like
islands and the stubble fields like deep water. Here he strolled
along the old ramparts of ancient fortifications that once had
been formidable, but now were only vision-like with their
charming mingling of broken grey walls and wayward vine
and ivy. From the broad coping on which he sat for a
moment, level with the rounded tops of clipped plane trees, he
saw the esplanade far below lying in shadow. Here and there
a yellow sunbeam crept in and lay upon the fallen yellow
leaves, and from the height he looked down and saw that the
townsfolk were walking to and fro in the cool of the evening.
He could just hear the sound of their slow footfalls, and the
murmur of their voices floated up to him through the gaps
between the trees. The figures looked like shadows as he caught
glimpses of their quiet movements far below.

He sat there for some time pondering, bathed in the waves
of murmurs and half-lost echoes that rose to his ears, muffled

by the leaves of the plane trees. The whole town, and the little hill out of which it grew as naturally as an ancient wood, seemed to him like a being lying there half asleep on the plain and crooning to itself as it dozed.

And, presently, as he sat lazily melting into its dream, a sound of horns and strings and wood instruments rose to his ears, and the town band began to play at the far end of the crowded terrace below to the accompaniment of a very soft, deep-throated drum. Vezin was very sensitive to music, knew about it intelligently, and had even ventured, unknown to his friends, upon the composition of quiet melodies with low-running chords which he played to himself with the soft pedal when no one was about. And this music floating up through the trees from an invisible and doubtless very picturesque band of the townspeople wholly charmed him. He recognized nothing that they played, and it sounded as though they were simply improvising without a conductor. No definitely marked time ran through the pieces, which ended and began oddly after the fashion of wind through an Aeolian harp. It was part of the place and scene, just as the dying sunlight and faintly-breathing wind were part of the scene and hour, and the mellow notes of old-fashioned plaintive horns, pierced here and there by the sharper strings, all half smothered by the continuous booming of the deep drum, touched his soul with a curiously potent spell that was almost too engrossing to be quite pleasant.

There was a certain queer sense of bewitchment in it all. The music seemed to him oddly unartificial. It made him think of trees swept by the wind, of night breezes singing among wires and chimney-stacks, or in the rigging of invisible ships; or – and the simile leaped up in his thoughts with a sudden sharpness of suggestion – a chorus of animals, of wild creatures, somewhere in desolate places of the world, crying and singing as animals will, to the moon. He could fancy he heard the wailing, half-human cries of cats upon the tiles at night, rising and falling with weird intervals of sound, and this music, muffled by distance and the trees, made him think of a queer company of these creatures on some roof far away in the sky, uttering their solemn music to one another and the moon in chorus.

It was, he felt at the time, a singular image to occur to him, yet it expressed his sensation pictorially better than anything else. The instruments played such impossibly odd intervals, and the crescendos and diminuendos were so very suggestive of cat-land on the tiles at night, rising swiftly, dropping without warning to deep notes again, and all in such strange confusion of discords and accords. But, at the same time a plaintive sweetness resulted on the whole, and the discords of these half-broken instruments were so singular that they did not distress his musical soul like fiddles out of tune.

He listened a long time, wholly surrendering himself as his character was, and then strolled homewards in the dusk as the air grew chilly.

'There was nothing to alarm?' put in Dr Silence briefly.

'Absolutely nothing,' said Vezin; 'but you know it was all so fantastical and charming that my imagination was profoundly impressed. Perhaps, too,' he continued, gently explanatory, 'it was this stirring of my imagination that caused other impressions; for, as I walked back, the spell of the place began to steal over me in a dozen ways, though all intelligible ways. But there were other things I could not account for in the least, even then.'

'Incidents, you mean?'

'Hardly incidents, I think. A lot of vivid sensations crowded themselves upon my mind and I could trace them to no causes. It was just after sunset and the tumbled old buildings traced magical outlines against an opalescent sky of gold and red. The dusk was running down the twisted streets. All round the hill the plain pressed in like a dim sea, its level rising with the darkness. The spell of this kind of scene, you know, can be very moving, and it was so that night. Yet I felt that what came to me had nothing directly to do with the mystery and wonder of the scene.'

'Not merely the subtle transformations of the spirit that

come with beauty,' put in the doctor, noticing his hesitation.

'Exactly,' Vezin went on, duly encouraged and no longer so fearful of our smiles at his expense. 'The impressions came from somewhere else. For instance, down the busy main street where men and women were bustling home from work, shopping at stalls and barrows, idly gossiping in groups, and all the rest of it, I saw that I aroused no interest and that no one turned to stare at me as a foreigner and stranger. I was utterly ignored, and my presence among them excited no special interest or attention.

'And then, quite suddenly, it dawned upon me with conviction that all the time this indifference and inattention were merely feigned. Everybody as a matter of fact was watching me closely. Every movement I made was known and observed. Ignoring me was all a pretence – an elaborate pretence.'

He paused a moment and looked at us to see if we were smiling, and then continued, reassured –

'It is useless to ask me how I noticed this, because I simply cannot explain it. But the discovery gave me something of a shock. Before I got back to the inn, however, another curious thing rose up strongly in my mind and forced my recognition of it as true. And this, too, I may as well say at once, was equally inexplicable to me. I mean I can only give you the fact, as fact it was to me.'

The little man left his chair and stood on the mat before the fire. His diffidence lessened from now onwards, and he lost himself again in the magic of the old adventure. His eyes shone a little already as he talked.

'Well,' he went on, his soft voice rising somewhat with his excitement, 'I was in a shop when it came to me first – though the idea must have been at work for a long time subconsciously to appear in so complete a form all at once. I was buying socks, I think,' he laughed, 'and struggling with my dreadful French, when it struck me that the woman in the shop did not care two pins whether I bought anything or not. She was indifferent whether she made a sale or did not make a sale. She was only pretending to sell.

'This sounds a very small and fanciful incident to build upon what follows. But really it was not small. I mean it was the spark that lit the line of powder and ran along to the big blaze in my mind.

'For the whole town, I suddenly realized, was something other than I so far saw it. The real activities and interests of the people were elsewhere and otherwise than appeared. Their true lives lay somewhere out of sight behind the scenes. Their busy-ness was but the outward semblance that masked their actual purposes. They bought and sold, and ate and drank, and walked about the streets, yet all the while the main stream of their existence lay somewhere beyond my ken, underground, in secret places. In the shops and at the stalls they did not care whether I purchased their articles or not; at the inn, they were indifferent to my staying or going; their life lay remote from my own, springing from hidden, mysterious sources, coursing out of sight, unknown. It was all a great elaborate pretence, assumed possibly for my benefit, or possibly for purposes of their own. But the main current of their energies ran elsewhere. I almost felt as an unwelcome foreign substance might be expected to feel when it has found its way into the human system and the whole body organizes itself to eject it or to absorb it. The town was doing this very thing to me.

'This bizarre notion presented itself forcibly to my mind as I walked home to the inn, and I began busily to wonder wherein the true life of this town could lie and what were the actual interests and activities of its hidden life.

'And, now that my eyes were partly opened, I noticed other things too that puzzled me, first of which, I think, was the extraordinary silence of the whole place. Positively, the town was muffled. Although the streets were paved with cobbles the people moved about silently, softly, with padded feet, like cats. Nothing made noise. All was hushed, subdued, muted. The very voices were quiet, low-pitched like purring. Nothing clamourous, vehement or emphatic seemed able to live in the drowsy atmosphere of soft dreaming that soothed this little hill-town into its sleep. It was like the woman at the inn – an outward repose screening intense inner activity and purpose.

'Yet there was no sign of lethargy or sluggishness anywhere about it. The people were active and alert. Only a magical and uncanny softness lay over them all like a spell.'

Vezin passed his hand across his eyes for a moment as though the memory had become very vivid. His voice had run off into a whisper so that we heard the last part with difficulty. He was telling a true thing obviously, yet something that he both liked and hated telling.

'I went back to the inn,' he continued presently in a louder voice, 'and dined. I felt a new strange world about me. My old world of reality receded. Here, whether I liked it or no, was something new and incomprehensible. I regretted having left the train so impulsively. An adventure was upon me, and I loathed adventures as foreign to my nature. Moreover, this was the beginning apparently of an adventure somewhere deep within me, in a region I could not check or measure, and a feeling of alarm mingled itself with my wonder – alarm for the stability of what I had for forty years recognized as my "personality".

'I went upstairs to bed, my mind teeming with thoughts that were unusual to me, and of rather a haunting description. By way of relief I kept thinking of that nice, prosaic noisy train and all those wholesome, blustering passengers. I almost wished I were with them again. But my dreams took me elsewhere. I dreamed of cats, and soft-moving creatures, and the silence of life in a dim muffled world beyond the senses.'

2

Vezin stayed on from day to day, indefinitely, much longer than he had intended. He felt in a kind of dazed, somnolent condition. He did nothing in particular, but the place fascinated him and he could not decide to leave. Decisions were always very difficult for him and he sometimes wondered how he had ever brought himself to the point of leaving the train. It seemed as though some one else must have arranged it for him, and once or twice his thoughts ran to the swarthy Frenchman who had sat opposite. If only he could have understood that long sentence ending so strangely with '*à cause du sommeil et à cause des chats*.' He wondered what it all meant.

Meanwhile the hushed softness of the town held him prisoner and he sought in his muddling, gentle way to find out where the mystery lay, and what it was all about. But his limited French and his constitutional hatred of active investigation made it hard for him to buttonhole anybody and ask questions. He was content to observe, and watch, and remain negative.

The weather held on calm and hazy, and this just suited him. He wandered about the town till he knew every street and alley. The people suffered him to come and go without let or hindrance, though it became clearer to him every day that he was never free himself from observation. The town watched him as a cat watches a mouse. And he got no nearer to finding out what they were all so busy with or where the main stream of their activities lay. This remained hidden. The people were as soft and mysterious as cats.

But that he was continually under observation became more evident from day to day.

For instance, when he strolled to the end of the town and entered a little green public garden beneath the ramparts and seated himself upon one of the empty benches in the sun, he was quite alone – at first. Not another seat was occupied; the little park was empty, the paths deserted. Yet, within ten minutes of his coming, there must have been fully twenty persons scattered about him, some strolling aimlessly along the gravel walks, staring at the flowers, and others seated on the wooden benches enjoying the sun like himself. None of them appeared to take any notice of him; yet he understood quite well they had all come there to watch. They kept him under close observation. In the street they had seemed busy enough, hurrying upon various errands; yet these were suddenly all forgotten and they had nothing to do but loll and laze in the sun, their duties unremembered. Five minutes after he left, the garden was again deserted, the seats vacant. But in the crowded street it was the same thing again; he was never alone. He was ever in their thoughts.

By degrees, too, he began to see how it was he was so cleverly watched, yet without the appearance of it. The people did nothing *directly*. They behaved *obliquely*. He laughed in his mind as the thought thus clothed itself in words, but the phrase exactly described it. They looked at him from angles which naturally should have led their sight in another direction altogether. Their movements were oblique, too, so far as these concerned himself. The straight, direct thing was not their way evidently. They did nothing obviously. If he entered a shop to buy, the woman walked instantly away and busied herself with something at the farther end of the counter, though answering at once when he spoke, showing that she knew he was there and that this was only her way of attending to him. It was the fashion of the cat she followed. Even in the dining-room of the inn, the be-whiskered and courteous waiter, lithe and silent in all his movements, never seemed able to come straight to his table for an order or a dish. He came by zigzags, indirectly, vaguely, so that he appeared to be going to another table altogether, and only turned suddenly at the last moment, and was there beside him.

Vezin smiled curiously to himself as he described how he began to realize these things. Other tourists there were none in the hostel, but he recalled the figures of one or two old men, inhabitants, who took their *déjeuner* and dinner there, and remembered how fantastically they entered the room in similar fashion. First, they paused in the doorway, peering about the room, and then, after a temporary inspection, they came in, as it were, sideways, keeping close to the walls so that he wondered which table they were making for, and at the last minute making almost a little quick run to their particular seats. And again he thought of the ways and methods of cats.

Other small incidents, too, impressed him as all part of this queer, soft town with its muffled, indirect life, for the way some of the people appeared and disappeared with extraordinary swiftness puzzled him exceedingly. It may have been all perfectly natural, he knew, yet he could not make it out how the alleys swallowed them up and shot them forth in a second of time when there were no visible doorways or openings near enough to explain the phenomenon. Once he followed two elderly women who, he felt, had been particularly examining him from across the street – quite near the inn this was – and saw them turn the corner a few feet only in front of him. Yet when he sharply followed on their heels he saw nothing but an utterly deserted alley stretching in front of him with no sign of a living thing. And the only opening through which they could have escaped was a porch some fifty yards away, which not the swiftest human runner could have reached in time.

And in just such sudden fashion people appeared when he never expected them. Once when he heard a great noise of fighting going on behind a low wall, and hurried up to see what was going on, what should he see but a group of girls and women engaged in vociferous conversation which instantly hushed itself to the normal whispering note of the town when his head appeared over the wall. And even then none of them turned to look at him directly, but slunk off with the most unaccountable rapidity into doors and sheds across the yard. And their voices, he thought, had sounded so like, so strangely like, the angry snarling of fighting animals, almost of cats.

The whole spirit of the town, however, continued to evade him as something elusive, protean, screened from the outer world, and at the same time intensely, genuinely vital; and, since he now formed part of its life, this concealment puzzled and irritated him; more – it began rather to frighten him.

Out of the mists that slowly gathered about his ordinary surface thoughts, there rose again the idea that the inhabitants were waiting for him to declare himself, to take an attitude, to do this, or to do that; and that when he had done so they in their turn would at length make some direct response, accepting or rejecting him. Yet the vital matter concerning which his decision was awaited came no nearer to him.

Once or twice he purposely followed little processions or groups of the citizens in order to find out, if possible, on what purpose they were bent; but they always discovered him in time and dwindled away, each individual going his or her own way. It was always the same: he never could learn what their main interest was. The cathedral was ever empty, the old church of St Martin, at the other end of the town, deserted. They shopped because they had to, and not because they wished to. The booths stood neglected, the stalls unvisited, the little cafés desolate. Yet the streets were always full, the townsfolk ever on the bustle.

'Can it be,' he thought to himself, yet with a deprecating laugh that he should have dared to think anything so odd, 'can it be that these people are people of the twilight, that they live only at night their real life, and come out honestly only with the dusk? That during the day they make a sham though brave pretence, and after the sun is down their true life begins? Have they the souls of night-things, and is the whole blessed town in the hands of the cats?'

The fancy somehow electrified him with little shocks of shrinking and dismay. Yet, though he affected to laugh, he knew that he was beginning to feel more than uneasy, and that strange forces were tugging with a thousand invisible cords at the very centre of his being. Something utterly remote from his ordinary life, something that had not waked for years, began faintly to stir in his soul, sending feelers abroad into his brain and heart, shaping queer thoughts and penetrating even into certain of his minor actions. Something exceedingly vital to himself, to his soul, hung in the balance.

And, always when he returned to the inn about the hour of sunset, he saw the figures of the townsfolk stealing through the dusk from their shop doors, moving sentry-wise to and fro at the corners of the streets, yet always vanishing silently like shadows at his near approach. And as the inn invariably closed its doors at ten o'clock he had never yet found the opportunity he rather half-heartedly sought to see for himself what account the town could give of itself at night.

'– *à cause du sommeil et à cause des chats*' – the words now rang in his ears more and more often, though still as yet without any definite meaning.

Moreover, something made him sleep like the dead.

3

It was, I think, on the fifth day – though in this detail his story sometimes varied – that he made a definite discovery which increased his alarm and brought him up to a rather sharp climax. Before that he had already noticed that a change was going forward and certain subtle transformations being brought about in his character which modified several of his minor habits. And he had affected to ignore them. Here, however, was something he could no longer ignore; and it startled him.

At the best of times he was never very positive, always negative rather, compliant and acquiescent; yet, when necessity arose he was capable of reasonably vigorous action and could take a strongish decision. The discovery he now made that brought him up with such a sharp turn was that this power had positively dwindled to nothing. He found it impossible to make up his mind. For, on this fifth day, he realized that he had stayed long enough in the town and that for reasons he could only vaguely define to himself it was wiser *and safer* that he should leave.

And he found that he could not leave!

This is difficult to describe in words, and it was more by gesture and the expression of his face that he conveyed to Dr Silence the state of impotence he had reached. All this spying and watching, he said, had as it were spun a net about his feet so that he was trapped and powerless to escape; he felt like a fly that had blundered into the intricacies of a great web; he was caught, imprisoned, and could not get away. It was a distressing sensation. A numbness had crept over his will till it had become almost incapable of decision. The mere thought of vigorous action – action towards escape – began to terrify him. All the currents of his life had turned inwards upon himself, striving to bring to the surface something that lay buried almost beyond reach, determined to force his recognition of something he had long forgotten – forgotten years upon years, centuries almost ago. It seemed as though a window deep within his being would presently open and reveal an entirely new world, yet somehow a world that was not unfamiliar. Beyond that, again, he fancied a great curtain hung; and when that too rolled up he would see still farther into this region and at last understand something of the secret life of these extraordinary people.

'Is this why they wait and watch?' he asked himself with rather a shaking heart, 'for the time when I shall join them – or refuse to join them? Does the decision rest with me after all, and not with them?'

And it was at this point that the sinister character of the adventure first really declared itself, and he became genuinely alarmed. The stability of his rather fluid personality was at stake, he felt, and something in his heart turned coward.

Why otherwise should he have suddenly taken to walking stealthily, silently, making as little sound as possible, for ever looking behind him? Why else should he have moved almost on tiptoe about the passages of the practically deserted inn, and when he was abroad have found himself deliberately taking advantage of what cover presented itself? And why, if he was not afraid, should the wisdom of staying indoors after sundown have suddenly occurred to him as eminently desirable? Why, indeed?

And, when John Silence gently pressed him for an explanation of these things, he admitted apologetically that he had none to give.

'It was simply that I feared something might happen to me unless I kept a sharp look-out. I felt afraid. It was instinctive,' was all he could say. 'I got the impression that the whole town was after me – wanted me for something; and that if it got me I should lose myself, or at least the Self I knew, in some unfamiliar state of consciousness. But I am not a psychologist, you know,' he added meekly, 'and I cannot define it better than that.'

It was while lounging in the courtyard half an hour before the evening meal that Vezin made this discovery, and he at once went upstairs to his quiet room at the end of the winding passage to think it over alone. In the yard it was empty enough, true, but there was always the possibility that the big woman whom he dreaded would come out of some door, with her pretence of knitting, to sit and watch him. This had happened several times, and he could not endure the sight of her. He still remembered his original fancy, bizarre though it was, that she would spring upon him the moment his back was turned and land with one single crushing leap upon his neck. Of course it was nonsense, but then it haunted him, and once an idea begins to do that it ceases to be nonsense. It has clothed itself in reality.

He went upstairs accordingly. It was dusk, and the oil lamps had not yet been lit in the passages. He stumbled over the uneven surface of the ancient flooring, passing the dim outlines of doors along the corridor – doors that he had never once seen opened – rooms that seemed never occupied. He moved, as his habit now was, stealthily and on tiptoe.

Half-way down the last passage to his own chamber there was a sharp turn, and it was just here, while groping round the walls with outstretched hands, that his fingers touched something that was not wall – something that moved. It was soft and warm in texture, indescribably fragrant, and about the height of his shoulder; and he immediately thought of a furry, sweet-smelling kitten. The next minute he knew it was something quite different.

Instead of investigating, however, – his nerves must have

been too overwrought for that, he said, – he shrank back as closely as possible against the wall on the other side. The thing, whatever it was, slipped past him with a sound of rustling, and retreating with light footsteps down the passage behind him, was gone. A breath of warm, scented air was wafted to his nostrils.

Vezin caught his breath for an instant and paused, stock-still, half leaning against the wall – and then almost ran down the remaining distance and entered his room with a rush, locking the door hurriedly behind him. Yet it was not fear that made him run: it was excitement, pleasurable excitement. His nerves were tingling, and a delicious glow made itself felt all over his body. In a flash it came to him that this was just what he had felt twenty-five years ago as a boy when he was in love for the first time. Warm currents of life ran all over him and mounted to his brain in a whirl of soft delight. His mood was suddenly become tender, melting, loving.

The room was quite dark, and he collapsed upon the sofa by the window, wondering what had happened to him and what it all meant. But the only thing he understood clearly in that instant was that something in him had swiftly, magically changed: he no longer wished to leave, or to argue with himself about leaving. The encounter in the passage-way had changed all that. The strange perfume of it still hung about him, bemusing his heart and mind. For he knew that it was a girl who had passed him, a girl's face that his fingers had brushed in the darkness, and he felt in some extraordinary way as though he had been actually kissed by her, kissed full upon the lips.

Trembling, he sat upon the sofa by the window and struggled to collect his thoughts. He was utterly unable to understand how the mere passing of a girl in the darkness of a narrow passage-way could communicate so electric a thrill to his whole being that he still shook with the sweetness of it. Yet, there it was! And he found it as useless to deny as to attempt analysis. Some ancient fire had entered his veins, and now ran coursing through his blood; and that he was forty-

five instead of twenty did not matter one little jot. Out of all
the inner turmoil and confusion emerged the one salient fact
that the mere atmosphere, the merest casual touch, of this
girl, unseen, unknown in the darkness, had been sufficient to
stir dormant fires in the centre of his heart, and rouse his
whole being from a state of feeble sluggishness to one of tearing and tumultuous excitement.

After a time, however, the number of Vezin's years began
to assert their cumulative power; he grew calmer; and when
a knock came at length upon his door and he heard the waiter's
voice suggesting that dinner was nearly over, he pulled himself together and slowly made his way downstairs into the
dining-room.

Every one looked up as he entered, for he was very late, but
he took his customary seat in the far corner and began to
eat. The trepidation was still in his nerves, but the fact that he
had passed through the courtyard and hall without catching
sight of a petticoat served to calm him a little. He ate so fast
that he had almost caught up with the current stage of the
table d'hôte, when a slight commotion in the room drew his
attention.

His chair was so placed that the door and the greater portion of the long *salle à manger* were behind him, yet it was not
necessary to turn round to know that the same person he had
passed in the dark passage had now come into the room. He
felt the presence long before he heard or saw any one. Then
he became aware that the old men, the only other guests,
were rising one by one in their places, and exchanging greetings with some one who passed among them from table to
table. And when at length he turned with his heart beating
furiously to ascertain for himself, he saw the form of a young
girl, lithe and slim, moving down the centre of the room and
making straight for his own table in the corner. She moved
wonderfully, with sinuous grace, like a young panther, and
her approach filled him with such delicious bewilderment that
he was utterly unable to tell at first what her face was like, or
discover what it was about the whole presentment of the

creature that filled him anew with trepidation and delight.

'Ah, Ma'mselle est de retour!' he heard the old waiter murmur at his side, and he was just able to take in that she was the daughter of the proprietress, when she was upon him, and he heard her voice. She was addressing him. Something of red lips he saw and laughing white teeth, and stray wisps of fine dark hair about the temples; but all the rest was a dream in which his own emotions rose like a thick cloud before his eyes and prevented his seeing accurately, or knowing exactly what he did. He was aware that she greeted him with a charming little bow; that her beautiful large eyes looked searchingly into his own; that the perfume he had noticed in the dark passage again assailed his nostrils, and that she was bending a little towards him and leaning with one hand on the table at his side. She was quite close to him – that was the chief thing he knew – explaining that she had been asking after the comfort of her mother's guests, and was now introducing herself to the latest arrival – himself.

'M'sieur has already been here a few days,' he heard the waiter say; and then her own voice, sweet as singing, replied –

'Ah, but M'sieur is not going to leave us just yet, I hope. My mother is too old to look after the comfort of our guests properly, but now I am here I will remedy all that.' She laughed deliciously. 'M'sieur shall be well looked after.'

Vezin, struggling with his emotion and desire to be polite, half rose to acknowledge the pretty speech, and to stammer some sort of reply, but as he did so his hand by chance touched her own that was resting upon the table, and a shock that was for all the world like a shock of electricity, passed from her skin into his body. His soul wavered and shook deep within him. He caught her eyes fixed upon his own with a look of most curious intentness, and the next moment he knew that he had sat down wordless again on his chair, that the girl was already half-way across the room, and that he was trying to eat his salad with a dessert-spoon and a knife.

Longing for her return, and yet dreading it, he gulped down the remainder of his dinner, and then went at once to his bedroom to be alone with his thoughts. This time the passages were lighted, and he suffered no exciting contretemps; yet the winding corridor was dim with shadows, and the last portion, from the bend of the walls onwards, seemed longer than he had ever known it. It ran downhill like the pathway on a mountain side, and as he tiptoed softly down it he felt that by rights it ought to have led him clean out of the house into the heart of a great forest. The world was singing with him. Strange fancies filled his brain, and once in the room, with the door securely locked, he did not light the candles, but sat by the open window thinking long, long thoughts that came unbidden in troops to his mind.

4

This part of the story he told to Dr Silence, without special coaxing, it is true, yet with much stammering embarrassment. He could not in the least understand, he said, how the girl had managed to affect him so profoundly, and even before he had set eyes upon her. For her mere proximity in the darkness had been sufficient to set him on fire. He knew nothing of enchantments, and for years had been a stranger to anything approaching tender relations with any member of the opposite sex, for he was encased in shyness, and realized his overwhelming defects only too well. Yet this bewitching young creature came to him deliberately. Her manner was unmistakable, and she sought him out on every possible occasion. Chaste and sweet she was undoubtedly, yet frankly inviting; and she won him utterly with the first glance of her shining eyes, even if she had not already done so in the dark merely by the magic of her invisible presence.

'You felt she was altogether wholesome and good?' queried the doctor. 'You had no reaction of any sort – for instance, of alarm?'

Vezin looked up sharply with one of his inimitable little

apologetic smiles. It was some time before he replied. The
mere memory of the adventure had suffused his shy face with
blushes, and his brown eyes sought the floor again before he
answered.

'I don't think I can quite say that,' he explained presently.
'I acknowledged certain qualms, sitting up in my room afterwards. A conviction grew upon me that there was something
about her – how shall I express it? – well, something unholy.
It is not impurity in any sense, physical or mental, that I mean,
but something quite indefinable that gave me a vague sensation
of the creeps. She drew me, and at the same time repelled me,
more than – than –'

He hesitated, blushing furiously, and unable to finish the
sentence.

'Nothing like it has ever come to me before or since,' he
concluded, with lame confusion. 'I suppose it was, as you suggested just now, something of an enchantment. At any rate, it
was strong enough to make me feel that I would stay in that
awful little haunted town for years if only I could see her
every day, hear her voice, watch her wonderful movements,
and sometimes, perhaps, touch her hand.'

'Can you explain to me what you felt was the source of her
power?' John Silence asked, looking purposely anywhere but
at the narrator.

'I am surprised that *you* should ask me such a question,'
answered Vezin, with the nearest approach to dignity he could
manage. 'I think no man can describe to another convincingly
wherein lies the magic of the woman who ensnares him. I certainly cannot. I can only say this slip of a girl bewitched me,
and the mere knowledge that she was living and sleeping in
the same house filled me with an extraordinary sense of delight.

'But there's one thing I can tell you,' he went on earnestly,
his eyes aglow, 'namely, that she seemed to sum up and syn-
thesize in herself all the strange hidden forces that operated so
mysteriously in the town and its inhabitants. She had the silken
movements of the panther, going smoothly, silently to and fro,

and the same indirect, oblique methods as the townsfolk, screening, like them, secret purposes of her own – purposes that I was sure had *me* for their objective. She kept me, to my terror and delight, ceaselessly under observation, yet so carelessly, so consummately, that another man less sensitive, if I may say so' – he made a deprecating gesture – 'or less prepared by what had gone before, would never have noticed it at all. She was always still, always reposeful, yet she seemed to be everywhere at once, so that I never could escape from her. I was continually meeting the stare and laughter of her great eyes, in the corners of the rooms, in the passages, calmly looking at me through the windows, or in the busiest parts of the public streets.'

Their intimacy, it seems, grew very rapidly after this first encounter which had so violently disturbed the little man's equilibrium. He was naturally very prim, and prim folk live mostly in so small a world that anything violently unusual may shake them clean out of it, and they therefore instinctively distrust originality. But Vezin began to forget his primness after a while. The girl was always modestly behaved, and as her mother's representative she naturally had to do with the guests in the hotel. It was not out of the way that a spirit of camaraderie should spring up. Besides, she was young, she was charmingly pretty, she was French, and – she obviously liked him.

At the same time, there was something indescribable – a certain indefinable atmosphere of other places, other times – that made him try hard to remain on his guard, and sometimes made him catch his breath with a sudden start. It was all rather like a delirious dream, half delight, half dread, he confided in a whisper to Dr Silence; and more than once he hardly knew quite what he was doing or saying, as though he were driven forward by impulses he scarcely recognized as his own.

And though the thought of leaving presented itself again and again to his mind, it was each time with less insistence, so that he stayed on from day to day, becoming more and more a part of the sleepy life of this dreamy medieval town, losing more and more of his recognizable personality. Soon, he felt, the Curtain within would roll up with an awful rush, and he would find himself suddenly admitted into the secret purposes of the hidden life that lay behind it all. Only, by that time, he would have become transformed into an entirely different being.

And, meanwhile, he noticed various little signs of the intention to make his stay attractive to him: flowers in his bedroom, a more comfortable arm-chair in the corner, and even special little extra dishes on his private table in the dining-room. Conversations, too, with 'Mademoiselle Ilsé' became more and more frequent and pleasant, and although they seldom travelled beyond the weather, or the details of the town, the girl, he noticed, was never in a hurry to bring them to an end, and often contrived to interject little odd sentences that he never properly understood, yet felt to be significant.

And it was these stray remarks, full of a meaning that evaded him, that pointed to some hidden purpose of her own and made him feel uneasy. They all had to do, he felt sure, with reasons for his staying on in the town indefinitely.

'And has M'sieur not even yet come to a decision?' she said softly in his ear, sitting beside him in the sunny yard before *déjeuner*, the acquaintance having progressed with significant rapidity. 'Because, if it's so difficult, we must all try together to help him!'

The question startled him, following upon his own thoughts. It was spoken with a pretty laugh, and a stray bit of hair across one eye, as she turned and peered at him half roguishly. Possibly he did not quite understand the French of it, for her near presence always confused his small knowledge of the language distressingly. Yet the words, and her manner, and something else that lay behind it all in her mind, frightened him. It gave such point to his feeling that the town was waiting for him to make his mind up on some important matter.

At the same time, her voice, and the fact that she was there so close beside him in her soft dark dress, thrilled him inexpressibly.

'It is true I find it difficult to leave,' he stammered, losing his way deliciously in the depths of her eyes, 'and especially now that Mademoiselle Ilsé has come.'

He was surprised at the success of his sentence, and quite delighted with the little gallantry of it. But at the same time he could have bitten his tongue off for having said it.

'Then after all you like our little town, or you would not be pleased to stay on,' she said, ignoring the compliment.

'I am enchanted with it, and enchanted with you,' he cried, feeling that his tongue was somehow slipping beyond the control of his brain. And he was on the verge of saying all manner of other things of the wildest description, when the girl sprang lightly up from her chair beside him, and made to go.

'It is *soupe à l'oignon* today!' she cried, laughing back at him through the sunlight, 'and I must go and see about it. Otherwise, you know, M'sieur will not enjoy his dinner, and then, perhaps, he will leave us!'

He watched her cross the courtyard, moving with all the grace and lightness of the feline race, and her simple black dress clothed her, he thought, exactly like the fur of the same supple species. She turned once to laugh at him from the porch with the glass door, and then stopped a moment to speak to her mother, who sat knitting as usual in her corner seat just inside the hall-way.

But how was it, then, that the moment his eye fell upon this ungainly woman, the pair of them appeared suddenly as other than they were? Whence came that transforming dignity and sense of power that enveloped them both as by magic? What was it about that massive woman that made her appear instantly regal, and set her on a throne in some dark and dreadful scenery, wielding a sceptre over the red glare of some tempestuous orgy? And why did this slender stripling of a girl, graceful as a willow, lithe as a young leopard, assume suddenly an air of sinister majesty, and move with flame and smoke about her head, and the darkness of night beneath her feet?

Vezin caught his breath and sat there transfixed. Then,

almost simultaneously with its appearance, the queer notion vanished again, and the sunlight of day caught them both, and he heard her laughing to her mother about the *soupe à l'oignon*, and saw her glancing back at him over her dear little shoulder with a smile that made him think of a dew-kissed rose bending lightly before summer airs.

And, indeed, the onion soup was particularly excellent that day, because he saw another cover laid at his small table and, with fluttering heart, heard the waiter murmur by way of explanation that 'Ma'mselle Ilsé would honour M'sieur today at *déjeuner*, as her custom sometimes is with her mother's guests.'

So actually she sat by him all through that delirious meal, talking quietly to him in easy French, seeing that he was well looked after, mixing the salad-dressing, and even helping him with her own hand. And, later in the afternoon, while he was smoking in the courtyard, longing for a sight of her as soon as her duties were done, she came again to his side, and when he rose to meet her, she stood facing him a moment, full of a perplexing sweet shyness before she spoke –

'My mother thinks you ought to know more of the beauties of our little town, and *I* think so too! Would M'sieur like me to be his guide, perhaps? I can show him everything, for our family has lived here for many generations.'

She had him by the hand, indeed, before he could find a single word to express his pleasure, and led him, all unresisting, out into the street, yet in such a way that it seemed perfectly natural she should do so, and without the faintest suggestion of boldness or immodesty. Her face glowed with the pleasure and interest of it, and with her short dress and tumbled hair she looked every bit the charming child of seventeen that she was, innocent and playful, proud of her native town, and alive beyond her years to the sense of its ancient beauty.

So they went over the town together, and she showed him what she considered its chief interest: the tumble-down old house where her forebears had lived; the sombre, aristocratic-looking mansion where her mother's family dwelt for centuries, and the ancient market-place where several hundred years before the witches had been burnt by the score. She kept up a lively running stream of talk about it all, of which he understood not a fiftieth part as he trudged along by her side, cursing his forty-five years and feeling all the yearnings of his early manhood revive and jeer at him. And, as she talked, England and Surbiton seemed very far away indeed, almost in another age of the world's history. Her voice touched something immeasurably old in him, something that slept deep. It lulled the surface parts of his consciousness to sleep, allowing what was far more ancient to awaken. Like the town, with its elaborate pretence of modern active life, the upper layers of his being became dulled, soothed, muffled, and what lay underneath began to stir in its sleep. That big Curtain swayed a little to and fro. Presently it might lift altogether. . . .

He began to understand a little better at last. The mood of the town was reproducing itself in him. In proportion as his ordinary external self became muffled, that inner secret life, that was far more real and vital, asserted itself. And this girl was surely the high-priestess of it all, the chief instrument of its accomplishment. New thoughts, with new interpretations, flooded his mind as she walked beside him through the winding streets, while the picturesque old gabled town, softly coloured in the sunset, had never appeared to him so wholly wonderful and seductive.

And only one curious incident came to disturb and puzzle him, slight in itself, but utterly inexplicable, bringing white terror into the child's face and a scream to her laughing lips. He had merely pointed to a column of blue smoke that rose from the burning autumn leaves and made a picture against the red roofs, and had then run to the wall and called her to his side to watch the flames shooting here and there through the heap of rubbish. Yet at the sight of it, as though taken by surprise, her face had altered dreadfully, and she had turned and run like the wind, calling out wild sentences to him as she ran, of which he had not understood a single word, except that the fire apparently frightened her, and she wanted to get quickly away from it, and to get him away too.

Yet five minutes later she was as calm and happy again as though nothing had happened to alarm or waken troubled thoughts in her, and they had both forgotten the incident.

They were leaning over the ruined ramparts together listening to the weird music of the band as he had heard it the first day of his arrival. It moved him again profoundly as it had done before, and somehow he managed to find his tongue and his best French. The girl leaned across the stones close beside him. No one was about. Driven by some remorseless engine within he began to stammer something – he hardly knew what – of his strange admiration for her. Almost at the first word she sprang lightly off the wall and came up smiling in front of him, just touching his knees as he sat there. She was hatless as usual, and the sun caught her hair and one side of her cheek and throat.

'Oh, I'm *so* glad!' she cried, clapping her little hands softly in his face, 'so very glad, because that means that if you like me you must also like what I do, and what I belong to.'

Already he regretted bitterly having lost control of himself. Something in the phrasing of her sentence chilled him. He knew the fear of embarking upon an unknown and dangerous sea.

'You will take part in our real life, I mean,' she added softly, with an indescribable coaxing of manner, as though she noticed his shrinking. 'You will come back to us.'

Already this slip of a child seemed to dominate him; he felt the power coming over him more and more; something emanated from her that stole over his senses and made him aware that her personality, for all its simple grace, held forces that were stately, imposing, august. He saw her again moving through smoke and flame amid broken and tempestuous scenery, alarmingly strong, her terrible mother by her side. Dimly this shone through her smile and appearance of charming innocence.

'You will, I know,' she repeated, holding him with her eyes.

They were quite alone up there on the ramparts, and the sensation that she was overmastering him stirred a wild sensuousness in his blood. The mingled abandon and reserve in her attracted him furiously, and all of him that was man rose up and resisted the creeping influence, at the same time acclaiming it with the full delight of his forgotten youth. An irresistible desire came to him to question her, to summon what still remained to him of his own little personality in an effort to retain the right to his normal self.

The girl had grown quiet again, and was now leaning on the broad wall close beside him, gazing out across the darkening plain, her elbows on the coping, motionless as a figure carved in stone. He took his courage in both hands.

'Tell me, Ilsé,' he said, unconsciously imitating her own purring softness of voice, yet aware that he was utterly in earnest, 'what is the meaning of this town, and what is this real life you speak of? And why is it that the people watch me from morning to night? Tell me what it all means? And, tell me,' he added more quickly with passion in his voice, 'what you really are – yourself?'

She turned her head and looked at him through half-closed eyelids, her growing inner excitement betraying itself by the faint colour that ran like a shadow across her face.

'It seems to me,' – he faltered oddly under her gaze – 'that I have some right to know –'

Suddenly she opened her eyes to the full. 'You love me, then?' she asked softly.

'I swear,' he cried impetuously, moved as by the force of a rising tide, 'I never felt before – I have never known any other girl who –'

'Then you *have* the right to know,' she calmly interrupted his confused confession; 'for love shares all secrets.'

She paused, and a thrill like fire ran swiftly through him. Her words lifted him off the earth, and he felt a radiant happiness, followed almost the same instant in horrible contrast by the thought of death. He became aware that she had turned her eyes upon his own and was speaking again.

'The real life I speak of,' she whispered, 'is the old, old life within, the life of long ago, the life to which you, too, once belonged, and to which you still belong.'

A faint wave of memory troubled the deeps of his soul as her low voice sank into him. What she was saying he knew instinctively to be true, even though he could not as yet understand its full purport. His present life seemed slipping from him as he listened, merging his personality in one that was far older and greater. It was this loss of his present self that brought to him the thought of death.

'You came here,' she went on, 'with the purpose of seeking it, and the people felt your presence and are waiting to know what you decide, whether you will leave them without having found it, or whether –'

Her eyes remained fixed upon his own, but her face began to change, growing larger and darker with an expression of age.

'It is their thoughts constantly playing about your soul that makes you feel they watch you. They do not watch you with their eyes. The purposes of their inner life are calling to you, seeking to claim you. You were all part of the same life long, long ago, and now they want you back again among them.'

Vezin's timid heart sank with dread as he listened; but the girl's eyes held him with a net of joy so that he had no wish to escape. She fascinated him, as it were, clean out of his normal self.

'Alone, however, the people could never have caught and held you,' she resumed. 'The motive force was not strong enough; it has faded through all these years. But I' – she paused a moment and looked at him with complete confidence in her splendid eyes – 'I possess the spell to conquer you and hold you: the spell of old love. I can win you back again and make you live the old life with me, for the force of the ancient tie between us, if I choose to use it, is irresistible. And I do choose to use it. I still want you. And you, dear soul of my dim past' – she pressed closer to him so that her breath passed across his eyes, and her voice positively sang – 'I mean to have you, for you love me and are utterly at my mercy.'

Vezin heard, and yet did not hear; understood, yet did not understand. He had passed into a condition of exaltation. The world was beneath his feet, made of music and flowers, and he was flying somewhere far above it through the sunshine of pure delight. He was breathless and giddy with the wonder of her words. They intoxicated him. And, still, the terror of it all, the dreadful thought of death, pressed ever behind her sentences. For flames shot through her voice out of black smoke and licked at his soul.

And they communicated with one another, it seemed to him, by a process of swift telepathy, for his French could never have compassed all he said to her. Yet she understood perfectly, and what she said to him was like the recital of verses long since known. And the mingled pain and sweetness of it as he listened were almost more than his little soul could hold.

'Yet I came here wholly by chance –' he heard himself saying.

'No,' she cried with passion, 'you came here because I called you. I have called to you for years, and you came with the whole force of the past behind you. You had to come, for I own you, and I claim you.'

She rose again and moved closer, looking at him with a certain insolence in the face – the insolence of power.

The sun had set behind the towers of the old cathedral and the darkness rose up from the plain and enveloped them. The music of the band had ceased. The leaves of the plane trees hung motionless, but the chill of the autumn evening rose about them and made Vezin shiver. There was no sound but the sound of their voices and the occasional soft rustle of the girl's dress. He could hear the blood rushing in his ears. He scarcely realized where he was or what he was doing. Some terrible magic of the imagination drew him deeply down into the tombs of his own being, telling him in no unfaltering voice that her words shadowed forth the truth. And this simple little French maid, speaking beside him with so strange authority, he saw curiously alter into quite another being. As he stared into her eyes, the picture in his mind grew and lived, dressing itself vividly to his inner vision with a degree of reality he was compelled to acknowledge. As once before, he saw her tall and stately, moving through wild and broken scenery of forests and mountain caverns, the glare of flames behind her head and clouds of shifting smoke about her feet. Dark leaves encircled her hair, flying loosely in the wind, and her limbs shone through the merest rags of clothing. Others were about her too, and ardent eyes on all sides cast delirious glances upon her, but her own eyes were always for One only, one whom she held by the hand. For she was leading the dance in some tempestuous orgy to the music of chanting voices, and the dance she led circled about a great and awful Figure on a throne, brooding over the scene through lurid vapours, while innumerable other wild faces and forms crowded furiously about her in the dance. But the one she held by the hand he knew to be himself, and the monstrous shape upon the throne he knew to be her mother.

The vision rose within him, rushing to him down the long years of buried time, crying aloud to him with the voice of memory reawakened. . . . And then the scene faded away and he saw the clear circle of the girl's eyes gazing steadfastly into his own, and she became once more the pretty little daughter of the innkeeper, and he found his voice again.

'And you,' he whispered tremblingly – 'you child of visions and enchantment, how is it that you so bewitch me that I loved you even before I saw?'

She drew herself up beside him with an air of rare dignity.

'The call of the Past,' she said; 'and besides,' she added proudly, 'in the real life I am a princess –'

'A princess!' he cried.

'– and my mother is a queen!'

At this, little Vezin utterly lost his head. Delight tore at his heart and swept him into sheer ecstasy. To hear that sweet singing voice, and to see those adorable little lips utter such things, upset his balance beyond all hope of control. He took her in his arms and covered her unresisting face with kisses.

But even while he did so, and while the hot passion swept him, he felt that she was soft and loathsome, and that her answering kisses stained his very soul. . . . And when, presently, she had freed herself and vanished into the darkness, he stood there, leaning against the wall in a state of collapse, creeping with horror from the touch of her yielding body, and inwardly raging at the weakness that he already dimly realized must prove his undoing.

And from the shadows of the old buildings into which she disappeared there rose in the stillness of the night a singular, long-drawn cry, which at first he took for laughter, but which later he was sure he recognized as the almost human wailing of a cat.

5

For a long time Vezin leant there against the wall, alone with his surging thoughts and emotions. He understood at length that he had done the one thing necessary to call down upon him the whole force of this ancient Past. For in those passionate kisses he had acknowledged the tie of olden days, and had revived it. And the memory of that soft impalpable caress in the darkness of the inn corridor came back to him with a shudder. The girl had first mastered him, and then led him to the one act that was necessary for her purpose. He had been waylaid, after the lapse of centuries – caught, and conquered.

Dimly he realized this, and sought to make plans for his escape. But, for the moment at any rate, he was powerless to manage his thoughts or will, for the sweet, fantastic madness of the whole adventure mounted to his brain like a spell, and he gloried in the feeling that he was utterly enchanted and moving in a world so much larger and wilder than the one he had ever been accustomed to.

The moon, pale and enormous, was just rising over the sea-like plain, when at last he rose to go. Her slanting rays drew all the houses into new perspective, so that their roofs, already glistening with dew, seemed to stretch much higher into the sky than usual, and their gables and quaint old towers lay far away in its purple reaches.

The cathedral appeared unreal in a silver mist. He moved softly, keeping to the shadows; but the streets were all deserted and very silent; the doors were closed, the shutters fastened. Not a soul was astir. The hush of night lay over everything; it was like a town of the dead, a churchyard with gigantic and grotesque tombstones.

Wondering where all the busy life of the day had so utterly disappeared to, he made his way to a back door that entered the inn by means of the stables, thinking thus to reach his room unobserved. He reached the courtyard safely and crossed it by keeping close to the shadow of the wall. He sidled down it, mincing along on tiptoe, just as the old men did when they entered the *salle à manger*. He was horrified to find himself doing this instinctively. A strange impulse came to him, catching him somehow in the centre of his body – an impulse to drop upon all fours and run swiftly and silently. He glanced upwards and the idea came to him to leap up upon the window-sill overhead instead of going round by the stairs. This occurred to him as the easiest, and most natural way. It was like the beginning of some horrible transformation of himself into something else. He was fearfully strung up.

The moon was higher now, and the shadows very dark along the side of the street where he moved. He kept among the deepest of them, and reached the porch with the glass doors.

But here there was light; the inmates, unfortunately, were still about. Hoping to slip across the hall unobserved and reach the stairs, he opened the door carefully and stole in. Then he saw that the hall was not empty. A large dark thing lay against the wall on his left. At first he thought it must be household articles. Then it moved, and he thought it was an immense cat, distorted in some way by the play of light and

111

shadow. Then it rose straight up before him and he saw that it was the proprietress.

What she had been doing in this position he could only venture a dreadful guess, but the moment she stood up and faced him he was aware of some terrible dignity clothing her about that instantly recalled the girl's strange saying that she was a queen. Huge and sinister she stood there under the little oil lamp; alone with him in the empty hall. Awe stirred in his heart, and the roots of some ancient fear. He felt that he must bow to her and make some kind of obeisance. The impulse was fierce and irresistible, as of long habit. He glanced quickly about him. There was no one there. Then he deliberately inclined his head towards her. He bowed.

'Enfin! M'sieur s'est donc décidé. C'est bien alors. J'en suis contente.'

Her words came to him sonorously as through a great open space.

Then the great figure came suddenly across the flagged hall at him and seized his trembling hands. Some overpowering force moved with her and caught him.

'On pourrait faire un p'tit tour ensemble, n'est-ce pas? Nous y allons cette nuit et il faut s'exercer un peu d'avance pour cela. Ilsé, Ilsé, viens donc ici. Viens vite!'

And she whirled him round in the opening steps of some dance that seemed oddly and horribly familiar. They made no sound on the stones, this strangely assorted couple. It was all soft and stealthy. And presently, when the air seemed to thicken like smoke, and a red glare as of flame shot through it, he was aware that some one else had joined them and that his hand the mother had released was now tightly held by the daughter. Ilsé had come in answer to the call, and he saw her with leaves of vervain twined in her dark hair, clothed in tattered vestiges of some curious garment, beautiful as the night, and horribly, odiously, loathsomely seductive.

'To the Sabbath! to the Sabbath!' they cried. 'On to the Witches' Sabbath!'

Up and down that narrow hall they danced, the women on

each side of him, to the wildest measure he had ever imagined, yet which he dimly, dreadfully remembered, till the lamp on the wall flickered and went out, and they were left in total darkness. And the devil woke in his heart with a thousand vile suggestions and made him afraid.

Suddenly they released his hands and he heard the voice of the mother cry that it was time, and they must go. Which way they went he did not pause to see. He only realized that he was free, and he blundered through the darkness till he found the stairs and then tore up them to his room as though all hell was at his heels.

He flung himself on the sofa, with his face in his hands, and groaned. Swiftly, reviewing a dozen ways of immediate escape, all equally impossible, he finally decided that the only thing to do for the moment was to sit quiet and wait. He must see what was going to happen. At least in the privacy of his own bedroom he would be fairly safe. The door was locked. He crossed over and softly opened the window which gave upon the courtyard and also permitted a partial view of the hall through the glass doors.

As he did so the hum and murmur of a great activity reached his ears from the streets beyond – the sound of footsteps and voices muffled by distance. He leaned out cautiously and listened. The moonlight was clear and strong now, but his own window was in shadow, the silver disc being still behind the house. It came to him irresistibly that the inhabitants of the town, who a little while before had all been invisible behind closed doors, were now issuing forth, busy upon some secret and unholy errand. He listened intently.

At first everything about him was silent, but soon he became aware of movements going on in the house itself. Rustlings and cheepings came to him across that still, moonlit yard. A concourse of living beings sent the hum of their activity into the night. Things were on the move everywhere. A biting, pungent odour rose through the air, coming he knew not whence. Presently his eyes became glued to the windows of the opposite wall where the moonshine fell in a soft blaze.

The roof overhead, and behind him, was reflected clearly in the panes of glass, and he saw the outlines of dark bodies moving with long footsteps over the tiles and along the coping. They passed swiftly and silently, shaped like immense cats, in an endless procession across the pictured glass, and then appeared to leap down to a lower level where he lost sight of them. He just caught the soft thudding of their leaps. Sometimes their shadows fell upon the white wall opposite, and then he could not make out whether they were the shadows of human beings or of cats. They seemed to change swiftly from one to the other. The transformation looked horribly real, for they leaped like human beings, yet changed swiftly in the air immediately afterwards, and dropped like animals.

The yard, too, beneath him, was now alive with the creeping movements of dark forms all stealthily drawing towards the porch with the glass doors. They kept so closely to the wall that he could not determine their actual shape, but when he saw that they passed on to the great congregation that was gathering in the hall, he understood that these were the creatures whose leaping shadows he had first seen reflected in the window-panes opposite. They were coming from all parts of the town, reaching the appointed meeting-place across the roofs and tiles, and springing from level to level till they came to the yard.

Then a new sound caught his ear, and he saw that the windows all about him were being softly opened, and that to each window came a face. A moment later figures began dropping hurriedly down into the yard. And these figures, as they lowered themselves down from the windows, were human, he saw; but once safely in the yard they fell upon all fours and changed in the swiftest possible second into – cats – huge, silent cats. They ran in streams to join the main body in the hall beyond.

So, after all, the rooms in the house had not been empty and unoccupied.

Moreover, what he saw no longer filled him with amazement. For he remembered it all. It was familiar. It had all happened before just so, hundreds of times, and he himself had taken part in it and known the wild madness of it all. The outline of the old building changed, the yard grew larger, and he seemed to be staring down upon it from a much greater height through smoky vapours. And, as he looked, half remembering, the old pains of long ago, fierce and sweet, furiously assailed him, and the blood stirred horribly as he heard the Call of the Dance again in his heart and tasted the ancient magic of Ilsé whirling by his side.

Suddenly he started back. A great lithe cat had leaped softly up from the shadows below on to the sill close to his face, and was staring fixedly at him with the eyes of a human. 'Come,' it seemed to say, 'come with us to the Dance! Change as of old! Transform yourself swiftly and come!' Only too well he understood the creature's soundless call.

It was gone again in a flash with scarcely a sound of its padded feet on the stones, and then others dropped by the score down the side of the house, past his very eyes, all changing as they fell and darting away rapidly, softly, towards the gathering point. And again he felt the dreadful desire to do likewise; to murmur the old incantation, and then drop upon hands and knees and run swiftly for the great flying leap into the air. Oh, how the passion of it rose within him like a flood, twisting his very entrails, sending his heart's desire flaming forth into the night for the old, old Dance of the Sorcerers at the Witches' Sabbath! The whirl of the stars was about him; once more he met the magic of the moon. The power of the wind, rushing from precipice and forest, leaping from cliff to cliff across the valleys, tore him away.... He heard the cries of the dancers and their wild laughter, and with this savage girl in his embrace he danced furiously about the dim Throne where sate the Figure with the sceptre of majesty....

Then, suddenly, all became hushed and still, and the fever died down a little in his heart. The calm moonlight flooded a courtyard empty and deserted. They had started. The procession was off into the sky. And he was left behind – alone.

Vezin tiptoed softly across the room and unlocked the door.

The murmur from the streets, growing momentarily as he advanced, met his ears. He made his way with the utmost caution down the corridor. At the head of the stairs he paused and listened. Below him, the hall where they had gathered was dark and still, but through opened doors and windows on the far side of the building came the sound of a great throng moving farther and farther into the distance.

He made his way down the creaking wooden stairs, dreading yet longing to meet some straggler who should point the way, but finding no one; across the dark hall, so lately thronged with living, moving things, and out through the opened front doors into the street. He could not believe that he was really left behind, really forgotten, that he had been purposely permitted to escape. It perplexed him.

Nervously he peered about him, and up and down the street; then, seeing nothing, advanced slowly down the pavement.

The whole town, as he went, showed itself empty and deserted, as though a great wind had blown everything alive out of it. The doors and windows of the houses stood open to the night; nothing stirred; moonlight and silence lay over all. The night lay about him like a cloak. The air, soft and cool, caressed his cheek like the touch of a great furry paw. He gained confidence and began to walk quickly, though still keeping to the shadowed side. Nowhere could he discover the faintest sign of the great unholy exodus he knew had just taken place. The moon sailed high over all in a sky cloudless and serene.

Hardly realizing where he was going, he crossed the open market-place and so came to the ramparts, whence he knew a pathway descended to the high road and along which he could make good his escape to one of the other little towns that lay to the northward, and so to the railway.

But first he paused and gazed out over the scene at his feet where the great plain lay like a silver map of some dream country. The still beauty of it entered his heart, increasing his sense of bewilderment and unreality. No air stirred, the leaves of the plane trees stood motionless, the near details were defined with the sharpness of day against dark shadows, and in the distance the fields and woods melted away into haze and shimmering mistiness.

But the breath caught in his throat and he stood stockstill as though transfixed when his gaze passed from the horizon and fell upon the near prospect in the depth of the valley at his feet. The whole lower slopes of the hill, that lay hid from the brightness of the moon, were aglow, and through the glare he saw countless moving forms, shifting thick and fast between the openings of the trees; while overhead, like leaves driven by the wind, he discerned flying shapes that hovered darkly one moment against the sky and then settled down with cries and weird singing through the branches into the region that was aflame.

Spellbound, he stood and stared for a time that he could not measure. And then, moved by one of the terrible impulses that seemed to control the whole adventure, he climbed swiftly upon the top of the broad coping, and balanced a moment where the valley gaped at his feet. But in that very instant, as he stood hovering, a sudden movement among the shadows of the houses caught his eye, and he turned to see the outline of a large animal dart swiftly across the open space behind him, and land with a flying leap upon the top of the wall a little lower down. It ran like the wind to his feet and then rose up beside him upon the ramparts. A shiver seemed to run through the moonlight, and his sight trembled for a second. His heart pulsed fearfully. Ilsé stood beside him, peering into his face.

Some dark substance, he saw, stained the girl's face and skin, shining in the moonlight as she stretched her hands towards him; she was dressed in wretched tattered garments that yet became her mightily; rue and vervain twined about her temples; her eyes glittered with unholy light. He only just controlled the wild impulse to take her in his arms and leap with her from their giddy perch into the valley below.

'See!' she cried, pointing with an arm on which the rags fluttered in the rising wind towards the forest aglow in the

117

distance. 'See where they await us! The woods are alive! Already the Great Ones are there, and the dance will soon begin! The slave is here! Anoint yourself and come!'

Though a moment before the sky was clear and cloudless, yet even while she spoke the face of the moon grew dark and the wind began to toss in the crests of the plane trees at his feet. Stray gusts brought the sounds of hoarse singing and crying from the lower slopes of the hill, and the pungent odour he had already noticed about the courtyard of the inn rose about him in the air.

'Transform, transform!' she cried again, her voice rising like a song. 'Rub well your skin before you fly. Come! Come with me to the Sabbath, to the madness of its furious delight, to the sweet abandonment of its evil worship! See! the Great Ones are there, and the terrible Sacraments prepared. The Throne is occupied. Anoint and come! Anoint and come!'

She grew to the height of a tree beside him, leaping upon the wall with flaming eyes and hair strewn upon the night. He too began to change swiftly. Her hands touched the skin of his face and neck, streaking him with the burning salve that sent the old magic into his blood with the power before which fades all that is good.

A wild roar came up to his ears from the heart of the wood, and the girl, when she heard it, leaped upon the wall in the frenzy of her wicked joy.

'Satan is there!' she screamed, rushing upon him and striving to draw him with her to the edge of the wall. 'Satan has come! The Sacraments call us! Come, with your dear apostate soul, and we will worship and dance till the moon dies and the world is forgotten!'

Just saving himself from the dreadful plunge, Vezin struggled to release himself from her grasp, while the passion tore at his reins and all but mastered him. He shrieked aloud, not knowing what he said, and then he shrieked again. It was the old impulses, the old awful habits instinctively finding voice; for though it seemed to him that he merely shrieked non-

118

sense, the words he uttered really had meaning in them, and were intelligible. It was the ancient call. And it was heard below. It was answered.

The wind whistled at the skirts of his coat as the air round him darkened with many flying forms crowding upwards out of the valley. The crying of hoarse voices smote upon his ears, coming closer. Strokes of wind buffeted him, tearing him this way and that along the crumbling top of the stone wall; and Ilsé clung to him with her long shining arms, smooth and bare, holding him fast about the neck. But not Ilsé alone, for a dozen of them surrounded him, dropping out of the air. The pungent odour of the anointed bodies stifled him, exciting him to the old madness of the Sabbath, the dance of the witches and sorcerers doing honour to the personified Evil of the world.

'Anoint and away! Anoint and away!' they cried in wild chorus about him. 'To the Dance that never dies! To the sweet and fearful fantasy of evil!'

Another moment and he would have yielded and gone, for his will turned soft and the flood of passionate memory all but overwhelmed him, when – so can a small thing alter the whole course of an adventure – he caught his foot upon a loose stone in the edge of the wall, and then fell with a sudden crash on to the ground below. But he fell towards the houses, in the open space of dust and cobble stones, and fortunately not into the gaping depth of the valley on the farther side.

And they, too, came in a tumbling heap about him, like flies upon a piece of food, but as they fell he was released for a moment from the power of their touch, and in that brief instant of freedom there flashed into his mind the sudden intuition that saved him. Before he could regain his feet he saw them scrabbling awkwardly back upon the wall, as though bat-like they could only fly by dropping from a height, and had no hold upon him in the open. Then, seeing them perched there in a row like cats upon a roof, all dark and singularly shapeless, their eyes like lamps, the sudden memory came back to him of Ilsé's terror at the sight of fire.

Quick as a flash he found his matches and lit the dry leaves that lay under the wall.

Dry and withered, they caught fire at once, and the wind carried the flame in a long line down the length of the wall, licking upwards as it ran; and with shrieks and wailings, the crowded row of forms upon the top melted away into the air on the other side, and were gone with a great rush and whirring of their bodies down into the heart of the haunted valley, leaving Vezin breathless and shaken in the middle of the deserted ground.

'Ilsé!' he called feebly; 'Ilsé!' for his heart ached to think that she was really gone to the great Dance without him, and that he had lost the opportunity of its fearful joy. Yet at the same time his relief was so great, and he was so dazed and troubled in mind with the whole thing, that he hardly knew what he was saying, and only cried aloud in the fierce storm of his emotion. . . .

The fire under the wall ran its course, and the moonlight came out again, soft and clear, from its temporary eclipse. With one last shuddering look at the ruined ramparts, and a feeling of horrid wonder for the haunted valley beyond, where the shapes still crowded and flew, he turned his face towards the town and slowly made his way in the direction of the hotel.

And as he went, a great wailing of cries, and a sound of howling, followed him from the gleaming forest below, growing fainter and fainter with the bursts of wind as he disappeared between the houses.

6

'It may seem rather abrupt to you, this sudden tame ending,' said Arthur Vezin, glancing with flushed face and timid eyes at Dr Silence sitting there with his notebook, 'but the fact is — er — from that moment my memory seems to have failed rather. I have no distinct recollection of how I got home or what precisely I did.

'It appears I never went back to the inn at all. I only dimly recollect racing down a long white road in the moonlight, past woods and villages, still and deserted, and then the dawn came up, and I saw the towers of a biggish town and so came to a station.

'But, long before that, I remember pausing somewhere on the road and looking back to where the hill-town of my adventure stood up in the moonlight, and thinking how exactly like a great monstrous cat it lay there upon the plain, its huge front paws lying down the two main streets, and the twin and broken towers of the cathedral marking its torn ears against the sky. That picture stays in my mind with the utmost vividness to this day.

'Another thing remains in my mind from that escape – namely, the sudden sharp reminder that I had not paid my bill, and the decision I made, standing there on the dusty highroad, that the small baggage I had left behind would more than settle for my indebtedness.

'For the rest, I can only tell you that I got coffee and bread at a café on the outskirts of this town I had come to, and soon after found my way to the station and caught a train later in the day. That same evening I reached London.'

'And how long altogether,' asked John Silence quietly, 'do you think you stayed in the town of the adventure?'

Vezin looked up sheepishly.

'I was coming to that,' he resumed, with apologetic wrigglings of his body. 'In London I found that I was a whole week out in my reckoning of time. I had stayed over a week in the town, and it ought to have been September 15th, – instead of which it was only September 10th!'

'So that, in reality, you had only stayed a night or two in the inn?' queried the doctor.

Vezin hesitated before replying. He shuffled upon the mat.

'I must have gained time somewhere,' he said at length –

'somewhere or somehow. I certainly had a week to my credit. I can't explain it. I can only give you the fact.'

'And this happened to you last year, since when you have never been back to the place?'

'Last autumn, yes,' murmured Vezin; 'and I have never dared to go back. I think I never want to.'

'And, tell me,' asked Dr Silence at length, when he saw that the little man had evidently come to the end of his words and had nothing more to say, 'had you ever read up the subject of the old witchcraft practices during the Middle Ages, or been at all interested in the subject?'

'Never!' declared Vezin emphatically. 'I had never given a thought to such matters so far as I know –'

'Or to the question of reincarnation, perhaps?'

'Never – before my adventure; but I have since,' he replied significantly.

There was, however, something still on the man's mind that he wished to relieve himself of by confession, yet could with difficulty bring himself to mention; and it was only after the sympathetic tactfulness of the doctor had provided numerous openings that he at length availed himself of one of them, and stammered that he would like to show him the marks he still had on his neck where, he said, the girl had touched him with her anointed hands.

He took off his collar after infinite fumbling hesitation, and lowered his shirt a little for the doctor to see. And there, on the surface of the skin, lay a faint reddish line across the shoulder and extending a little way down the back towards the spine. It certainly indicated exactly the position an arm might have taken in the act of embracing. And on the other side of the neck, slightly higher up, was a similar mark, though not quite so clearly defined.

'That was where she held me that night on the ramparts,' he whispered, a strange light coming and going in his eyes.

It was some weeks later when I again found occasion to consult John Silence concerning another extraordinary case that had come under my notice, and we fell to discussing Vezin's story. Since hearing it, the doctor had made investigations on his own account, and one of his secretaries had discovered that Vezin's ancestors had actually lived for generations in the very town where the adventure came to him. Two of them, both women, had been tried and convicted as witches, and had been burned alive at the stake. Moreover, it had not been difficult to prove that the very inn where Vezin stayed was built about 1700 upon the spot where the funeral pyres stood and the executions took place. The town was a sort of headquarters for all the sorcerers and witches of the entire region, and after conviction they were burnt there literally by scores.

'It seems strange,' continued the doctor, 'that Vezin should have remained ignorant of all this; but, on the other hand, it was not the kind of history that successive generations would have been anxious to keep alive, or to repeat to their children. Therefore I am inclined to think he still knows nothing about it.

'The whole adventure seems to have been a very vivid revival of the memories of an earlier life, caused by coming directly into contact with the living forces still intense enough to hang about the place, and, by a most singular chance too, with the very souls who had taken part with him in the events of that particular life. For the mother and daughter who impressed him so strangely must have been leading actors, with himself, in the scenes and practices of witchcraft which at that period dominated the imaginations of the whole country.

'One has only to read the histories of the times to know that these witches claimed the power of transforming themselves into various animals, both for the purposes of disguise and also to convey themselves swiftly to the scenes of their imaginary orgies. Lycanthropy, or the power to change themselves into wolves, was everywhere believed in, and the ability to transform themselves into cats by rubbing their bodies with a special salve or ointment provided by Satan himself, found equal credence. The witchcraft trials abound in evidences of such universal beliefs.'

Dr Silence quoted chapter and verse from many writers on the subject, and showed how every detail of Vezin's adventure had a basis in the practices of those dark days.

'But that the entire affair took place subjectively in the man's own consciousness, I have no doubt,' he went on, in reply to my questions; 'for my secretary, who has been to the town to investigate, discovered his signature in the visitors' book, and proved by it that he had arrived on September 8th, and left suddenly without paying his bill. He left two days later, and they still were in possession of his dirty brown bag and some tourist clothes. I paid a few francs in settlement of his debt, and have sent his luggage on to him. The daughter was absent from home, but the proprietress, a large woman very much as he described her, told my secretary that he had seemed a very strange, absent-minded kind of gentleman, and after his disappearance she had feared for a long time that he had met with a violent end in the neighbouring forest where he used to roam about alone.

'I should like to have obtained a personal interview with the daughter so as to ascertain how much was subjective and how much actually took place with her as Vezin told it. For her dread of fire and the sight of burning must, of course, have been the intuitive memory of her former painful death at the stake, and have thus explained why he fancied more than once that he saw her through smoke and flame.'

'And that mark on his skin, for instance?' I inquired.

'Merely the marks produced by hysterical brooding,' he replied, 'like the stigmata of the *religieuses,* and the bruises which appear on the bodies of hypnotised subjects who have been told to expect them. This is very common and easily explained. Only it seems curious that these marks should have remained so long in Vezin's case. Usually they disappear quickly.'

'Obviously he is still thinking about it all, brooding, and living it all over again,' I ventured.

'Probably. And this makes me fear that the end of his trouble is not yet. We shall hear of him again. It is a case, alas! I can do little to alleviate.'

Dr Silence spoke gravely and with sadness in his voice.

'And what do you make of the Frenchman in the train?' I asked further – 'the man who warned him against the place, *à cause du sommeil et à cause des chats?* Surely a very singular incident?'

'A *very* singular incident indeed,' he made answer slowly, 'and one I can only explain on the basis of a highly improbable coincidence –'

'Namely?'

'That the man was one who had himself stayed in the town and undergone there a similar experience. I should like to find this man and ask him. But the crystal is useless here, for I have no slightest clue to go upon, and I can only conclude that some singular psychic affinity, some force still active in his being out of the same past life, drew him thus to the personality of Vezin, and enabled him to fear what might happen to him, and thus to warn him as he did.

'Yes,' he presently continued, half talking to himself, 'I suspect in this case that Vezin was swept into the vortex of forces arising out of the intense activities of a past life, and that he lived over again a scene in which he had often played a leading part centuries before. For strong actions set up forces that are so slow to exhaust themselves, they may be said in a sense never to die. In this case they were not vital enough to render the illusion complete, so that the little man found himself caught in a very distressing confusion of the present and the past; yet he was sufficiently sensitive to recognize that it was true, and to fight against the degradation of returning, even in memory, to a former and lower state of development.

'Ah yes!' he continued, crossing the floor to gaze at the darkening sky, and seemingly quite oblivious of my presence, 'subliminal up-rushes of memory like this can be exceedingly painful, and sometimes exceedingly dangerous. I only trust that this gentle soul may soon escape from this obsession of a passionate and tempestuous past. But I doubt it, I doubt it.'

His voice was hushed with sadness as he spoke, and when he turned back into the room again there was an expression of profound yearning upon his face, the yearning of a soul whose desire to help is sometimes greater than his power.

The Nemesis of Fire

1

By some means which I never could fathom, John Silence always contrived to keep the compartment to himself, and as the train had a clear run of two hours before the first stop, there was ample time to go over the preliminary facts of the case. He had telephoned to me that very morning, and even through the disguise of the miles of wire the thrill of incalculable adventure had sounded in his voice.

'As if it were an ordinary country visit,' he called, in reply to my question; 'and don't forget to bring your gun.'

'With blank cartridges, I suppose?' for I knew his rigid principles with regard to the taking of life, and guessed that the guns were merely for some obvious purpose of disguise.

Then he thanked me for coming, mentioned the train, snapped down the receiver, and left me vibrating with the excitement of anticipation to do my packing. For the honour of accompanying Dr John Silence on one of his big cases was what many would have considered an empty honour – and risky. Certainly the adventure held all manner of possibilities, and I arrived at Waterloo with the feelings of a man who is about to embark on some dangerous and peculiar mission in which the dangers he expects to run will not be the ordinary dangers to life and limb, but of some secret character difficult to name and still more difficult to cope with.

'The Manor House has a high sound,' he told me, as we sat with our feet up and talked, 'but I believe it is little more than an overgrown farmhouse in the desolate heather country beyond D—, and its owner, Colonel Wragge, a retired soldier with a taste for books, lives there practically alone, I understand, with an elderly invalid sister. So you need not look forward to a lively visit, unless the case provides some excitement of its own.'

'Which is likely?'

By way of reply he handed me a letter marked 'Private'. It was dated a week ago, and signed 'Yours faithfully, Horace Wragge.'

'He heard of me, you see, through Captain Anderson,' the doctor explained modestly, as though his fame were not almost world-wide; 'you remember that Indian obsession case –'

I read the letter. Why it should have been marked private was difficult to understand. It was very brief, direct, and to the point. It referred by way of introduction to Captain Anderson, and then stated quite simply that the writer needed help of a peculiar kind and asked for a personal interview – a morning interview, since it was impossible for him to be absent from the house at night. The letter was dignified even to the point of abruptness, and it is difficult to explain how it managed to convey to me the impression of a strong man, shaken and perplexed. Perhaps the restraint of the wording, and the mystery of the affair had something to do with it; and the reference to the Anderson case, the horror of which lay still vivid in my memory, may have touched the sense of something rather ominous and alarming. But, whatever the cause, there was no doubt that an impression of serious peril rose somehow out of that white paper with the few lines of firm writing, and the spirit of a deep uneasiness ran between the words and reached the mind without any visible form of expression.

'And when you saw him –?' I asked, returning the letter as the train rushed clattering noisily through Clapham Junction.

'I have not seen him,' was the reply. 'The man's mind was charged to the brim when he wrote that; full of vivid mental pictures. Notice the restraint of it. For the main character of his case psychometry could be depended upon, and the scrap of paper his hand has touched is sufficient to give to another mind – a sensitive and sympathetic mind – clear mental pictures of what is going on. I think I have a very sound general idea of his problem.'

'So there may be excitement after all?'

John Silence waited a moment before he replied.

'Something very serious is amiss there,' he said gravely, at length. 'Some one – not himself, I gather, – has been meddling with a rather dangerous kind of gunpowder. So – yes, there may be excitement, as you put it.'

'And my duties?' I asked, with a decidedly growing interest. 'Remember, I am your "assistant".'

'Behave like an intelligent confidential secretary. Observe everything, without seeming to. Say nothing – nothing that means anything. Be present at all interviews. I may ask a good deal of you, for if my impressions are correct this is –'

He broke off suddenly.

'But I won't tell you my impressions yet,' he resumed after a moment's thought. 'Just watch and listen as the case proceeds. Form your own impressions and cultivate your intuitions. We come as ordinary visitors, of course,' he added, a twinkle showing for an instant in his eye; 'hence, the guns.'

Though disappointed not to hear more, I recognized the wisdom of his words and knew how valueless my impressions would be once the powerful suggestion of having heard his own lay behind them. I likewise reflected that intuition joined to a sense of humour was of more use to a man than double the quantity of mere 'brains', as such.

Before putting the letter away, however, he handed it back, telling me to place it against my forehead for a few moments and then describe any pictures that came spontaneously into my mind.

'Don't deliberately look for anything. Just imagine you see the inside of the eyelid, and wait for pictures that rise against its dark screen.'

I followed his instructions, making my mind as nearly a blank as possible. But no visions came. I saw nothing but the lines of light that pass to and fro like the changes of a kaleido-

scope across the blackness. A momentary sensation of warmth
came and went curiously.

'You see – what?' he asked presently.

'Nothing,' I was obliged to admit disappointedly; 'nothing
but the usual flashes of light one always sees. Only, perhaps,
they are more vivid than usual.'

He said nothing by way of comment or reply.

'And they group themselves now and then,' I continued,
with painful candour, for I longed to see the pictures he had
spoken of, 'group themselves into globes and round balls of fire,
and the lines that flash about sometimes look like triangles and
crosses – almost like geometrical figures. Nothing more.'

I opened my eyes again, and gave him back the letter.

'It makes my head hot,' I said, feeling somehow unworthy
for not seeing anything of interest. But the look in his eyes
arrested my attention at once.

'That sensation of heat is important,' he said significantly.

'It was certainly real, and rather uncomfortable,' I replied,
hoping he would expand and explain. 'There was a distinct
feeling of warmth – internal warmth somewhere – oppressive
in a sense.'

'That is interesting,' he remarked, putting the letter back
in his pocket, and settling himself in the corner with newspapers and books. He vouchsafed nothing more, and I knew
the uselessness of trying to make him talk. Following his
example I settled likewise with magazines into my corner. But
when I closed my eyes again to look for the flashing lights
and the sensation of heat, I found nothing but the usual
phantasmagoria of the day's events – faces, scenes, memories,
– and in due course I fell asleep and then saw nothing at all of
any kind.

When we left the train, after six hours' travelling, at a little
wayside station standing without trees in a world of sand and
heather, the late October shadows had already dropped their
sombre veil upon the landscape, and the sun dipped almost
out of sight behind the moorland hills. In a high dogcart, behind a fast horse, we were soon rattling across the undulating

stretches of an open and bleak country, the keen air stinging our cheeks and the scents of pine and bracken strong about us. Bare hills were faintly visible against the horizon, and the coachman pointed to a bank of distant shadows on our left where he told us the sea lay. Occasional stone farmhouses, standing back from the road among straggling fir trees, and large black barns that seemed to shift past us with a movement of their own in the gloom, were the only signs of humanity and civilization that we saw, until at the end of a bracing five miles the lights of the lodge gates flared before us and we plunged into a thick grove of pine trees that concealed the Manor House up to the moment of actual arrival.

Colonel Wragge himself met us in the hall. He was the typical army officer who had seen service, real service, and found himself in the process. He was tall and well built, broad in the shoulders, but lean as a greyhound, with grave eyes, rather stern, and a moustache turning grey. I judged him to be about sixty years of age, but his movements showed a suppleness of strength and agility that contradicted the years. The face was full of character and resolution, the face of a man to be depended upon, and the straight grey eyes, it seemed to me, wore a veil of perplexed anxiety that he made no attempt to disguise. The whole appearance of the man at once clothed the adventure with gravity and importance. A matter that gave such a man cause for serious alarm, I felt, must be something real and of genuine moment.

His speech and manner, as he welcomed us, were like his letter, simple and sincere. He had a nature as direct and undeviating as a bullet. Thus, he showed plainly his surprise that Dr Silence had not come alone.

'My confidential secretary, Mr Hubbard,' the doctor said, introducing me, and the steady gaze and powerful shake of the hand I then received were well calculated, I remember thinking, to drive home the impression that here was a man who was not to be trifled with, and whose perplexity must spring from some very real and tangible cause. And, quite obviously, he was relieved that we had come. His welcome was unmistakably genuine.

He led us at once into a room, half library, half smoking-room, that opened out of the low-ceilinged hall. The Manor House gave the impression of a rambling and glorified farm-house, solid, ancient, comfortable, and wholly unpretentious. And so it was. Only the heat of the place struck me as un-natural. This room with the blazing fire may have seemed un-comfortably warm after the long drive through the night air; yet it seemed to me that the hall itself, and the whole atmos-phere of the house, breathed a warmth that hardly belonged to well-filled grates or the pipes of hot air and water. It was not the heat of the greenhouse; it was an oppressive heat that somehow got into the head and mind. It stirred a curious sense of uneasiness in me, and I caught myself thinking of the sensation of warmth that had emanated from the letter in the train.

I heard him thanking Dr Silence for having come; there was no preamble, and the exchange of civilities was of the briefest description. Evidently here was a man who, like my companion, loved action rather than talk. His manner was straightforward and direct. I saw him in a flash: puzzled, wor-ried, harassed into a state of alarm by something he could not comprehend; forced to deal with things he would have pre-ferred to despise, yet facing it all with dogged seriousness and making no attempt to conceal that he felt secretly ashamed of his incompetence.

'So I cannot offer you much entertainment beyond that of my own company, and the queer business that has been going on here, and is still going on,' he said, with a slight inclination of the head towards me by way of including me in his con-fidence.

'I think, Colonel Wragge,' replied John Silence impres-sively, 'that we shall none of us find the time hang heavy. I gather we shall have our hands full.'

The two men looked at one another for the space of some seconds, and there was an indefinable quality in their silence which for the first time made me admit a swift question into my mind; and I wondered a little at my rashness in coming

with so little reflection into a big case of this incalculable
doctor. But no answer suggested itself, and to withdraw was,
of course, inconceivable. The gates had closed behind me
now, and the spirit of the adventure was already besieging my
mind with its advance guard of a thousand little hopes and
fears.

Explaining that he would wait till after dinner to discuss
anything serious, as no reference was ever made before his
sister, he led the way upstairs and showed us personally to our
rooms; and it was just as I was finishing dressing that a knock
came at my door and Dr Silence entered.

He was always what is called a serious man, so that even in
moments of comedy you felt he never lost sight of the profound gravity of life, but as he came across the room to me I
caught the expression of his face and understood in a flash
that he was now in his most grave and earnest mood. He
looked almost troubled. I stopped fumbling with my black tie
and stared.

'It *is* serious,' he said, speaking in a low voice, 'more so
even than I imagined. Colonel Wragge's control over his
thoughts concealed a great deal in my psychometrizing of the
letter. I looked in to warn you to keep yourself well in hand –
generally speaking.'

'Haunted house?' I asked, conscious of a distinct shiver
down my back.

But he smiled gravely at the question.

'Haunted House of Life more likely,' he replied, and a look
came into his eyes which I had only seen there when a human
soul was in the toils and he was thick in the fight of rescue.
He was stirred in the deeps.

'Colonel Wragge – or the sister?' I asked hurriedly, for the
gong was sounding.

'Neither directly,' he said from the door. 'Something far
older, something very, very remote indeed. This thing has to
do with the ages, unless I am mistaken greatly, the ages on
which the mists of memory have long lain undisturbed.'

He came across the floor very quickly with a finger on his

lips, looking at me with a peculiar searchingness of gaze.

'Are you aware yet of anything – odd here?' he asked in a whisper. 'Anything you cannot quite define, for instance. Tell me, Hubbard, for I want to know all your impressions. They may help me.'

I shook my head, avoiding his gaze, for there was something in the eyes that scared me a little. But he was so in earnest that I set my mind keenly searching.

'Nothing yet,' I replied truthfully, wishing I could confess to a real emotion; 'nothing but the strange heat of the place.'

He gave a little jump forward in my direction.

'The heat again, that's it!' he exclaimed, as though glad of my corroboration. 'And how would you describe it, perhaps?' he asked quickly, with a hand on the door knob.

'It doesn't seem like ordinary physical heat,' I said, casting about in my thoughts for a definition.

'More a mental heat,' he interrupted, 'a glowing of thought and desire, a sort of feverish warmth of the spirit. Isn't that it?'

I admitted that he had exactly described my sensations.

'Good!' he said, as he opened the door, and with an indescribable gesture that combined a warning to be ready with a sign of praise for my correct intuition, he was gone.

I hurried after him, and found the two men waiting for me in front of the fire.

'I ought to warn you,' our host was saying as I came in, 'that my sister, whom you will meet at dinner, is not aware of the real object of your visit. She is under the impression that we are interested in the same line of study – folklore – and that your researches have led to my seeking acquaintance. She comes to dinner in her chair, you know. It will be a great pleasure to her to meet you both. We have few visitors.'

So that on entering the dining-room we were prepared to find Miss Wragge already at her place, seated in a sort of bathchair. She was a vivacious and charming old lady, with smiling expression and bright eyes, and she chatted all through dinner with unfailing spontaneity. She had that face, unlined and fresh, that some people carry through life from the cradle to the grave; her smooth plump cheeks were all pink and white, and her hair, still dark, was divided into two glossy and sleek halves on either side of a careful parting. She wore gold-rimmed glasses, and at her throat was a large scarab of green jasper that made a very handsome brooch.

Her brother and Dr Silence talked little, so that most of the conversation was carried on between herself and me, and she told me a great deal about the history of the old house, most of which I fear I listened to with but half an ear.

'And when Cromwell stayed here,' she babbled on, 'he occupied the very rooms upstairs that used to be mine. But my brother thinks it safer for me to sleep on the ground floor now in case of fire.'

And this sentence has stayed in my memory only because of the sudden way her brother interrupted her and instantly led the conversation on to another topic. The passing reference to fire seemed to have disturbed him, and thenceforward he directed the talk himself.

It was difficult to believe that this lively and animated old lady, sitting beside me and taking so eager an interest in the affairs of life, was practically, we understood, without the use of her lower limbs, and that her whole existence for years had been passed between the sofa, the bed, and the bath-chair in which she chatted so naturally at the dinner-table. She made no allusion to her affliction until the dessert was reached, and then, touching a bell, she made us a witty little speech about leaving us 'like time, on noiseless feet', and was wheeled out of the room by the butler and carried off to her apartments at the other end of the house.

And the rest of us were not long in following suit, for Dr Silence and myself were quite as eager to learn the nature of our errand as our host was to impart it to us. He led us down a long flagged passage to a room at the very end of the house, a room provided with double doors, and windows, I saw, heavily shuttered. Books lined the walls on every side, and a large desk in the bow window was piled up with volumes, some open, some shut, some showing scraps of paper stuck between the leaves, and all smothered in a general cataract of untidy foolscap and loose half sheets.

'My study and workroom,' explained Colonel Wragge, with a delightful touch of innocent pride, as though he were a very serious scholar. He placed arm-chairs for us round the fire. 'Here,' he added significantly, 'we shall be safe from interruption and can talk securely.'

During dinner the manner of the doctor had been all that was natural and spontaneous, though it was impossible for me, knowing him as I did, not to be aware that he was subconsciously very keenly alert and already receiving upon the ultra-sensitive surface of his mind various and vivid impressions; and there was now something in the gravity of his face, as well as in the significant tone of Colonel Wragge's speech, and something, too, in the fact that we three were shut away in this private chamber about to listen to things probably strange, and certainly mysterious – something in all this that touched my imagination sharply and sent an undeniable thrill along my nerves. Taking the chair indicated by my host, I lit my cigar and waited for the opening of the attack, fully conscious that we were now too far gone in the adventure to admit of withdrawal, and wondering a little anxiously where it was going to lead.

What I expected precisely, it is hard to say. Nothing definite, perhaps. Only the sudden change was dramatic. A few hours before the prosaic atmosphere of Piccadilly was about me, and now I was sitting in a secret chamber of this remote old building waiting to hear an account of things that held possibly the genuine heart of terror. I thought of the dreary moors and hills outside, and the dark pine copses soughing in the wind of night; I remembered my companion's singular words up in my bedroom before dinner; and then I turned and noted carefully the stern countenance of the Colonel as he faced us and lit his big black cigar before speaking.

The threshold of an adventure, I reflected as I waited for

the first words, is always the most thrilling moment – until the climax comes.

But Colonel Wragge hesitated – mentally – a long time before he began. He talked briefly of our journey, the weather, the country, and other comparatively trivial topics, while he sought about in his mind for an appropriate entry into the subject that was uppermost in the thoughts of all of us. The fact was he found it a difficult matter to speak of at all, and it was Dr Silence who finally showed him the way over the hedge.

'Mr Hubbard will take a few notes when you are ready – you won't object,' he suggested; 'I can give my undivided attention in this way.'

'By all means,' turning to reach some of the loose sheets on the writing table, and glancing at me. He still hesitated a little, I thought. 'The fact is,' he said apologetically, 'I wondered if it was quite fair to trouble you so soon. The daylight might suit you better to hear what I have to tell. Your sleep, I mean, might be less disturbed, perhaps.'

'I appreciate your thoughtfulness,' John Silence replied with his gentle smile, taking command as it were from that moment, 'but really we are both quite immune. There is nothing, I think, that could prevent either of us sleeping, except – an outbreak of fire, or some such very physical disturbance.'

Colonel Wragge raised his eyes and looked fixedly at him. This reference to an outbreak of fire I felt sure was made with a purpose. It certainly had the desired effect of removing from our host's manner the last signs of hesitancy.

'Forgive me,' he said. 'Of course, I know nothing of your methods in matters of this kind – so, perhaps, you would like me to begin at once and give you an outline of the situation?'

Dr Silence bowed his agreement. 'I can then take my precautions accordingly,' he added calmly.

The soldier looked up for a moment as though he did not quite gather the meaning of these words; but he made no further comment and turned at once to tackle a subject on which he evidently talked with diffidence and unwillingness.

'It's all so utterly out of my line of things,' he began, puffing out clouds of cigar smoke between his words, 'and there's so little to tell with any real evidence behind it, that it's almost impossible to make a consecutive story for you. It's the total cumulative effect that is so – so disquieting.' He chose his words with care, as though determined not to travel one hair's breadth beyond the truth.

'I came into this place twenty years ago when my elder brother died,' he continued, 'but could not afford to live here then. My sister, whom you met at dinner, kept house for him till the end, and during all these years, while I was seeing service abroad, she had an eye to the place – for we never got a satisfactory tenant – and saw that it was not allowed to go to ruin. I myself took possession, however, only a year ago.

'My brother,' he went on, after a perceptible pause, 'spent much of his time away, too. He was a great traveller, and filled the house with stuff he brought home from all over the world. The laundry – a small detached building beyond the servants' quarters – he turned into a regular little museum. The curios and things I have cleared away – they collected dust and were always getting broken – but the laundry-house you shall see tomorrow.'

Colonel Wragge spoke with such deliberation and with so many pauses that this beginning took him a long time. But at this point he came to a full stop altogether. Evidently there was something he wished to say that cost him considerable effort. At length he looked up steadily into my companion's face.

'May I ask you – that is, if you won't think it strange,' he said, and a sort of hush came over his voice and manner, 'whether you have noticed anything at all unusual – anything queer, since you came into the house?'

Dr Silence answered without a moment's hesitation.

'I have,' he said. 'There is a curious sensation of heat in the place.'

'Ah!' exclaimed the other, with a slight start. 'You *have* noticed it. This unaccountable heat –'

'But its cause, I gather, is not in the house itself – but outside,' I was astonished to hear the doctor add.

Colonel Wragge rose from his chair and turned to unhook a framed map that hung upon the wall. I got the impression that the movement was made with the deliberate purpose of concealing his face.

'Your diagnosis, I believe, is amazingly accurate,' he said after a moment, turning round with the map in his hands. 'Though, of course, I can have no idea how you should guess –'

John Silence shrugged his shoulders expressively. 'Merely my impression,' he said. 'If you pay attention to impressions, and do not allow them to be confused by deductions of the intellect, you will often find them surprisingly, uncannily, accurate.'

Colonel Wragge resumed his seat and laid the map upon his knees. His face was very thoughtful as he plunged abruptly again into his story.

'On coming into possession,' he said, looking us alternately in the face, 'I found a crop of stories of the most extraordinary and impossible kind I had ever heard – stories which at first I treated with amused indifference, but later was forced to regard seriously, if only to keep my servants. These stories I thought I traced to the fact of my brother's death – and, in a way, I think so still.'

He leant forward and handed the map to Dr Silence.

'It's an old plan of the estate,' he explained, 'but accurate enough for our purpose, and I wish you would note the position of the plantations marked upon it, especially those near the house. That one,' indicating the spot with his finger, 'is called the Twelve Acre Plantation. It was just there, on the side nearest the house, that my brother and the head keeper met their deaths.'

He spoke as a man forced to recognize facts that he deplored, and would have preferred to leave untouched – things he personally would rather have treated with ridicule if possible. It made his words peculiarly dignified and impressive, and I listened with an increasing uneasiness as to the sort of help the doctor would look to me for later. It seemed as though I were a spectator of some drama of mystery in which any moment I might be summoned to play a part.

'It was twenty years ago,' continued the Colonel, 'but there was much talk about it at the time, unfortunately, and you may, perhaps, have heard of the affair. Stride, the keeper, was a passionate, hot-tempered man, but I regret to say, so was my brother, and quarrels between them seem to have been frequent.'

'I do not recall the affair,' said the doctor. 'May I ask what was the cause of death?' Something in his voice made me prick up my ears for the reply.

'The keeper, it was said, from suffocation. And at the in-quest the doctors averred that both men had been dead the same length of time when found.'

'And your brother?' asked John Silence, noticing the omission, and listening intently.

'Equally mysterious,' said our host, speaking in a low voice with effort. 'But there was one distressing feature I think I ought to mention. For those who saw the face – I did not see it myself – and though Stride carried a gun its chambers were undischarged –' He stammered and hesitated with confusion. Again that sense of terror moved between his words. He stuck.

'Yes,' said the chief listener sympathetically.

'My brother's face, they said, looked as though it had been scorched. It had been swept, as it were, by something that burned – blasted. It was, I am told, quite dreadful. The bodies were found lying side by side, faces downwards, both pointing away from the wood, as though they had been in the act of running, and not more than a dozen yards from its edge.'

Dr Silence made no comment. He appeared to be studying the map attentively.

'I did not see the face myself,' repeated the other, his man-ner somehow expressing the sense of awe he contrived to keep out of his voice, 'but my sister unfortunately did, and her present state I believe to be entirely due to the shock it gave to her nerves. She never can be brought to refer to it, naturally, and I am even inclined to think that the memory has mercifully been permitted to vanish from her mind. But she spoke of it at the time as a face swept by flame – blasted.'

John Silence looked up from his contemplation of the map, but with the air of one who wished to listen, not to speak, and presently Colonel Wragge went on with his account. He stood on the mat, his broad shoulders hiding most of the mantelpiece.

'They all centred about this particular plantation, these stories. That was to be expected, for the people here are as superstitious as Irish peasantry, and though I made one or two examples among them to stop the foolish talk, it had no effect, and new versions came to my ears every week. You may imagine how little good dismissals did, when I tell you that the servants dismissed themselves. It was not the house servants, but the men who worked on the estate outside. The keepers gave notice one after another, none of them with any reason I could accept; the foresters refused to enter the wood, and the beaters to beat in it. Word flew all over the countryside that Twelve Acre Plantation was a place to be avoided, day or night.

'There came a point,' the Colonel went on, now well in his swing, 'when I felt compelled to make investigations on my own account. I could not kill the thing by ignoring it; so I collected and analysed the stories at first hand. For this Twelve Acre Wood, you will see by the map, comes rather near home. Its lower end, if you will look, almost touches the end of the back lawn, as I will show you tomorrow, and its dense growth of pines forms the chief protection the house enjoys from the east winds that blow up from the sea. And in olden days, before my brother interfered with it and frightened all the game away, it was one of the best pheasant coverts on the whole estate.'

141

'And what form, if I may ask, did this interference take?' asked Dr Silence.

'In detail, I cannot tell you, for I do not know – except that I understand it was the subject of his frequent differences with the head keeper; but during the last two years of his life, when he gave up travelling and settled down here, he took a special interest in this wood, and for some unaccountable reason began to build a low stone wall round it. This wall was never finished, but you shall see the ruins tomorrow in the daylight.'

'And the result of your investigations – these stories, I mean?' the doctor broke in, anxious to keep him to the main issues.

'Yes, I'm coming to that,' he said slowly, 'but the wood first, for this wood out of which they grew like mushrooms has nothing in any way peculiar about it. It is very thickly grown, and rises to a clearer part in the centre, a sort of mound where there is a circle of large boulders – old Druid stones, I'm told. At another place there's a small pond. There's nothing distinctive about it that I could mention – just an ordinary pine-wood, a very ordinary pine-wood – only the trees are a bit twisted in the trunks, some of 'em, and very dense. Nothing more.

'And the stories? Well, none of them had anything to do with my poor brother, or the keeper, as you might have expected; and they were all odd – such odd things, I mean, to invent or imagine. I never could make out how these people got such notions into their heads.'

He paused a moment to relight his cigar.

'There's no regular path through it,' he resumed, puffing vigorously, 'but the fields round it are constantly used, and one of the gardeners whose cottage lies over that way declared he often saw moving lights in it at night, and luminous shapes like globes of fire over the tops of the trees, skimming and floating, and making a soft hissing sound – most of 'em said that, in fact – and another man saw shapes flitting in and out among the trees, things that were neither men nor animals, and all faintly luminous. No one ever pretended to see human forms – always queer, huge things they could not properly describe. Sometimes the whole wood was lit up, and one fellow – he's still here and you shall see him – has a most circumstantial yarn about having seen great stars lying on the ground round the edge of the wood at regular intervals –'

'What kind of stars?' put in John Silence sharply, in a sudden way that made me start.

'Oh, I don't know quite; ordinary stars, I think he said, only very large, and apparently blazing as though the ground was alight. He was too terrified to go close and examine, and he has never seen them since.'

He stooped and stirred the fire into a welcome blaze – welcome for its blaze of light rather than for its heat. In the room there was already a strange pervading sensation of warmth that was oppressive in its effect and far from comforting.

'Of course,' he went on, straightening up again on the mat, 'this was all commonplace enough – this seeing lights and figures at night. Most of these fellows drink, and imagination and terror between them may account for almost anything. But others saw things in broad daylight. One of the woodmen, a sober, respectable man, took the shortcut home to his midday meal, and swore he was followed the whole length of the wood by something that never showed itself, but dodged from tree to tree, always keeping out of sight, yet solid enough to make the branches sway and the twigs snap on the ground. And it made a noise, he declared – but really' – the speaker stopped and gave a short laugh – 'it's too absurd –'

'*Please!*' insisted the doctor; 'for it is these small details that give me the best clues always.'

'– it made a crackling noise, he said, like a bonfire. Those were his very words: like the crackling of a bonfire,' finished the soldier, with a repetition of his short laugh.

'Most interesting,' Dr Silence observed gravely. 'Please omit nothing.'

'Yes,' he went on, 'and it was soon after that the fires began – the fires in the wood. They started mysteriously burning in the patches of coarse white grass that cover the more open parts of the plantation. No one ever actually saw them start, but many, myself among the number, have seen them burning and smouldering. They are always small and circular in shape, and for all the world like a picnic fire. The head keeper has a dozen explanations, from sparks flying out of the house chimneys to the sunlight focusing through a dewdrop, but none of them, I must admit, convince me as being in the least likely or probable. They are most singular, I consider, most singular, these mysterious fires, and I am glad to say that they come only at rather long intervals and never seem to spread.

'But the keeper had other queer stories as well, and about things that are verifiable. He declared that no life ever willingly entered the plantation; more, that no life existed in it at all. No birds nested in the trees, or flew into their shade. He set countless traps, but never caught so much as a rabbit or a weasel. Animals avoided it, and more than once he had picked up dead creatures round the edges that bore no obvious signs of how they had met their death.

'Moreover, he told me one extraordinary tale about his retriever chasing some invisible creature across the field one day when he was out with his gun. The dog suddenly pointed at something in the field at his feet, and then gave chase, yelping like a mad thing. It followed its imaginary quarry to the borders of the wood, and then went in – a thing he had never known it to do before. The moment it crossed the edge – it is darkish in there even in daylight – it began fighting in the most frenzied and terrific fashion. It made him afraid to interfere, he said. And at last, when the dog came out, hanging its tail down and panting, he found something like white hair stuck to its jaws, and brought it to show me. I tell you these details because –'

'They are important, believe me,' the doctor stopped him. 'And you have it still, this hair?' he asked.

'It disappeared in the oddest way,' the Colonel explained. 'It was curious looking stuff, something like asbestos, and I sent it to be analysed by the local chemist. But either the man got wind of its origin, or else he didn't like the look of it for

The Nemesis of Fire

some reason, because he returned it to me and said it was neither animal, vegetable, nor mineral, so far as he could make out, and he didn't wish to have anything to do with it. I put it away in paper, but a week later, on opening the package – it was gone! Oh, the stories are simply endless. I could tell you hundreds all on the same lines.'

'And personal experiences of your own, Colonel Wragge?' asked John Silence earnestly, his manner showing the greatest possible interest and sympathy.

The soldier gave an almost imperceptible start. He looked distinctly uncomfortable.

'Nothing, I think,' he said slowly, 'nothing – er – I should like to rely on. I mean nothing I have the right to speak of, perhaps – yet.'

His mouth closed with a snap. Dr Silence, after waiting a little to see if he would add to his reply, did not seek to press him on the point.

'Well,' he resumed presently, and as though he would speak contemptuously, yet dared not, 'this sort of thing has gone on at intervals ever since. It spreads like wildfire, of course, mysterious chatter of this kind, and people began trespassing all over the estate, coming to see the wood, and making themselves a general nuisance. Notices of man-traps and spring-guns only seemed to increase their persistence; and – think of it,' he snorted, 'some local Research Society actually wrote and asked permission for one of their members to spend a night in the wood! Bolder fools, who didn't write for leave, came and took away bits of bark from the trees and gave them to clairvoyants, who invented in their turn a further batch of tales. There was simply no end to it all.'

'Most distressing and annoying, I can well believe,' interposed the doctor.

'Then suddenly the phenomena ceased as mysteriously as they had begun, and the interest flagged. The tales stopped. People got interested in something else. It all seemed to die out. This was last July. I can tell you exactly, for I've kept a diary more or less of what happened.'

'Ah!'

'But now, quite recently, within the past three weeks, it has all revived again with a rush – with a kind of furious attack, so to speak. It has really become unbearable. You may imagine what it means, and the general state of affairs, when I say that the possibility of leaving has occurred to me.'

'Incendiarism?' suggested Dr Silence, half under his breath, but not so low that Colonel Wragge did not hear him.

'By Jove, sir, you take the very words out of my mouth!' exclaimed the astonished man, glancing from the doctor to me and from me to the doctor, and rattling the money in his pocket as though some explanation of my friend's divining powers were to be found that way.

'It's only that you are thinking very vividly,' the doctor said quietly, 'and your thoughts form pictures in my mind before you utter them. It's merely a little elementary thought-reading.'

His intention, I saw, was not to perplex the good man, but to impress him with his powers so as to ensure obedience later.

'Good Lord! I had no idea –' He did not finish the sentence, and dived again abruptly into his narrative.

'I did not see anything myself, I must admit, but the stories of independent eye-witnesses were to the effect that lines of light, like streams of thin fire, moved through the wood and sometimes were seen to shoot out precisely as flames might shoot out – in the direction of this house. There,' he explained, in a louder voice that made me jump, pointing with a thick finger to the map, 'where the westerly fringe of the plantation comes up to the end of the lower lawn at the back of the house – where it links on to those dark patches, which are laurel shrubberies, running right up to the back premises – that's where these lights were seen. They passed from the wood to the shrubberies, and in this way reached the house itself. Like silent rockets, one man described them, rapid as lightning and exceedingly bright.'

'And this evidence you spoke of?'

'They actually reached the sides of the house. They've left

a mark of scorching on the walls – the walls of the laundry building at the other end. You shall see 'em tomorrow.' He pointed to the map to indicate the spot, and then straightened himself and glared about the room as though he had said something no one could believe and expected contradiction.

'Scorched – just as the faces were,' the doctor murmured, looking significantly at me.

'Scorched – yes,' repeated the Colonel, failing to catch the rest of the sentence in his excitement.

There was a prolonged silence in the room, in which I heard the gurgling of the oil in the lamp and the click of the coals and the heavy breathing of our host. The most unwelcome sensations were creeping about my spine, and I wondered whether my companion would scorn me utterly if I asked to sleep on the sofa in his room. It was eleven o'clock, I saw by the clock on the mantelpiece. We had crossed the dividing line and were now well in the movement of the adventure. The fight between my interest and my dread became acute. But, even if turning back had been possible, I think the interest would have easily gained the day.

'I have enemies, of course,' I heard the Colonel's rough voice break into the pause presently, 'and have discharged a number of servants –'

'It's not that,' put in John Silence briefly.

'You think not? In a sense I am glad, and yet – there are some things that can be met and dealt with –'

He left the sentence unfinished, and looked down at the floor with an expression of grim severity that betrayed a momentary glimpse of character. This fighting man loathed and abhorred the thought of an enemy he could not see and come to grips with. Presently he moved over and sat down in the chair between us. Something like a sigh escaped him. Dr Silence said nothing.

'My sister, of course, is kept in ignorance, as far as possible, of all this,' he said disconnectedly, and as if talking to himself. 'But even if she knew, she would find matter-of-fact explanations. I only wish I could. I'm sure they exist.'

There came then an interval in the conversation that was very significant. It did not seem a real pause, or the silence real silence, for both men continued to think so rapidly and strongly that one almost imagined their thoughts clothed themselves in words in the air of the room. I was more than a little keyed up with the strange excitement of all I had heard, but what stimulated my nerves more than anything else was the obvious fact that the doctor was clearly upon the trail of discovery. In his mind at that moment, I believe, he had already solved the nature of this perplexing psychical problem. His face was like a mask, and he employed the absolute minimum of gesture and words. All his energies were directed inwards, and by those incalculable methods and processes he had mastered with such infinite patience and study, I felt sure he was already in touch with the forces behind these singular phenomena and laying his deep plans for bringing them into the open, and then effectively dealing with them.

Colonel Wragge meanwhile grew more and more fidgety. From time to time he turned towards my companion, as though about to speak, yet always changing his mind at the last moment. Once he went over and opened the door suddenly, apparently to see if any one were listening at the keyhole, for he disappeared a moment between the two doors, and I then heard him open the outer one. He stood there for some seconds and made a noise as though he were sniffing the air like a dog. Then he closed both doors cautiously and came back to the fire-place. A strange excitement seemed growing upon him. Evidently he was trying to make up his mind to say something that he found it difficult to say. And John Silence, as I rightly judged, was waiting patiently for him to choose his own opportunity and his own way of saying it. At last he turned and faced us, squaring his great shoulders, and stiffening perceptibly.

Dr Silence looked up sympathetically.

'Your own experiences help me most,' he observed quietly.

'The fact is,' the Colonel said, speaking very low, 'this past week there have been outbreaks of fire in the house itself. Three separate outbreaks – and all – in my sister's room.'

'Yes,' the doctor said, as if this was just what he had expected to hear.

'Utterly unaccountable – all of them,' added the other, and then sat down. I began to understand something of the reason of his excitement. He was realizing at last that the 'natural' explanation he had held to all along was becoming impossible, and he hated it. It made him angry.

'Fortunately,' he went on, 'she was out each time and does not know. But I have made her sleep now in a room on the ground floor.'

'A wise precaution,' the doctor said simply. He asked one or two questions. The fire had started in the curtains – once by the window and once by the bed. The third time smoke had been discovered by the maid coming from the cupboard, and it was found that Miss Wragge's clothes hanging on the hooks were smouldering. The doctor listened attentively, but made no comment.

'And now can you tell me,' he said presently, 'what your own feeling about it is – your general impression?'

'It sounds foolish to say so,' replied the soldier, after a moment's hesitation, 'but I feel exactly as I have often felt on active service in my Indian campaigns: just as if the house and all in it were in a state of siege; as though a concealed enemy were encamped about us – in ambush somewhere.' He uttered a soft nervous laugh. 'As if the next sign of smoke would precipitate a panic – a dreadful panic.'

The picture came before me of the night shadowing the house, and the twisted pine trees he had described crowding about it, concealing some powerful enemy; and, glancing at the resolute face and figure of the old soldier, forced at length to his confession, I understood something of all he had been through before he sought the assistance of John Silence.

'And tomorrow, unless I am mistaken, is full moon,' said the doctor suddenly, watching the other's face for the effect of his apparently careless words.

Colonel Wragge gave an uncontrollable start, and his face for the first time showed unmistakable pallor.

'What in the world –?' he began, his lip quivering.

'Only that I am beginning to see light in this extraordinary affair,' returned the other calmly, 'and, if my theory is correct, each month when the moon is at the full should witness an increase in the activity of the phenomena.'

'I don't see the connexion,' Colonel Wragge answered almost savagely, 'but I am bound to say my diary bears you out.' He wore the most puzzled expression I have ever seen upon an honest face, but he abhorred this additional corroboration of an explanation that perplexed him.

'I confess,' he repeated, 'I cannot see the connexion.'

'Why should you?' said the doctor, with his first laugh that evening. He got up and hung the map upon the wall again. 'But I do – because these things are my special study – and let me add that I have yet to come across a problem that is not natural, and has not a natural explanation. It's merely a question of how much one knows – and admits.'

Colonel Wragge eyed him with a new and curious respect in his face. But his feelings were soothed. Moreover, the doctor's laugh and change of manner came as a relief to all, and broke the spell of grave suspense that had held us so long. We all rose and stretched our limbs, and took little walks about the room.

'I am glad, Dr Silence, if you will allow me to say so, that you are here,' he said simply, 'very glad indeed. And now I fear I have kept you both up very late,' with a glance to include me, 'for you must be tired, and ready for your beds. I have told you all there is to tell,' he added, 'and tomorrow you must feel perfectly free to take any steps you think necessary.'

The end was abrupt, yet natural, for there was nothing more to say, and neither of these men talked for mere talking's sake.

Out in the cold and chilly hall he lit our candles and took us upstairs. The house was at rest and still, every one asleep. We moved softly. Through the windows on the stairs we saw the moonlight falling across the lawn, throwing deep shadows. The nearer pine trees were just visible in the distance, a wall of impenetrable blackness.

Our host came for a moment to our rooms to see that we had everything. He pointed to a coil of strong rope lying beside the window, fastened to the wall by means of an iron ring. Evidently it had been recently put in.

'I don't think we shall need it,' Dr Silence said, with a smile.

'I trust not,' replied our host gravely. 'I sleep quite close to you across the landing,' he whispered, pointing to his door, 'and if you – if you want anything in the night you will know where to find me.'

He wished us pleasant dreams and disappeared down the passage into his room, shading the candle with his big muscular hand from the draughts.

John Silence stopped me a moment before I went.

'You know what it is?' I asked, with an excitement that even overcame my weariness.

'Yes,' he said, 'I'm almost sure. And you?'

'Not the smallest notion.'

He looked disappointed, but not half as disappointed as I felt.

'Egypt,' he whispered, 'Egypt!'

2

Nothing happened to disturb me in the night – nothing, that is, except a nightmare in which Colonel Wragge chased me amid thin streaks of fire, and his sister always prevented my escape by suddenly rising up out of the ground in her chair – dead. The deep baying of dogs woke me once, just before the dawn, it must have been, for I saw the window frame against the sky; there was a flash of lightning, too, I thought, as I turned over in bed. And it was warm, for October oppressively warm.

It was after eleven o'clock when our host suggested going

out with the guns, these, we understood, being a somewhat thin disguise for our true purpose. Personally, I was glad to be in the open air, for the atmosphere of the house was heavy with presentiment. The sense of impending disaster hung over all. Fear stalked the passages, and lurked in the corners of every room. It was a house haunted, but really haunted; not by some vague shadow of the dead, but by a definite though incalculable influence that was actively alive, and dangerous. At the least smell of smoke the entire household quivered. An odour of burning, I was convinced, would paralyse all the inmates. For the servants, though professedly ignorant by the master's unspoken orders, yet shared the common dread; and the hideous uncertainty, joined with this display of so spiteful and calculated a spirit of malignity, provided a kind of black doom that draped not only the walls, but also the minds of the people living within them.

Only the bright and cheerful vision of old Miss Wragge being pushed about the house in her noiseless chair, chatting and nodding briskly to every one she met, prevented us from giving way entirely to the depression which governed the majority. The sight of her was like a gleam of sunshine through the depths of some ill-omened wood, and just as we went out I saw her being wheeled along by her attendant into the sunshine of the back lawn, and caught her cheery smile as she turned her head and wished us good sport.

The morning was October at its best. Sunshine glistened on the dew-drenched grass and on leaves turned golden-red. The dainty messengers of coming hoar-frost were already in the air, asearch for permanent winter quarters. From the wide moors that everywhere swept up against the sky, like a purple sea splashed by the occasional grey of rocky clefts, there stole down the cool and perfumed wind of the west. And the keen taste of the sea ran through all like a master-flavour, borne over the spaces perhaps by the seagulls that cried and circled high in the air.

But our host took little interest in this sparkling beauty, and had no thought of showing off the scenery of his property,

His mind was otherwise intent, and, for that matter, so were our own.

'Those bleak moors and hills stretch unbroken for hours,' he said, with a sweep of the hand; 'and over there, some four miles,' pointing in another direction, 'lies S— Bay, a long, swampy inlet of the sea, haunted by myriads of seabirds. On the other side of the house are the plantations and pine-woods. I thought we would get the dogs and go first to the Twelve Acre Wood I told you about last night. It's quite near.'

We found the dogs in the stable, and I recalled the deep baying of the night when a fine bloodhound and two great Danes leaped out to greet us. Singular companions for guns, I thought to myself, as we struck out across the fields and the great creatures bounded and ran beside us, nose to ground.

The conversation was scanty. John Silence's grave face did not encourage talk. He wore the expression I knew well – that look of earnest solicitude which meant that his whole being was deeply absorbed and preoccupied. Frightened, I had never seen him, but anxious often – it always moved me to witness it – and he was anxious now.

'On the way back you shall see the laundry building,' Colonel Wragge observed shortly, for he, too, found little to say. 'We shall attract less attention then.'

Yet not all the crisp beauty of the morning seemed able to dispel the feelings of uneasy dread that gathered increasingly about our minds as we went.

In a very few minutes a clump of pine trees concealed the house from view, and we found ourselves on the outskirts of a densely-grown plantation of conifers. Colonel Wragge stopped abruptly, and, producing a map from his pocket, explained once more very briefly its position with regard to the house. He showed how it ran up almost to the walls of the laundry building – though at the moment beyond our actual view – and pointed to the windows of his sister's bedroom where the fires had been. The room, now empty, looked straight on to the wood. Then, glancing nervously about him, and calling the dogs to heel, he proposed that we should enter the plantation and make as thorough examination of it as we thought worth while. The dogs, he added, might perhaps be persuaded to accompany us a little way – and he pointed to where they cowered at his feet – but he doubted it. 'Neither voice nor whip will get them very far, I'm afraid,' he said. 'I know by experience.'

'If you have no objection,' replied Dr Silence, with decision, and speaking almost for the first time, 'we will make our examination alone – Mr Hubbard and myself. It will be best so.'

His tone was absolutely final, and the Colonel acquiesced so politely that even a less intuitive man than myself must have seen that he was genuinely relieved.

'You doubtless have good reasons,' he said.

'Merely that I wish to obtain my impressions uncoloured. This delicate clue I am working on might be so easily blurred by the thought-currents of another mind with strongly pre-conceived ideas.'

'Perfectly. I understand,' rejoined the soldier, though with an expression of countenance that plainly contradicted his words. 'Then I will wait here with the dogs; and we'll have a look at the laundry on our way home.'

I turned once to look back as we clambered over the low stone wall built by the late owner, and saw his straight, soldierly figure standing in the sunlit field watching us with a curiously intent look on his face. There was something to me incongruous, yet distinctly pathetic, in the man's efforts to meet all far-fetched explanations of the mystery with contempt, and at the same time in his stolid, unswerving investigation of it all. He nodded at me and made a gesture of farewell with his hand. That picture of him, standing in the sunshine with his big dogs, steadily watching us, remains with me to this day.

Dr Silence led the way in among the twisted trunks, planted closely together in serried ranks, and I followed sharp at his heels. The moment we were out of sight he turned and put down his gun against the roots of a big tree, and I did likewise.

'We shall hardly want these cumbersome weapons of murder,' he observed, with a passing smile.

'You are sure of your clue, then?' I asked at once, bursting with curiosity, yet fearing to betray it lest he should think me unworthy. His own methods were so absolutely simple and untheatrical.

'I am sure of my clue,' he answered gravely. 'And I think we have come just in time. You shall know in due course. For the present – be content to follow and observe. And think steadily. The support of your mind will help me.'

His voice had that quiet mastery in it which leads men to face death with a sort of happiness and pride. I would have followed him anywhere at that moment. At the same time his words conveyed a sense of dread seriousness. I caught the thrill of his confidence; but also, in this broad light of day, I felt the measure of alarm that lay behind.

'You still have no strong impressions?' he asked. 'Nothing happened in the night, for instance? No vivid dreamings?'

He looked closely for my answer, I was aware.

'I slept almost an unbroken sleep. I was tremendously tired, you know, and, but for the oppressive heat –'

'Good! You still notice the heat, then,' he said to himself, rather than expecting an answer. 'And the lightning?' he added, 'that lightning out of a clear sky – that flashing – did you notice *that*?'

I answered truly that I thought I had seen a flash during a moment of wakefulness, and he then drew my attention to certain facts before moving on.

'You remember the sensation of warmth when you put the letter to your forehead in the train; the heat generally in the house last evening, and, as you now mention, in the night. You heard, too, the Colonel's stories about the appearances of fire in this wood and in the house itself, and the way his brother and the gamekeeper came to their deaths twenty years ago.'

I nodded, wondering what in the world it all meant.

'And you get no clue from these facts?' he asked, a trifle surprised.

I searched every corner of my mind and imagination for some inkling of his meaning, but was obliged to admit that I understood nothing so far.

'Never mind; you will later. And now,' he added, 'we will go over the wood and see what we can find.'

His words explained to me something of his method. We were to keep our minds alert and report to each other the least fancy that crossed the picture-gallery of our thoughts. Then, just as we started, he turned again to me with a final warning.

'And, for your safety,' he said earnestly, 'imagine *now* – and for that matter, imagine always until we leave this place – imagine with the utmost keenness, that you are surrounded by a shell that protects you. Picture yourself inside a protective envelope, and build it up with the most intense imagination you can evoke. Pour the whole force of your thought and will into it. Believe vividly all through this adventure that such a shell, constructed of your thought, will and imagination, surrounds you completely, and that nothing can pierce it to attack.'

He spoke with dramatic conviction, gazing hard at me as though to enforce his meaning, and then moved forward and began to pick his way over the rough, tussocky ground into the wood. And meanwhile, knowing the efficacy of his prescription, I adopted it to the best of my ability.

The trees at once closed about us like the night. Their branches met overhead in a continuous tangle, their stems crept closer and closer, the brambly undergrowth thickened and multiplied. We tore our trousers, scratched our hands, and our eyes filled with fine dust that made it most difficult to avoid the clinging, prickly network of branches and creepers. Coarse white grass that caught our feet like string grew here and there in patches. It crowned the lumps of peaty growth that stuck up like human heads, fantastically dressed, thrusting up at us out of the ground with crests of dead hair. We stumbled and floundered among them. It was hard going, and I could well conceive it impossible to find a way at all in the night-time. We jumped, when possible, from tussock to tussock, and it seemed as though we were springing among heads on a battlefield, and that this dead white grass concealed eyes that turned to stare as we passed.

Here and there the sunlight shot in with vivid spots of white light, dazzling the sight, but only making the surrounding gloom deeper by contrast. And on two occasions we passed dark circular places in the grass where fires had eaten their mark and left a ring of ashes. Dr Silence pointed to them, but without comment and without pausing, and the sight of them woke in me a singular realization of the dread that lay so far only just out of sight in this adventure.

It was exhausting work, and heavy going. We kept close together. The warmth, too, was extraordinary. Yet it did not seem the warmth of the body due to violent exertion, but rather an inner heat of the mind that laid glowing hands of fire upon the heart and set the brain in a kind of steady blaze. When my companion found himself too far in advance, he waited for me to come up. The place had evidently been untouched by hand of man, keeper, forester or sportsman, for many a year; and my thoughts, as we advanced painfully, were not unlike the state of the wood itself – dark, confused, full of a haunting wonder and the shadow of fear.

By this time all signs of the open field behind us were hid. No single gleam penetrated. We might have been groping in the heart of some primeval forest. Then, suddenly, the brambles and tussocks and string-like grass came to an end; the trees opened out; and the ground began to slope upwards towards a large central mound. We had reached the middle of the plantation, and before us stood the broken Druid stones our host had mentioned. We walked easily up the little hill, between the sparser stems, and, resting upon one of the ivy-covered boulders, looked round upon a comparatively open space, as large, perhaps, as a small London Square.

Thinking of the ceremonies and sacrifices this rough circle of prehistoric monoliths might have witnessed, I looked up into my companion's face with an unspoken question. But he read my thought and shook his head.

'Our mystery has nothing to do with these dead symbols,' he said, 'but with something perhaps even more ancient, and of another country altogether.'

'Egypt?' I said half under my breath, hopelessly puzzled, but recalling his words in my bedroom.

He nodded. Mentally I still floundered, but he seemed intensely preoccupied and it was no time for asking questions; so while his words circled unintelligibly in my mind I looked round at the scene before me, glad of the opportunity to recover breath and some measure of composure. But hardly had I time to notice the twisted and contorted shapes of many of the pine trees close at hand when Dr Silence leaned over and touched me on the shoulder. He pointed down the slope. And the look I saw in his eyes keyed up every nerve in my body to its utmost pitch.

A thin, almost imperceptible column of blue smoke was rising among the trees some twenty yards away at the foot of the mound. It curled up and up, and disappeared from sight among the tangled branches overhead. It was scarcely thicker than the smoke from a small brand of burning wood.

'Protect yourself! Imagine your shell strongly,' whispered the doctor sharply, 'and follow me closely.'

He rose at once and moved swiftly down the slope towards the smoke, and I followed, afraid to remain alone. I heard the soft crunching of our steps on the pine needles. Over his shoulder I watched the thin blue spiral, without once taking my eyes off it. I hardly know how to describe the peculiar sense of vague horror inspired in me by the sight of that streak of smoke pencilling its way upwards among the dark trees. And the sensation of increasing heat as we approached was phenomenal. It was like walking towards a glowing yet invisible fire.

As we drew nearer his pace slackened. Then he stopped and pointed, and I saw a small circle of burnt grass upon the ground. The tussocks were blackened and smouldering, and from the centre rose this line of smoke, pale, blue, steady. Then I noticed a movement of the atmosphere beside us, as if the warm air were rising and the cooler air rushing in to take its place: a little centre of wind in the stillness. Overhead the boughs stirred and trembled where the smoke disappeared. Otherwise, not a tree sighed, not a sound made itself heard. The wood was still as a graveyard. A horrible idea came to me that the course of nature was about to change without warning, *had* changed a little already, that the sky would drop, or the surface of the earth crash inwards like a broken bubble. Something, certainly, reached up to the citadel of my reason, causing its throne to shake.

John Silence moved forward again. I could not see his face, but his attitude was plainly one of resolution, of muscles and mind ready for vigorous action. We were within ten feet of the blackened circle when the smoke of a sudden ceased to rise, and vanished. The tail of the column disappeared in the air above, and at the same instant it seemed to me that the sensation of heat passed from my face, and the motion of the wind was gone. The calm spirit of the fresh October day resumed command.

Side by side we advanced and examined the place. The grass was smouldering, the ground still hot. The circle of burned earth was a foot to a foot and a half in diameter. It looked like an ordinary picnic fire-place. I bent down cautiously to look, but in a second I sprang back with an involuntary cry of alarm, for, as the doctor stamped on the ashes to prevent them spreading, a sound of hissing rose from the spot as though he had kicked a living creature. This hissing was faintly audible in the air. It moved past us, away towards the thicker portion of the wood in the direction of our field, and in a second Dr Silence had left the fire and started in pursuit.

And then began the most extraordinary hunt of invisibility I can ever conceive.

He went fast even at the beginning, and, of course, it was perfectly obvious that he was following something. To judge by the poise of his head he kept his eyes steadily at a certain level – just above the height of a man – and the consequence was he stumbled a good deal over the roughness of the ground.

The hissing sound had stopped. There was no sound of any kind, and what he saw to follow was utterly beyond me. I only know, that in mortal dread of being left behind, and with a biting curiosity to see whatever there was to be seen, I followed as quickly as I could, and even then barely succeeded in keeping up with him.

And, as we went, the whole mad jumble of the Colonel's stories ran through my brain, touching a sense of frightened laughter that was only held in check by the sight of this earnest, hurrying figure before me. For John Silence at work inspired me with a kind of awe. He looked so diminutive among these giant twisted trees, while yet I knew that his purpose and his knowledge were so great, and even in hurry he was dignified. The fancy that we were playing some queer, exaggerated game together met the fact that we were two men dancing upon the brink of some possible tragedy, and the mingling of the two emotions in my mind was both grotesque and terrifying.

He never turned in his mad chase, but pushed rapidly on, while I panted after him like a figure in some unreasoning nightmare. And, as I ran, it came upon me that he had been aware all the time, in his quiet, internal way, of many things that he had kept for his own secret consideration; he had been watching, waiting, planning from the very moment we entered the shade of the wood. By some inner, concentrated process of mind, dynamic if not actually magical, he had been in direct contact with the source of the whole adventure, the very essence of the real mystery. And now the forces were moving to a climax. Something was about to happen, something important, something possibly dreadful. Every nerve, every sense, every significant gesture of the plunging figure before me proclaimed the fact just as surely as the skies, the winds, and the face of the earth tell the birds the time to migrate and warn the animals that danger lurks and they must move.

In a few moments we reached the foot of the mound and entered the tangled undergrowth that lay between us and the sunlight of the field. Here the difficulties of fast travelling increased a hundredfold. There were brambles to dodge, low boughs to dive under, and countless tree trunks closing up to make a direct path impossible. Yet Dr Silence never seemed to falter or hesitate. He went, diving, jumping, dodging, ducking, but ever in the same main direction, following a clean trail. Twice I tripped and fell, and both times, when I picked myself up again, I saw him ahead of me, still forcing a way like a dog after its quarry. And sometimes, like a dog, he stopped and pointed – human pointing it was, psychic pointing – and each time he stopped to point I heard the faint high hissing in the air beyond us. The instinct of an infallible dowser possessed him, and he made no mistakes.

At length, abruptly, I caught up with him, and found that we stood at the edge of the shallow pond Colonel Wragge had mentioned in his account the night before. It was long and narrow, filled with dark brown water, in which the trees were dimly reflected. Not a ripple stirred its surface.

'Watch!' he cried out, as I came up. 'It's going to cross. It's bound to betray itself. The water is its natural enemy, and we shall see the direction.'

And, even as he spoke, a thin line like the track of a water-spider, shot swiftly across the shiny surface; there was a ghost of steam in the air above; and immediately I became aware of an odour of burning.

Dr Silence turned and shot a glance at me that made me think of lightning. I began to shake all over.

'Quick!' he cried with excitement, 'to the trail again! We must run round. It's going to the house!'

The alarm in his voice quite terrified me. Without a false step I dashed round the slippery banks and dived again at his heels into the sea of bushes and tree trunks. We were now in the thick of the very dense belt that ran round the outer edge of the plantation, and the field was near; yet so dark was the tangle that it was some time before the first shafts of white sunlight became visible. The doctor now ran in zigzags. He was following something that dodged and doubled quite wonderfully, yet had begun, I fancied, to move more slowly than before.

161

'Quick!' he cried. 'In the light we shall lose it!'

I still saw nothing, heard nothing, caught no suggestion of a trail; yet this man, guided by some interior divining that seemed infallible, made no false turns, though how we failed to crash headlong into the trees has remained a mystery to me ever since. And then, with a sudden rush, we found ourselves on the skirts of the wood with the open field lying in bright sunshine before our eyes.

'Too late!' I heard him cry, a note of anguish in his voice. 'It's out – and, by God, it's making for the house!'

I saw the Colonel standing in the field with his dogs where we had left him. He was bending double, peering into the wood where he heard us running, and he straightened up like a bent whip released. John Silence dashed past, calling him to follow.

'We shall lose the trail in the light,' I heard him cry as he ran. 'But quick! We may yet get there in time!'

That wild rush across the open field, with the dogs at our heels, leaping and barking, and the elderly Colonel behind us running as though for his life, shall I ever forget it? Though I had only vague ideas of the meaning of it all, I put my best foot forward, and, being the youngest of the three, I reached the house an easy first. I drew up, panting, and turned to wait for the others. But, as I turned, something moving a little distance away caught my eye, and in that moment I swear I experienced the most overwhelming and singular shock of surprise and terror I have ever known, or can conceive as possible.

For the front door was open, and the waist of the house being narrow, I could see through the hall into the dining-room beyond, and so out on to the back lawn, and there I saw no less a sight than the figure of Miss Wragge – running. Even at that distance it was plain that she had seen me, and was coming fast towards me, running with the frantic gait of a terror-stricken woman. She had recovered the use of her legs.

Her face was a livid grey, as of death itself, but the general expression was one of laughter, for her mouth was gaping, and her eyes, always bright, shone with the light of a wild merriment that seemed the merriment of a child, yet was singularly ghastly. And that very second, as she fled past me into her brother's arms behind, I smelt again most unmistakably the odour of burning, and to this day the smell of smoke and fire can come very near to turning me sick with the memory of what I had seen.

Fast on her heels, too, came the terrified attendant, more mistress of herself, and able to speak – which the old lady could not do – but with a face almost, if not quite, as fearful.

'We were down by the bushes in the sun,' – she gasped and screamed in reply to Colonel Wragge's distracted questionings, – 'I was wheeling the chair as usual when she shrieked and leaped – I don't know exactly – I was too frightened to see – Oh, my God! she jumped clean out of the chair – *and ran!* There was a blast of hot air from the wood, and she hid her face and jumped. She didn't make a sound – she didn't cry out, or make a sound. She just ran.'

But the nightmare horror of it all reached the breaking point a few minutes later, and while I was still standing in the hall temporarily bereft of speech and movement; for while the doctor, the Colonel and the attendant were half-way up the staircase, helping the fainting woman to the privacy of her room, and all in a confused group of dark figures, there sounded a voice behind me, and I turned to see the butler, his face dripping with perspiration, his eyes starting out of his head.

'The laundry's on fire!' he cried; 'the laundry building's a-caught!'

I remember his odd expression 'a-caught', and wanting to laugh, but finding my face rigid and inflexible.

'The devil's about again, s'help me Gawd!' he cried, in a voice thin with terror, running about in circles.

And then the group on the stairs scattered as at the sound of a shot, and the Colonel and Dr Silence came down three steps at a time, leaving the afflicted Miss Wragge to the care of her single attendant.

We were out across the front lawn in a moment and round

the corner of the house, the Colonel leading, Silence and I at his heels, and the portly butler puffing some distance in the rear, getting more and more mixed in his addresses to God and the devil; and the moment we passed the stables we saw a wicked-looking volume of smoke pouring out of the narrow windows, and the frightened women-servants and grooms running hither and thither, calling aloud as they ran.

The arrival of the master restored order instantly, and this retired soldier, poor thinker perhaps, but capable man of action, had the matter in hand from the start. He issued orders like a martinet, and, almost before I could realize it, there were streaming buckets on the scene and a line of men and women formed between the building and the stable pump.

'Inside,' I heard John Silence cry, and the Colonel followed him through the door, while I was just quick enough at their heels to hear him add, 'the smoke's the worst part of it. There's no fire yet, I think.'

And, true enough, there was no fire. The interior was thick with smoke, but it speedily cleared and not a single bucket was used upon the floor or walls. The air was stifling, the heat fearful.

'There's precious little to burn in here; it's all stone,' the Colonel exclaimed, coughing. But the doctor was pointing to the wooden covers of the great cauldron in which the clothes were washed, and we saw that these were smouldering and charred. And when we sprinkled half a bucket of water on them the surrounding bricks hissed and fizzed and sent up clouds of steam. Through the open door and windows this passed out with the rest of the smoke, and we three stood there on the brick floor staring at the spot and wondering, each in our own fashion, how in the name of natural law the place could have caught fire or smoked at all. And each was silent – myself from sheer incapacity and befuddlement, the Colonel from the quiet pluck that faces all things yet speaks little, and John Silence from the intense mental grapplings with this latest manifestation of a profound problem that called for concentration of thought rather than for any words.

There was really nothing to say. The facts were indisputable. Colonel Wragge was the first to utter.

'My sister,' he said briefly, and moved off. In the yard I heard him sending the frightened servants about their business in an excellently matter-of-fact voice, scolding some one roundly for making such a big fire and letting the flues get over-heated, and paying no heed to the stammering reply that no fire had been lit there for several days. Then he dispatched a groom on horseback for the local doctor.

Then Dr Silence turned and looked at me. The absolute control he possessed, not only over the outward expression of emotion by gesture, change of colour, light in the eyes, and so forth, but also, as I well knew, over its very birth in his heart, the mask-like face of the dead he could assume at will, made it extremely difficult to know at any given moment what was at work in his inner consciousness. But now, when he turned and looked at me, there was no sphinx-expression there, but rather the keen, triumphant face of a man who had solved a dangerous and complicated problem, and saw his way to a clean victory.

'*Now* do you guess?' he asked quietly, as though it were the simplest matter in the world, and ignorance were impossible.

I could only stare stupidly and remain silent. He glanced down at the charred cauldron-lids, and traced a figure in the air with his finger. But I was too excited, or too mortified, or still too dazed, perhaps, to see what it was he outlined, or what it was he meant to convey. I could only go on staring and shaking my puzzled head.

'A fire-elemental,' he cried, 'a fire-elemental of the most powerful and malignant kind –'

'A what?' thundered the voice of Colonel Wragge behind us, having returned suddenly and overheard.

'It's a fire-elemental,' repeated Dr Silence more calmly, but with a note of triumph in his voice he could not keep out, 'and a fire-elemental enraged.'

The light began to dawn in my mind at last. But the Colonel

– who had never heard the term before, and was besides feeling considerably worked-up for a plain man with all this mystery he knew not how to grapple with – the Colonel stood, with the most dumbfounded look ever seen on a human countenance, and continued to roar, and stammer, and stare.

'And why,' he began, savage with the desire to find something visible he could fight – 'why, in the name of all the blazes –?' and then stopped as John Silence moved up and took his arm.

'There, my dear Colonel Wragge,' he said gently, 'you touch the heart of the whole thing. You ask "Why". That is precisely our problem.' He held the soldier's eyes firmly with his own. 'And that, too, I think, we shall soon know. Come and let us talk over a plan of action – that room with the double doors, perhaps.'

The word 'action' calmed him a little, and he led the way, without further speech, back into the house, and down the long stone passage to the room where we had heard his stories on the night of our arrival. I understood from the doctor's glance that my presence would not make the interview easier for our host, and I went upstairs to my own room – shaking.

But in the solitude of my room the vivid memories of the last hour revived so mercilessly that I began to feel I should never in my whole life lose the dreadful picture of Miss Wragge running – that dreadful human climax after all the non-human mystery in the wood – and I was not sorry when a servant knocked at my door and said that Colonel Wragge would be glad if I would join them in the little smoking-room.

'I think it is better you should be present,' was all Colonel Wragge said as I entered the room. I took the chair with my back to the window. There was still an hour before lunch, though I imagine that the usual divisions of the day hardly found a place in the thoughts of any one of us.

The atmosphere of the room was what I might call electric. The Colonel was positively bristling; he stood with his back to the fire, fingering an unlit black cigar, his face flushed, his being obviously roused and ready for action. He hated this

The Nemesis of Fire

mystery. It was poisonous to his nature, and he longed to meet something face to face – something he could gauge and fight. Dr Silence, I noticed at once, was sitting before the map of the estate which was spread upon a table. I knew by his expression the state of his mind. He was in the thick of it all, knew it, delighted in it, and was working at high pressure. He recognized my presence with a lifted eyelid, and the flash of the eyes, contrasted with his stillness and composure, told me volumes.

'I was about to explain to our host briefly what seems to me afoot in all this business,' he said without looking up, 'when he asked that you should join us so that we can all work together.' And, while signifying my assent, I caught myself wondering what quality it was in the calm speech of this undemonstrative man that was so full of power, so charged with the strange, virile personality behind it and that seemed to inspire us with his own confidence as by a process of radiation.

'Mr Hubbard,' he went on gravely, turning to the soldier, 'knows something of my methods, and in more than one – er – interesting situation has proved of assistance. What we want now' – and here he suddenly got up and took his place on the mat beside the Colonel, and looked hard at him – 'is men who have self-control, who are sure of themselves, whose minds at the critical moment will emit positive forces, instead of the wavering and uncertain currents due to negative feelings – due, for instance, to fear.'

He looked at us each in turn. Colonel Wragge moved his feet farther apart, and squared his shoulders; and I felt guilty but said nothing, conscious that my latent store of courage was being deliberately hauled to the front. He was winding me up like a clock.

'So that, in what is yet to come,' continued our leader, 'each of us will contribute his share of power, and ensure success for my plan.'

'I'm not afraid of anything I can *see*,' said the Colonel bluntly.

'I'm ready,' I heard myself say, as it were automatically,

167

'for anything,' and then added, feeling the declaration was lamely insufficient, 'and everything.'

Dr Silence left the mat and began walking to and fro about the room, both hands plunged deep into the pockets of his shooting-jacket. Tremendous vitality streamed from him. I never took my eyes off the small, moving figure; small, yes, – and yet somehow making me think of a giant plotting the destruction of worlds. And his manner was gentle, as always, soothing almost, and his words uttered quietly without emphasis or emotion. Most of what he said was addressed, though not too obviously, to the Colonel.

'The violence of this sudden attack,' he said softly, pacing to and fro beneath the bookcase at the end of the room, 'is due, of course, partly to the fact that tonight the moon is at the full' – here he glanced at me for a moment – 'and partly to the fact that we have all been so deliberately concentrating upon the matter. Our thinking, our investigation, has stirred it into unusual activity. I mean that the intelligent force behind these manifestations has realized that someone is busied about its destruction. And it is now on the defensive: more, it is aggressive.'

'But "it" – what is "it"?' began the soldier, fuming. 'What, in the name of all that's dreadful, *is* a fire-elemental?'

'I cannot give you at this moment,' replied Dr Silence, turning to him, but undisturbed by the interruption, 'a lecture on the nature and history of magic, but can only say that an Elemental is the active force behind the elements, – whether earth, air, water, *or fire*, – it is impersonal in its essential nature, but can be focused, personified, ensouled, so to say, by those who know how – by magicians, if you will – for certain purposes of their own, much in the same way that steam and electricity can be harnessed by the practical man of this century.

'Alone, these blind elemental energies can accomplish little, but governed and directed by the trained will of a powerful manipulator they may become potent activities for good or evil. They are the basis of all magic, and it is the motive behind them that constitutes the magic "black" or "white"; they can be the vehicles of curses or of blessings, for a curse is nothing more than the thought of a violent will perpetuated. And in such cases – cases like this – the conscious, directing will of the mind that is using the elemental stands always behind the phenomena –'

'You think that my brother –!' broke in the Colonel, aghast.

'Has nothing whatever to do with it – directly. The fire-elemental that has here been tormenting you and your household was sent upon its mission long before you, or your family, or your ancestors, or even the nation you belong to – unless I am much mistaken – was even in existence. We will come to that a little later; after the experiment I propose to make we shall be more positive. At present I can only say we have to deal now, not only with the phenomenon of Attacking Fire merely, but with the vindictive and enraged intelligence that is directing it from behind the scenes – vindicative and enraged,' – he repeated the words.

'That explains –' began Colonel Wragge, seeking furiously for words he could not find quickly enough.

'Much,' said John Silence, with a gesture to restrain him.

He stopped a moment in the middle of his walk, and a deep silence came down over the little room. Through the windows the sunlight seemed less bright, the long line of dark hills less friendly, making me think of a vast wave towering to heaven and about to break and overwhelm us. Something formidable had crept into the world about us. For, undoubtedly, there was a disquieting thought, holding terror as well as awe, in the picture his words conjured up: the conception of a human will reaching its deathless hand, spiteful and destructive, down through the ages, to strike the living and afflict the innocent.

'But what *is* its object?' burst out the soldier, unable to restrain himself longer in the silence. 'Why does it come from that plantation? And why should it attack us, or anyone in particular?' Questions began to pour from him in a stream.

'All in good time,' the doctor answered quietly, having let him run on for several minutes. 'But I must first discover positively what, or who, it is that directs this particular fire-elemental. And, to do that, we must first' – he spoke with slow deliberation – 'seek to capture – to confine by visibility – to limit its sphere in a concrete form.'

'Good heavens almighty!' exclaimed the soldier, mixing his words in his unfeigned surprise.

'Quite so,' pursued the other calmly; 'for in so doing I think we can release it from the purpose that binds it, restore it to its normal condition of latent fire, and also' – he lowered his voice perceptibly – 'also discover the face and form of the Being that ensouls it.'

'The man behind the gun!' cried the Colonel, beginning to understand something, and leaning forward so as not to miss a single syllable.

'I mean that in the last resort, before it returns to the womb of potential fire, it will probably assume the face and figure of its Director, of the man of magical knowledge who originally bound it with his incantations and sent it forth upon its mission of centuries.'

The soldier sat down and gasped openly in his face, breathing hard; but it was a very subdued voice that framed the question.

'And how do you propose to make it visible? How capture and confine it? What d'ye mean, Dr John Silence?'

'By furnishing it with the materials for a form. By the process of materialization simply. Once limited by dimensions, it will become slow, heavy, visible. We can then dissipate it. Invisible fire, you see, is dangerous and incalculable; locked up in a form we can perhaps manage it. We must betray it – to its death.'

'And this material?' we asked in the same breath, although I think I had already guessed.

'Not pleasant, but effective,' came the quiet reply; 'the exhalations of freshly-spilled blood.'

'Not human blood!' cried Colonel Wragge, starting up from his chair with a voice like an explosion. I thought his eyes would start from their sockets.

The face of Dr Silence relaxed in spite of himself, and his spontaneous little laugh brought a welcome though momentary relief.

'The days of human sacrifice, I hope, will never come again,' he explained. 'Animal blood will answer the purpose, and we can make the experiment as pleasant as possible. Only, the blood must be freshly spilled and strong with the vital emanations that attract this peculiar class of elemental creature. Perhaps – perhaps if some pig on the estate is ready for the market –'

He turned to hide a smile; but the passing touch of comedy found no echo in the mind of our host, who did not understand how to change quickly from one emotion to another. Clearly he was debating many things laboriously in his honest brain. But, in the end, the earnestness and scientific disinterestedness of the doctor, whose influence over him was already very great, won the day, and he presently looked up more calmly, and observed shortly that he thought perhaps the matter could be arranged.

'There are other and pleasanter methods,' Dr Silence went on to explain, 'but they require time and preparation, and things have gone much too far, in my opinion, to admit of delay. And the process need cause you no distress: we sit round the bowl and await results. Nothing more. The emanations of blood – which, as Levi says, is the first incarnation of the universal fluid – furnish the materials out of which the creatures of discarnate life, spirits if you prefer, can fashion themselves a temporary appearance. The process is old, and lies at the root of all blood sacrifice. It was known to the priests of Baal, and it is known to the modern ecstasy dancers who cut themselves to produce objective phantoms who dance with them. And the least gifted clairvoyant could tell you that the forms to be seen in the vicinity of slaughter-houses, or hovering above the deserted battlefield, are – well, simply beyond all description. I do not mean,' he added, noticing the uneasy fidgeting of his host, 'that anything in our laundry-experiment need appear to terrify us, for this case seems a

171

comparatively simple one, and it is only the vindictive character of the intelligence directing this fire-elemental that causes
anxiety and makes for personal danger.'

'It is curious,' said the Colonel, with a sudden rush of words,
drawing a deep breath, and as though speaking of things dis-
tasteful to him, 'that during my years among the Hill Tribes
of Northern India I came across – personally came across –
instances of the sacrifices of blood to certain deities being
stopped suddenly, and all manner of disasters happening until
they were resumed. Fires broke out in the huts, and even on
the clothes, of the natives – and – and I admit I have read, in
the course of my duties,' – he made a gesture towards his
books and heavily laden table, – 'of the Yezidis of Syria evok-
ing phantoms by means of cutting their bodies with knives
during their whirling dances – enormous globes of fire which
turned into monstrous and terrible forms – and I remember
an account somewhere, too, how the emaciated forms and
pallid countenances of the spectres, that appeared to the Em-
peror Julian, claimed to be the true Immortals, and told him
to renew the sacrifices of blood "for the fumes of which, since
the establishment of Christianity, they had been pining" –
that these were in reality the phantoms evoked by the rites of
blood.'

Both Dr Silence and myself listened in amazement, for this
sudden speech was so unexpected, and betrayed so much
more knowledge than we had either of us suspected in the old
soldier.

'Then perhaps you have read, too,' said the doctor, 'how
the Cosmic Deities of savage races, elemental in their nature,
have been kept alive through many ages by these blood rites?'

'No,' he answered; 'that is new to me.'

'In any case,' Dr Silence added, 'I am glad you are not
wholly unfamiliar with the subject, for you will now bring
more sympathy, and therefore more help, to our experiment.
For, of course, in this case, we only want the blood to tempt
the creature from its lair and enclose it in a form –'

'I quite understand. And I only hesitated just now,' he

went on, his words coming much more slowly, as though he felt he had already said too much, 'because I wished to be quite sure it was no mere curiosity, but an actual sense of necessity that dictated this horrible experiment.'

'It is your safety, and that of your household, and of your sister, that is at stake,' replied the doctor. 'Once I have *seen*, I hope to discover whence this elemental comes, and what its real purpose is.'

Colonel Wragge signified his assent with a bow.

'And the moon will help us,' the other said, 'for it will be full in the early hours of the morning, and this kind of elemental-being is always most active at the period of full moon. Hence, you see, the clue furnished by your diary.'

So it was finally settled. Colonel Wragge would provide the materials for the experiment, and we were to meet at midnight. How he would contrive at that hour – but that was his business. I only know we both realized that he would keep his word, and whether a pig died at midnight, or at noon, was after all perhaps only a question of the sleep and personal comfort of the executioner.

'Tonight, then, in the laundry,' said Dr Silence finally, to clinch the plan; 'we three alone – and at midnight, when the household is asleep and we shall be free from disturbance.'

He exchanged significant glances with our host, who, at that moment, was called away by the announcement that the family doctor had arrived, and was ready to see him in his sister's room.

For the remainder of the afternoon John Silence disappeared. I had my suspicions that he made a secret visit to the plantation and also to the laundry building; but, in any case, we saw nothing of him, and he kept strictly to himself. He was preparing for the night, I felt sure, but the nature of his preparations I could only guess. There was movement in his room, I heard, and an odour like incense hung about the door, and knowing that he regarded rites as the vehicles of energies, my guesses were probably not far wrong.

Colonel Wragge, too, remained absent the greater part of

the afternoon, and, deeply afflicted, had scarcely left his sister's bedside, but in response to my inquiry when we met for a moment at tea-time, he told me that although she had moments of attempted speech, her talk was quite incoherent and hysterical, and she was still quite unable to explain the nature of what she had seen. The doctor, he said, feared she had recovered the use of her limbs, only to lose that of her memory, and perhaps even of her mind.

'Then the recovery of her legs, I trust, may be permanent, at any rate,' I ventured, finding it difficult to know what sympathy to offer. And he replied with a curious short laugh, 'Oh yes; about that there can be no doubt whatever.'

And it was due merely to the chance of my overhearing a fragment of conversation – unwillingly, of course – that a little further light was thrown upon the state in which the old lady actually lay. For, as I came out of my room, it happened that Colonel Wragge and the doctor were going downstairs together, and their words floated up to my ears before I could make my presence known by so much as a cough.

'Then you must find a way,' the doctor was saying with decision; 'for I cannot insist too strongly upon that – and at all costs she must be kept quiet. These attempts to go out must be prevented – if necessary, by force. This desire to visit some wood or other she keeps talking about is, of course, hysterical in nature. It cannot be permitted for a moment.'

'It shall not be permitted,' I heard the soldier reply, as they reached the hall below.

'It has impressed her mind for some reason –' the doctor went on, by way evidently of soothing explanation, and then the distance made it impossible for me to hear more.

At dinner Dr Silence was still absent, on the public plea of a headache, and though food was sent to his room, I am inclined to believe he did not touch it, but spent the entire time fasting.

We retired early, desiring that the household should do likewise, and I must confess that at ten o'clock when I bid my host a temporary good night, and sought my room to make what mental preparation I could, I realized in no very pleasant fashion that it was a singular and formidable assignation, this midnight meeting in the laundry building, and that there were moments in every adventure of life when a wise man, and one who knew his own limitations, owed it to his dignity to withdraw discreetly. And, but for the character of our leader, I probably should have then and there offered the best excuse I could think of, and have allowed myself quietly to fall asleep and wait for an exciting story in the morning of what had happened. But with a man like John Silence, such a lapse was out of the question, and I sat before my fire counting the minutes and doing everything I could think of to fortify my resolution and fasten my will at the point where I could be reasonably sure that my self-control would hold against all attacks of men, devils, or elementals.

3

At a quarter before midnight, clad in a heavy ulster, and with slippered feet, I crept cautiously from my room and stole down the passage to the top of the stairs. Outside the doctor's door I waited a moment to listen. All was still; the house in utter darkness; no gleam of light beneath any door; only, down the length of the corridor, from the direction of the sick-room, came faint sounds of laughter and incoherent talk that were not things to reassure a mind already half a-tremble, and I made haste to reach the hall and let myself out through the front door into the night.

The air was keen and frosty, perfumed with night smells, and exquisitely fresh; all the million candles of the sky were alight, and a faint breeze rose and fell with far-away sighings in the tops of the pine trees. My blood leaped for a moment in the spaciousness of the night, for the splendid stars brought courage; but the next instant, as I turned the corner of the house, moving stealthily down the gravel drive, my spirits sank again ominously. For, yonder, over the funereal plumes of the Twelve Acre Plantation, I saw the broken, yellow disc of the half-moon just rising in the east, staring down like some vast Being come to watch upon the progress of our doom. Seen through the distorting vapours of the earth's atmosphere, her face looked weirdly unfamiliar, her usual expression of benignant vacancy somehow a-twist. I slipped along by the shadows of the wall, keeping my eyes upon the ground.

The laundry-house, as already described, stood detached from the other offices, with laurel shrubberies crowding thickly behind it, and the kitchen-garden so close on the other side that the strong smells of soil and growing things came across almost heavily. The shadows of the haunted plantation, hugely lengthened by the rising moon behind them, reached to the very walls and covered the stone tiles of the roof with a dark pall. So keenly were my senses alert at this moment that I believe I could fill a chapter with the endless small details of the impression I received – shadows, odour, shapes, sounds – in the space of the few seconds I stood and waited before the closed wooden door.

Then I became aware of some one moving towards me through the moonlight, and the figure of John Silence, without overcoat and bareheaded, came quickly and without noise to join me. His eyes, I saw at once, were wonderfully bright, and so marked was the shining pallor of his face that I could hardly tell when he passed from the moonlight into the shade.

He passed without a word, beckoning me to follow, and then pushed the door open, and went in.

The chill air of the place met us like that of an underground vault; and the brick floor and white-washed walls, streaked with damp and smoke, threw back the cold in our faces. Directly opposite gaped the black throat of the huge open fireplace, the ashes of wood fires still piled and scattered about the hearth, and on either side of the projecting chimney-column were the deep recesses holding the big twin cauldrons for boiling clothes. Upon the lids of these cauldrons stood the two little oil lamps, shaded red, which gave all the light there was, and immediately in front of the fireplace there was a small circular table with three chairs set about it. Overhead, the narrow slit windows, high up the walls, pointed to a dim network of wooden rafters half lost among the shadows, and then came the dark vault of the roof. Cheerless and unalluring, for all the red light, it certainly was, reminding me of some unused conventicle, bare of pews or pulpit, ugly and severe, and I was forcibly struck by the contrast between the normal uses to which the place was ordinarily put, and the strange and medieval purpose which had brought us under its roof tonight.

Possibly an involuntary shudder ran over me, for my companion turned with a confident look to reassure me, and he was so completely master of himself that I at once absorbed from his abundance, and felt the chinks of my failing courage beginning to close up. To meet his eye in the presence of danger was like finding a mental railing that guided and supported thought along the giddy edges of alarm.

'I am quite ready,' I whispered, turning to listen for approaching footsteps.

He nodded, still keeping his eye on mine. Our whispers sounded hollow as they echoed overhead among the rafters.

'I'm glad you are here,' he said. 'Not all would have the courage. Keep your thoughts controlled, and imagine the protective shell round you – round your *inner* being.'

'I'm all right,' I repeated, cursing my chattering teeth.

He took my hand and shook it, and the contact seemed to shake into me something of his supreme confidence. The eyes and hands of a strong man can touch the soul. I think he guessed my thought, for a passing smile flashed about the corners of his mouth.

'You will feel more comfortable,' he said, in a low tone, 'when the chain is complete. The Colonel we can count on, of course. Remember, though,' he added warningly, 'he may perhaps become controlled – possessed – when the thing comes, because he won't know how to resist. And to explain the business to such a man –!' He shrugged his shoulders

177

expressively. 'But it will only be temporary, and I will see that no harm comes to him.'

He glanced round at the arrangements with approval.

'Red light,' he said, indicating the shaded lamps, 'has the lowest rate of vibration. Materializations are dissipated by strong light – won't form, or hold together – in rapid vibrations.'

I was not sure that I approved altogether of this dim light, for in complete darkness there is something protective – the knowledge that one cannot be seen, probably – which a half-light destroys, but I remembered the warning to keep my thoughts steady, and forbore to give them expression.

There was a step outside, and the figure of Colonel Wragge stood in the doorway. Though entering on tiptoe, he made considerable noise and clatter, for his free movements were impeded by the burden he carried, and we saw a large yellow-ish bowl held out at arm's length from his body, the mouth covered with a white cloth. His face, I noted, was rigidly composed. He, too, was master of himself. And, as I thought of this old soldier moving through the long series of alarms, worn with watching and wearied with assault, unenlightened yet undismayed, even down to the dreadful shock of his sister's terror, and still showing the dogged pluck that persists in the face of defeat, I understood what Dr Silence meant when he described him as a man 'to be counted on'.

I think there was nothing beyond the rigidity of his stern features, and a certain greyness of the complexion, to betray the turmoil of the emotions that was doubtless going on within; and the quality of these two men, each in his own way, so keyed me up that, by the time the door was shut and we had exchanged silent greetings, all the latent courage I possessed was well to the fore, and I felt as sure of myself as I knew I ever could feel.

Colonel Wragge set the bowl carefully in the centre of the table.

'Midnight,' he said shortly, glancing at his watch, and we all three moved to our chairs.

There, in the middle of that cold and silent place, we sat, with the vile bowl before us, and a thin, hardly perceptible steam rising through the damp air from the surface of the white cloth and disappearing upwards the moment it passed beyond the zone of red light and entered the deep shadows thrown forward by the projecting wall of chimney.

The doctor had indicated our respective places, and I found myself seated with my back to the door and opposite the black hearth. The Colonel was on my left, and Dr Silence on my right, both half facing me, the latter more in shadow than the former. We thus divided the little table into even sections, and sitting back in our chairs we awaited events in silence.

For something like an hour I do not think there was even the faintest sound within those four walls and under the canopy of that vaulted roof. Our slippers made no scratching on the gritty floor, and our breathing was suppressed almost to nothing; even the rustle of our clothes as we shifted from time to time upon our seats was inaudible. Silence smothered us absolutely – the silence of night, of listening, the silence of a haunted expectancy. The very gurgling of the lamps was too soft to be heard, and if light itself had sound, I do not think we should have noticed the silvery tread of the moonlight as it entered the high narrow windows and threw upon the floor the slender traces of its pallid footsteps.

Colonel Wragge and the doctor, and myself too for that matter, sat thus like figures of stone, without speech and without gesture. My eyes passed in ceaseless journeys from the bowl to their faces, and from their faces to the bowl. They might have been masks, however, for all the signs of life they gave; and the light steaming from the horrid contents beneath the white cloth had long ceased to be visible.

Then presently, as the moon rose higher, the wind rose with it. It sighed, like the lightest of passing wings, over the roof; it crept most softly round the walls; it made the brick floor like ice beneath our feet. With it I saw mentally the desolate moorland flowing like a sea about the old house, the treeless

179

expanse of lonely hills, the nearer copses, sombre, and mysterious in the night. *The* plantation, too, in particular I saw, and imagined I heard the mournful whisperings that must now be a-stirring among its tree-tops as the breeze played down between the twisted stems. In the depth of the room behind us the shafts of moonlight met and crossed in a growing network.

It was after an hour of this wearing and unbroken attention, and I should judge about one o'clock in the morning, when the baying of the dogs in the stable-yard first began, and I saw John Silence move suddenly in his chair and sit up in an attitude of attention. Every force in my being instantly leaped into the keenest vigilance. Colonel Wragge moved too, though slowly, and without raising his eyes from the table before him.

The doctor stretched his arm out and took the white cloth from the bowl.

It was perhaps imagination that persuaded me the red glare of the lamps grew fainter and the air over the table before us thickened. I had been expecting something for so long that the movement of my companions, and the lifting of the cloth, may easily have caused the momentary delusion that something hovered in the air before my face, touching the skin of my cheeks with a silken run. But it was certainly not a delusion that the Colonel looked up at the same moment and glanced over his shoulder, as though his eyes followed the movements of something to and fro about the room, and that he then buttoned his overcoat more tightly about him and his eyes sought my own face first, and then the doctor's. And it was no delusion that his face seemed somehow to have turned dark, become spread as it were with a shadowy blackness. I saw his lips tighten and his expression grow hard and stern, and it came to me then with a rush that, of course, this man had told us but a part of the experiences he had been through in the house, and that there was much more he had never been able to bring himself to reveal at all. I felt sure of it. The way he turned and stared about him betrayed a familiarity with other things than those he had described to us. It was not merely a sight of fire he looked for; it was a sight of something alive, intelligent, something able to evade his searching; it was *a person*. It was the watch for the ancient Being who sought to obsess him.

And the way in which Dr Silence answered his look – though it was only by a glance of subtlest sympathy – confirmed my impression.

'We may be ready now,' I heard him say in a whisper, and I understood that his words were intended as a steadying warning, and braced myself mentally to the utmost of my power.

Yet long before Colonel Wragge had turned to stare about the room, and long before the doctor had confirmed my impression that things were at last beginning to stir, I had become aware in most singular fashion that the place held more than our three selves. With the rising of the wind this increase to our numbers had first taken place. The baying of the hounds almost seemed to have signalled it. I cannot say how it may be possible to realize that an empty place has suddenly become – not empty, when the new arrival is nothing that appeals to any one of the senses; for this recognition of an 'invisible', as of the change in the balance of personal forces in a human group, is indefinable and beyond proof. Yet it is unmistakable. And I knew perfectly well at what given moment the atmosphere within these four walls became charged with the presence of other living beings besides ourselves. And, on reflection, I am convinced that both my companions knew it too.

'Watch the light,' said the doctor under his breath, and then I knew too that it was no fancy of my own that had turned the air darker, and the way he turned to examine the face of our host sent an electric thrill of wonder and expectancy shivering along every nerve in my body.

Yet it was no kind of terror that I experienced, but rather a sort of mental dizziness, and a sensation as of being suspended in some remote and dreadful altitude where things might happen, indeed were about to happen, that had never before happened within the ken of man. Horror may have formed an ingredient, but it was not chiefly horror, and in no sense ghostly horror.

Uncommon thoughts kept beating on my brain like tiny hammers, soft yet persistent, seeking admission, their un-bidden tide began to wash along the far fringes of my mind, the currents of unwonted sensations to rise over the remote frontiers of my consciousness. I was aware of thoughts, and the fantasies of thoughts, that I never knew before existed. Portions of my being stirred that had never stirred before, and things ancient and inexplicable rose to the surface and beck-oned me to follow. I felt as though I were about to fly off, at some immense tangent, into an outer space hitherto unknown even in dreams. And so singular was the result produced upon me that I was uncommonly glad to anchor my mind, as well as my eyes, upon the masterful personality of the doctor at my side, for there, I realized, I could draw always upon the forces of sanity and safety.

With a vigorous effort of will I returned to the scene before me, and tried to focus my attention, with steadier thoughts, upon the table, and upon the silent figures seated round it. And then I saw that certain changes had come about in the place where we sat.

The patches of moonlight on the floor, I noted, had become curiously shaded; the faces of my companions opposite were not so clearly visible as before; and the forehead and cheeks of Colonel Wragge were glistening with perspiration. I realized further, that an extraordinary change had come about in the temperature of the atmosphere. The increased warmth had a painful effect, not alone on Colonel Wragge, but upon all of us. It was oppressive and unnatural. We gasped figuratively as well as actually.

'You are the first to feel it,' said Dr Silence in low tones, looking across at him. 'You are in more intimate touch, of course –'

The Colonel was trembling, and appeared to be in consider-able distress. His knees shook, so that the shuffling of his slip-pered feet became audible. He inclined his head to show that he had heard, but made no other reply. I think, even then, he was sore put to it to keep himself in hand. I knew what he was struggling against. As Dr Silence had warned me, he was about to be obsessed, and was savagely, though vainly, resisting.

But, meanwhile, a curious and whirling sense of exhilaration began to come over me. The increasing heat was delightful, bringing a sensation of intense activity, of thoughts pouring through the mind at high speed, of vivid pictures in the brain, of fierce desires and lightning energies alive in every part of the body. I was conscious of no physical distress, such as the Colonel felt, but only of a vague feeling that it might all grow suddenly too intense – that I might be consumed – that my personality as well as my body might become resolved into the flame of pure spirit. I began to live at a speed too intense to last. It was as if a thousand ecstasies besieged me –

'Steady!' whispered the voice of John Silence in my ear, and I looked up with a start to see that the Colonel had risen from his chair. The doctor rose too. I followed suit, and for the first time saw down into the bowl. To my amazement and horror I saw that the contents were troubled. The blood was astir with movement.

The rest of the experiment was witnessed by us standing. It came, too, with a curious suddenness. There was no more dreaming, for me at any rate.

I shall never forget the figure of Colonel Wragge standing there beside me, upright and unshaken, squarely planted on his feet, looking about him, puzzled beyond belief, yet full of a fighting anger. Framed by the white walls, the red glow of the lamps upon his streaming cheeks, his eyes glowing against the deathly pallor of his skin, breathing hard and making convulsive efforts of hands and body to keep himself under control, his whole being roused to the point of savage fighting, yet with nothing visible to get at anywhere – he stood there, immovable against odds. And the strange contrast of the pale skin and the burning face I had never seen before, or wish to see again.

But what has left an even sharper impression on my memory was the blackness that then began crawling over his face, obliterating the features, concealing their human outline, and hiding him inch by inch from view. This was my first realization that the process of materialization was at work. His visage became shrouded. I moved from one side to the other to keep him in view, and it was only then I understood that, properly speaking, the blackness was not upon the countenance of Colonel Wragge, but that something had inserted itself between me and him, thus screening his face with the effect of a dark veil. Something that apparently rose through the floor was passing slowly into the air above the table and above the bowl. The blood in the bowl, moreover, was considerably less than before.

And, with this change in the air before us, there came at the same time a further change, I thought, in the face of the soldier. One-half was turned towards the red lamps, while the other caught the pale illumination of the moonlight falling aslant from the high windows, so that it was difficult to estimate this change with accuracy of detail. But it seemed to me that, while the features – eyes, nose, mouth – remained the same, the life informing them had undergone some profound transformation. The signature of a new power had crept into the face and left its traces there – an expression dark, and in some unexplained way, terrible.

Then suddenly he opened his mouth and spoke, and the sound of his changed voice, deep and musical though it was, made me cold and set my heart beating with uncomfortable rapidity. The Being, as he had dreaded, was already in control of his brain, using his mouth.

'I see a blackness like the blackness of Egypt before my face,' said the tones of this unknown voice that seemed half his own and half another's. 'And out of this darkness they come, they come.'

I gave a dreadful start. The doctor turned to look at me for an instant, and then turned to centre his attention upon the figure of our host, and I understood in some intuitive fashion that he was there to watch over the strangest contest man ever saw – to watch over and, if necessary, to protect.

'He is being controlled – possessed,' he whispered to me through the shadows. His face wore a wonderful expression, half triumph, half admiration.

Even as Colonel Wragge spoke, it seemed to me that this visible darkness began to increase, pouring up thickly out of the ground by the hearth, rising up in sheets and veils, shrouding our eyes and faces. It stole up from below – an awful blackness that seemed to drink in all the radiations of light in the building, leaving nothing but the ghost of a radiance in their place. Then, out of this rising sea of shadows, issued a pale and spectral light that gradually spread itself about us, and from the heart of this light I saw the shapes of fire crowd and gather. And these were not human shapes, or the shapes of anything I recognized as alive in the world, but outlines of fire that traced globes, triangles, crosses, and the luminous bodies of various geometrical figures. They grew bright, faded, and then grew bright again with an effect almost of pulsation. They passed swiftly to and fro through the air, rising and falling, and particularly in the immediate neighbourhood of the Colonel, often gathering about his head and shoulders, and even appearing to settle upon him like giant insects of flame. They were accompanied, moreover, by a faint sound of hissing – the same sound we had heard that afternoon in the plantation.

'The fire-elementals that precede their master,' the doctor said in an undertone. 'Be ready.'

And while this weird display of the shapes of fire alternately flashed and faded, and the hissing echoed faintly among the dim rafters overhead, we heard the awful voice issue at intervals from the lips of the afflicted soldier. It was a voice of power, splendid in some way I cannot describe, and with a certain sense of majesty in its cadences, and, as I listened to it with quickly-beating heart, I could fancy it was some ancient voice of Time itself, echoing down immense corridors of stone, from the depths of vast temples, from the very heart of mountain tombs.

'I have seen my divine Father, Osiris,' thundered the great

tones. 'I have scattered the gloom of the night. I have burst through the earth, and am one with the starry Deities!'

Something grand came into the soldier's face. He was staring fixedly before him, as though seeing nothing.

'Watch,' whispered Dr Silence in my ear, and his whisper seemed to come from very far away.

Again the mouth opened and the awesome voice issued forth.

'Thoth,' it boomed, 'has loosened the bandages of Set which fettered my mouth. I have taken my place in the great winds of heaven.'

I heard the little wind of night, with its mournful voice of ages, sighing round the walls and over the roof.

'Listen!' came from the doctor at my side, and the thunder of the voice continued –

'I have hidden myself with you, O ye stars that never diminish. I remember my name – in – the – House – of – Fire!'

The voice ceased and the sound died away. Something about the face and figure of Colonel Wragge relaxed, I thought. The terrible look passed from his face. The Being that obsessed him was gone.

'The great Ritual,' said Dr Silence aside to me, very low, 'the Book of the Dead. Now it's leaving him. Soon the blood will fashion it a body.'

Colonel Wragge, who had stood absolutely motionless all this time, suddenly swayed, so that I thought he was going to fall – and, but for the quick support of the doctor's arm, he probably would have fallen, for he staggered as in the beginning of collapse.

'I am drunk with the wine of Osiris,' he cried – and it was half with his own voice this time – 'but Horus, the Eternal Watcher, is about my path – for – safety.' The voice dwindled and failed, dying away into something almost like a cry of distress.

'Now, watch closely,' said Dr Silence, speaking loud, 'for after the cry will come the Fire!'

I began to tremble involuntarily; an awful change had come

without warning into the air; my legs grew weak as paper beneath my weight and I had to support myself by leaning on the table. Colonel Wragge, I saw, was also leaning forward with a kind of droop. The shapes of fire had vanished, all but his face was lit by the red lamps and the pale shifting moonlight rose behind him like mist.

We were both gazing at the bowl, now almost empty; the Colonel stooped so low I feared every minute he would lose his balance and drop into it; and the shadow, that had so long been in process of forming, now at length began to assume material outline in the air before us.

Then John Silence moved forward quickly. He took his place between us and the shadow. Erect, formidable, absolute master of the situation, I saw him stand there, his face calm and almost smiling, and fire in his eyes. His protective influence was astounding and incalculable. Even the abhorrent dread I felt at the sight of the creature growing into life and substance before us, lessened in some way so that I was able to keep my eyes fixed on the air above the bowl without too vivid a terror.

But as it took shape, rising out of nothing as it were, and growing momentarily more defined in outline, a period of utter and wonderful silence settled down upon the building and all it contained. A hush of ages, like the sudden centre of peace at the heart of the travelling cyclone, descended through the night, and out of this hush, as out of the emanations of the steaming blood, issued the form of the ancient being who had first sent the elemental of fire upon its mission. It grew and darkened and solidified before our eyes. It rose from just beyond the table so that the lower portions remained invisible, but I saw the outline limn itself upon the air, as though slowly revealed by the rising of a curtain. It apparently had not then quite concentrated to the normal proportions, but was spread out on all sides into space, huge, though rapidly condensing, for I saw the colossal shoulders, the neck, the lower portion of the dark jaws, the terrible mouth, and then the teeth and lips – and, as the veil seemed to lift further upon the tremendous

187

face – I saw the nose and cheek bones. In another moment I should have looked straight into the eyes –

But what Dr Silence did at that moment was so unexpected, and took me so by surprise, that I have never yet properly understood its nature, and he has never yet seen fit to explain in detail to me. He uttered some sound that had a note of command in it – and, in so doing, stepped forward and intervened between me and the face. The figure, just nearing completeness, he therefore hid from my sight – and I have always thought purposely hid from my sight.

'The fire!' he cried out. 'The fire! Beware!'

There was a sudden roar as of flame from the very mouth of the pit, and for the space of a single second all grew light as day. A blinding flash passed across my face, and there was heat for an instant that seemed to shrivel skin, and flesh, and bone. Then came steps, and I heard Colonel Wragge utter a great cry, wilder than any human cry I have ever known. The heat sucked all the breath out of my lungs with a rush, and the blaze of light, as it vanished, swept my vision with it into enveloping darkness.

When I recovered the use of my senses a few moments later I saw that Colonel Wragge, with a face of death, its whiteness strangely stained, had moved closer to me. Dr Silence stood beside him, an expression of triumph and success in his eyes. The next minute the soldier tried to clutch me with his hand. Then he reeled, staggered, and, unable to save himself, fell with a great crash upon the brick floor.

After the sheet of flame, a wind raged round the building as though it would lift the roof off, but then passed as suddenly as it came. And in the intense calm that followed I saw that the form had vanished, and the doctor was stooping over Colonel Wragge upon the floor, trying to lift him to a sitting position.

'Light,' he said quietly, 'more light. Take the shades off.'

Colonel Wragge sat up and the glare of the unshaded lamps fell upon his face. It was grey and drawn, still running heat, and there was a look in the eyes and about the corners of the mouth that seemed in this short space of time to have added years to its age. At the same time, the expression of effort and anxiety had left it. It showed relief.

'Gone!' he said, looking up at the doctor in a dazed fashion, and struggling to his feet. 'Thank God! it's gone at last.' He stared round the laundry as though to find out where he was. 'Did it control me – take possession of me? Did I talk nonsense?' he asked bluntly. 'After the heat came, I remember nothing –'

'You'll feel yourself again in a few minutes,' the doctor said. To my infinite horror I saw that he was surreptitiously wiping sundry dark stains from the face. 'Our experiment has been a success and –'

He gave me a swift glance to hide the bowl, standing between me and our host while I hurriedly stuffed it down under the lid of the nearest cauldron.

'– and none of us the worse for it,' he finished.

'And fires?' he asked, still dazed, 'there'll be no more fires?'

'It is dissipated – partly, at any rate,' replied Dr Silence cautiously.

'And the man behind the gun,' he went on, only half realizing what he was saying, I think; 'have you discovered *that*?'

'A form materialized,' said the doctor briefly. 'I know for certain now what the directing intelligence was behind it all.'

Colonel Wragge pulled himself together and got upon his feet. The words conveyed no clear meaning to him yet. But his memory was returning gradually, and he was trying to piece together the fragments into a connected whole. He shivered a little, for the place had grown suddenly chilly. The air was empty again, lifeless.

'You feel all right again now,' Dr Silence said, in the tone of a man stating a fact rather than asking a question.

'Thanks to you – both, yes.' He drew a deep breath, and mopped his face, and even attempted a smile. He made me think of a man coming from the battlefield with the stains of fighting still upon him, but scornful of his wounds. Then he turned gravely towards the doctor with a question in his eyes. Memory had returned and he was himself again.

'Precisely what I expected,' the doctor said calmly; 'a fire-elemental sent upon its mission in the days of Thebes, centuries before Christ, and tonight, for the first time all these thousands of years, released from the spell that originally bound it.'

We stared at him in amazement, Colonel Wragge opening his lips for words that refused to shape themselves.

'And, if we dig,' he continued significantly, pointing to the floor where the blackness had poured up, 'we shall find some underground connexion – tunnel most likely – leading to the Twelve Acre Wood. It was made by – your predecessor.'

'A tunnel made by my brother!' gasped the soldier. 'Then my sister should know – she lived here with him –' He stopped suddenly.

John Silence inclined his head slowly. 'I think so,' he said quietly. 'Your brother, no doubt, was as much tormented as you have been,' he continued after a pause in which Colonel Wragge seemed deeply preoccupied with his thoughts, 'and tried to find peace by burying it in the wood, and surrounding the wood then, like a large magic circle, with the enchantments of the old formulae. So the stars the man saw blazing –'

'But burying *what*?' asked the soldier faintly, stepping backwards towards the support of the wall.

Dr Silence regarded us both intently for a moment before he replied. I think he weighed in his mind whether to tell us now, or when the investigation was absolutely complete.

'The mummy,' he said softly, after a moment; 'the mummy that your brother took from its resting-place of centuries, and brought home – here.'

Colonel Wragge dropped down upon the nearest chair, hanging breathlessly on every word. He was far too amazed for speech.

'The mummy of some important person – a priest most likely – protected from disturbance and desecration by the ceremonial magic of the time. For they understood how to attach to the mummy, to lock up with it in the tomb, an elemental force that would direct itself even after ages upon anyone who dared to molest it. In this case it was an elemental of fire.'

Dr Silence crossed the floor and turned out the lamps one by one. He had nothing more to say for the moment. Following his example, I folded the table together and took up the chairs, and our host, still dazed and silent, mechanically obeyed him and moved to the door.

We removed all traces of the experiment, taking the empty bowl back to the house concealed beneath an ulster.

The air was cool and fragrant as we walked to the house, the stars beginning to fade overhead and a fresh wind of early morning blowing up out of the east where the sky was already hinting of the coming day. It was after five o'clock.

Stealthily we entered the front hall and locked the door, and as we went on tiptoe upstairs to our rooms, the Colonel, peering at us over his candle as he nodded good night, whispered that if we were ready the digging should be begun that very day.

Then I saw him steal along to his sister's room and disappear.

4

But not even the mysterious references to the mummy, or the prospect of a revelation by digging, were able to hinder the reaction that followed the intense excitement of the past twelve hours, and I slept the sleep of the dead, dreamless and undisturbed. A touch on the shoulder woke me, and I saw Dr Silence standing beside the bed, dressed to go out.

'Come,' he said, 'it's tea-time. You've slept the best part of a dozen hours.'

I sprang up and made a hurried toilet, while my companion sat and talked. He looked fresh and rested, and his manner was even quieter than usual.

'Colonel Wragge has provided spades and pick-axes. We're

going out to unearth this mummy at once,' he said; 'and there's no reason we should not get away by the morning train.'

'I'm ready to go tonight, if you are,' I said honestly.

But Dr Silence shook his head.

'I must see this through to the end,' he said gravely, and in a tone that made me think he still anticipated serious things, perhaps. He went on talking while I dressed.

'This case is really typical of all stories of mummy-haunting, and none of them are cases to trifle with,' he explained, 'for the mummies of important people – kings, priests, magicians – were laid away with profoundly significant ceremonial, and were very effectively protected, as you have seen, against desecration, and especially against destruction.

'The general belief,' he went on, anticipating my questions, 'held, of course, that the perpetuity of the mummy guaranteed that of its Ka – the owner's spirit – but it is not improbable that the magical embalming was also used to retard reincarnation, the preservation of the body preventing the return of the spirit to the toil and discipline of earth-life; and, in any case, they knew how to attach powerful guardian-forces to keep off trespassers. And any one who dared to remove the mummy, or especially to unwind it – well,' he added, with meaning, 'you have seen – and you *will* see.'

I caught his face in the mirror while I struggled with my collar. It was deeply serious. There could be no question that he spoke of what he believed and knew.

'The traveller-brother who brought it here must have been haunted too,' he continued, 'for he tried to banish it by burial in the wood, making a magic circle to enclose it. Something of genuine ceremonial he must have known, for the stars the man saw were of course the remains of the still flaming penta-grams he traced at intervals in the circle. Only he did not know enough, or possibly was ignorant that the mummy's guardian was a fire-force. Fire cannot be enclosed by fire, though, as you saw, it can be released by it.'

'Then that awful figure in the laundry?' I asked, thrilled to find him so communicative.

'Undoubtedly the actual Ka of the mummy operating always behind its agent, the elemental, and most likely thousands of years old.'

'And Miss Wragge –?' I ventured once more.

'Ah, Miss Wragge,' he repeated with increased gravity, 'Miss Wragge –'

A knock at the door brought a servant with word that tea was ready, and the Colonel had sent to ask if we were coming down. The thread was broken. Dr Silence moved to the door and signed to me to follow. But his manner told me that in any case no real answer would have been forthcoming to my question.

'And the place to dig in,' I asked, unable to restrain my curiosity, 'will you find it by some process of divination or – ?'

He paused at the door and looked back at me, and with that he left me to finish my dressing.

It was growing dark when the three of us silently made our way to the Twelve Acre Plantation; the sky was overcast, and a black wind came out of the east. Gloom hung about the old house and the air seemed full of sighings. We found the tools ready laid at the edge of the wood, and each shouldering his piece, we followed our leader at once in among the trees. He went straight forward for some twenty yards and then stopped. At his feet lay the blackened circle of one of the burned places. It was just discernible against the surrounding white grass.

'There are three of these,' he said, 'and they all lie in a line with one another. Any one of them will tap the tunnel that connects the laundry – the former Museum – with the chamber where the mummy now lies buried.'

He at once cleared away the burnt grass and began to dig; we all began to dig. While I used the pick, the others shovelled vigorously. No one spoke. Colonel Wragge worked the hardest of the three. The soil was light and sandy, and there were only a few snake-like roots and occasional loose stones to delay us. The pick made short work of these. And meanwhile the darkness settled about us and the biting wind swept roaring through the trees overhead.

Then, quite suddenly, without a cry, Colonel Wragge disappeared up to his neck.

'The tunnel!' cried the doctor, helping to drag him out, red, breathless, and covered with sand and perspiration. 'Now, let me lead the way.' And he slipped down nimbly into the hole, so that a moment later we heard his voice, muffled by sand and distance, rising up to us.

'Hubbard, you come next, and then Colonel Wragge – if he wishes,' we heard.

'I'll follow you, of course,' he said, looking at me as I scrambled in.

The hole was bigger now, and I got down on all-fours in a channel not much bigger than a large sewer-pipe and found myself in total darkness. A minute later a heavy thud, followed by a cataract of loose sand, announced the arrival of the Colonel.

'Catch hold of my heel,' called Dr Silence, 'and Colonel Wragge can take yours.'

In this slow, laborious fashion we wormed our way along a tunnel that had been roughly dug out of the shifting sand, and was shored up clumsily by means of wooden pillars and posts. Any moment, it seemed to me, we might be buried alive. We could not see an inch before our eyes, but had to grope our way feeling the pillars and the walls. It was difficult to breathe, and the Colonel behind me made but slow progress, for the cramped position of our bodies was very severe.

We had travelled in this way for ten minutes, and gone perhaps as much as ten yards, when I lost my grasp of the doctor's heel.

'Ah!' I heard his voice, sounding above me somewhere. He was standing up in a clear space, and the next moment I was standing beside him. Colonel Wragge came heavily after, and he too rose up and stood. Then Dr Silence produced his candles and we heard preparations for striking matches.

Yet even before there was light, an indefinable sensation of awe came over us all. In this hole in the sand, some three feet under ground, we stood side by side, cramped and huddled, struck suddenly with an overwhelming apprehension of something ancient, something formidable, something incalculably wonderful, that touched in each one of us a sense of the sublime and the terrible even before we could see an inch before our faces. I know not how to express in language this singular emotion that caught us here in utter darkness, touching no sense directly, it seemed, yet with the recognition that before us in the blackness of this underground night there lay something that was mighty with the mightiness of long past ages.

I felt Colonel Wragge press in closely to my side, and I understood the pressure and welcomed it. No human touch, to me at least, has ever been more eloquent.

Then the match flared, a thousand shadows fled on black wings, and I saw John Silence fumbling with the candle, his face lit up grotesquely by the flickering light below it.

I had dreaded this light, yet when it came there was apparently nothing to explain the profound sensations of dread that preceded it. We stood in a small vaulted chamber in the sand, the sides and roof shored with bars of wood, and the ground laid roughly with what seemed to be tiles. It was six feet high, so that we could all stand comfortably, and may have been ten feet long by eight feet wide. Upon the wooden pillars at the side I saw that Egyptian hieroglyphics had been rudely traced by burning.

Dr Silence lit three candles and handed one to each of us. He placed a fourth in the sand against the wall on his right, and another to mark the entrance to the tunnel. We stood and stared about us, instinctively holding our breath.

'Empty, by God!' exclaimed Colonel Wragge. His voice trembled with excitement. And then, as his eyes rested on the ground, he added, 'And footsteps – look – footsteps in the sand!'

Dr Silence said nothing. He stooped down and began to make a search of the chamber, and as he moved, my eyes followed his crouching figure and noted the queer distorted shadows that poured over the walls and ceiling after him. Here and there thin trickles of loose sand ran fizzing down the sides. The atmosphere, heavily charged with faint yet pungent odours, lay utterly still, and the flames of the candles might have been painted on the air for all the movement they betrayed.

And, as I watched, it was almost necessary to persuade myself forcibly that I was only standing upright with difficulty in this little sand-hole of a modern garden in the south of England, for it seemed to me that I stood, as in vision, at the entrance of some vast rock-hewn Temple far, far down the river of Time. The illusion was powerful, and persisted. Granite columns, that rose to heaven, piled themselves about me, majestically uprearing, and a roof like the sky itself spread above a line of colossal figures that moved in shadowy procession along endless and stupendous aisles. This huge and splendid fantasy, borne I knew not whence, possessed me so vividly that I was actually obliged to concentrate my attention upon the small stooping figure of the doctor, as he groped about the walls, in order to keep the eye of imagination on the scene before me.

But the limited space rendered a long search out of the question, and his footsteps, instead of shuffling through loose sand, presently struck something of a different quality that gave forth a hollow and resounding echo. He stooped to examine more closely.

He was standing exactly in the centre of the little chamber when this happened, and he at once began scraping away the sand with his feet. In less than a minute a smooth surface became visible – the surface of a wooden covering. The next thing I saw was that he had raised it and was peering down into a space below. Instantly, a strong odour of nitre and bitumen, mingled with the strange perfume of unknown and powdered aromatics, rose up from the uncovered space and filled the vault, stinging the throat and making the eyes water and smart.

'The mummy!' whispered Dr Silence, looking up into our

faces over his candle; and as he said the word I felt the soldier lurch against me, and heard his breathing in my very ear.

'The mummy!' he repeated under his breath, as we pressed forward to look.

It is difficult to say exactly why the sight should have stirred in me so prodigious an emotion of wonder and veneration, for I have had not a little to do with mummies, have unwound scores of them, and even experimented magically with not a few. But there was something in the sight of that grey and silent figure, lying in its modern box of lead and wood at the bottom of this sandy grave, swathed in the bandages of centuries and wrapped in the perfumed linen that the priests of Egypt had prayed over with their mighty enchantments thousands of years before – something in the sight of it lying there and breathing its own spice-laden atmosphere even in the darkness of its exile in this remote land, something that pierced to the very core of my being and touched that root of awe which slumbers in every man near the birth of tears and the passion of true worship.

I remember turning quickly from the Colonel, lest he should see my emotion, yet fail to understand its cause, turn and clutch John Silence by the arm, and then fall trembling to see that he, too, had lowered his head and was hiding his face in his hands.

A kind of whirling storm came over me, rising out of I know not what utter deeps of memory, and in a whiteness of vision I heard the magical old chauntings from the Book of the Dead, and saw the Gods pass by in dim procession, the mighty, immemorial Beings who were yet themselves only the personified attributes of the true Gods, the God with the Eyes of Fire, the God with the Face of Smoke. I saw again Anubis, the dog-faced deity, and the children of Horus, eternal watcher of the ages, as they swathed Osiris, the first mummy of the world, in the scented and mystic bands, and I tasted again something of the ecstasy of the justified soul as it embarked in the golden Boat of Ra, and journeyed onwards to rest in the fields of the blessed.

And then, as Dr Silence, with infinite reverence, stooped and touched the still face, so dreadfully staring with its painted eyes, there rose again to our nostrils wave upon wave of this perfume of thousands of years, and time fled backwards like a thing of naught, showing me in haunted panorama the most wonderful dream of the whole world.

A gentle hissing became audible in the air, and the doctor moved quickly backwards. It came close to our faces and then seemed to play about the walls and ceiling.

'The last of the Fire – still waiting for its full accomplishment,' he muttered; but I heard both words and hissing as things far away, for I was still busy with the journeys of the soul through the Seven Halls of Death, listening for echoes of the grandest ritual ever known to men.

The earthen plates covered with hieroglyphics still lay beside the mummy, and round it, carefully arranged at the points of the compass, stood the four jars with the heads of the hawk, the jackal, the cynocephalus, and man, the jars in which were placed the hair, the nail parings, the heart, and other special portions of the body. Even the amulets, the mirror, the blue clay statues of the Ka, and the lamp with seven wicks were there. Only the sacred scarabaeus was missing.

'Not only has it been torn from its ancient resting-place,' I heard Dr Silence saying in a solemn voice as he looked at Colonel Wragge with fixed gaze, 'but it has been partially unwound,' – he pointed to the wrappings of the breast – 'and – the scarabaeus has been removed from the throat.'

The hissing, that was like the hissing of an invisible flame, had ceased; only from time to time we heard it as though it passed backwards and forwards in the tunnel; and we stood looking into each other's faces without speaking.

Presently Colonel Wragge made a great effort and braced himself. I heard the sound catch in his throat before the words actually became audible.

'My sister,' he said, very low. And then there followed a long pause, broken at length by John Silence.

'It must be replaced,' he said significantly,

'I knew nothing,' the soldier said, forcing himself to speak the words he hated saying. 'Absolutely nothing.'

'It must be returned,' repeated the other, 'if it is not now too late. For I fear – I fear –'

Colonel Wragge made a movement of assent with his head.

'It shall be,' he said.

The place was still as the grave.

I do not know what it was then that made us all three turn round with so sudden a start, for there was no sound audible to my ears, at least.

The doctor was on the point of replacing the lid over the mummy, when he straightened up as if he had been shot.

'There's something coming,' said Colonel Wragge under his breath, and the doctor's eyes, peering down the small opening of the tunnel, showed me the true direction.

A distant shuffling noise became distinctly audible coming from a point about half-way down the tunnel we had so laboriously penetrated.

'It's the sand falling in,' I said, though I knew it was foolish.

'No,' said the Colonel calmly, in a voice that seemed to have the ring of iron, 'I've heard it for some time past. It is something alive – and it is coming nearer.'

He stared about him with a look of resolution that made his face almost noble. The horror in his heart was overmastering, yet he stood there prepared for anything that might come.

'There's no other way out,' John Silence said.

He leaned the lid against the sand, and waited. I knew by the mask-like expression of his face, the pallor, and the steadiness of the eyes, that he anticipated something that might be very terrible – appalling.

The Colonel and myself stood on either side of the opening. I still held my candle and was ashamed of the way it shook, dripping the grease all over me; but the soldier had set his into the sand just behind his feet.

Thoughts of being buried alive, of being smothered like rats in a trap, of being caught and done to death by some invisible and merciless force we could not grapple with, rushed into my mind. Then I thought of fire – of suffocation – of being roasted alive. The perspiration began to pour from my face.

'Steady!' came the voice of Dr Silence to me through the vault.

For five minutes, that seemed fifty, we stood waiting, looking from each other's faces to the mummy, and from the mummy to the hole, and all the time the shuffling sound, soft and stealthy, came gradually nearer. The tension, for me at least, was very near the breaking point when at last the cause of the disturbance reached the edge. It was hidden for a moment just behind the broken rim of soil. A jet of sand, shaken by the close vibration, trickled down on to the ground; I have never in my life seen anything fall with such laborious leisure. The next second, uttering a cry of curious quality, it came into view.

And it was far more distressingly horrible than anything I had anticipated.

For the sight of some Egyptian monster, some god of the tombs, or even of some demon of fire, I think I was already half prepared; but when, instead, I saw the white visage of Miss Wragge framed in that round opening of sand, followed by her body crawling on all-fours, her eyes bulging and reflecting the yellow glare of the candles, my first instinct was to turn and run like a frantic animal seeking a way of escape.

But Dr Silence, who seemed no whit surprised, caught my arm and steadied me, and we both saw the Colonel then drop upon his knees and come thus to a level with his sister. For more than a whole minute, as though struck in stone, the two faces gazed silently at each other: hers, for all the dreadful emotion in it, more like a gargoyle than anything human; and his, white and blank with an expression that was beyond either astonishment or alarm. She looked up; he looked down. It was a picture in a nightmare, and the candle, stuck in the sand close to the hole, threw upon it the glare of impromptu footlights.

John Silence moved forward and spoke in a voice that was very low, yet perfectly calm and natural.

'I am glad you have come,' he said. 'You are the one person whose presence at this moment is most required. And I hope that you may yet be in time to appease the anger of the Fire, and to bring peace again to your household, and,' he added lower still so that no one heard it but myself, *'safety to yourself.'*

And while her brother stumbled backwards, crushing a candle into the sand in his awkwardness, the old lady crawled further into the vaulted chamber and slowly rose upon her feet.

At the sight of the wrapped figure of the mummy I was fully prepared to see her scream and faint, but on the contrary, to my complete amazement, she merely bowed her head and dropped quietly upon her knees. Then, after a pause of more than a minute, she raised her eyes to the roof and her lips began to mutter as in prayer. Her right hand, meanwhile, which had been fumbling for some time at her throat, suddenly came away, and before the gaze of us all she held it out, palm upwards, over the grey and ancient figure outstretched below. And in it we beheld glistening the green jasper of the stolen scarabaeus.

Her brother, leaning heavily against the wall behind, uttered a sound that was half cry, half exclamation, but John Silence, standing directly in front of her, merely fixed his eyes on her and pointed downwards to the staring face below.

'Replace it,' he said sternly, 'where it belongs.'

Miss Wragge was kneeling at the feet of the mummy when this happened. We three men all had our eyes riveted on what followed. Only the reader who by some remote chance may have witnessed a line of mummies, freshly laid from their tombs upon the sand, slowly stir and bend as the heat of the Egyptian sun warms their ancient bodies into the semblance of life, can form any conception of the ultimate horror we experienced when the silent figure before us moved in its grave of lead and sand. Slowly, before our eyes, it writhed, and, with a faint rustling of the immemorial cerements, rose up, and, through sightless and bandaged eyes, stared across the yellow candle-light at the woman who had violated it.

I tried to move – her brother tried to move – but the sand seemed to hold our feet. I tried to cry – her brother tried to cry – but the sand seemed to fill our lungs and throat. We could only stare – and, even so, the sand seemed to rise like a desert storm and cloud our vision. . . .

And when I managed at length to open my eyes again, the mummy was lying once more upon its back, motionless, the shrunken and painted face upturned towards the ceiling, and the old lady had tumbled forward and was lying in the semblance of death with her head and arms upon its crumbling body.

But upon the wrappings of the throat I saw the green jasper of the sacred scarabaeus shining again like a living eye.

Colonel Wragge and the doctor recovered themselves long before I did, and I found myself helping them clumsily and unintelligently to raise the frail body of the old lady, while John Silence carefully replaced the covering over the grave and scraped back the sand with his foot, while he issued brief directions.

I heard his voice as in a dream; but the journey back along that cramped tunnel, weighted by a dead woman, blinded with sand, suffocated with heat, was in no sense a dream. It took us the best part of half an hour to reach the open air. And, even then, we had to wait a considerable time for the appearance of Dr Silence. We carried her undiscovered into the house and up to her own room.

'The mummy will cause no further disturbance,' I heard Dr Silence say to our host later that evening as we prepared to drive for the night train, 'provided always,' he added significantly, 'that you, and yours, cause *it* no disturbance.'

It was in a dream, too, that we left.

'You did not see her face, I know,' he said to me as we wrapped our rugs about us in the empty compartment. And when I shook my head, quite unable to explain the instinct that had come to me not to look, he turned towards me, his face pale, and genuinely sad.

'Scorched and blasted,' he whispered.

More about Penguins and Pelicans

Penguinews, which appears every month, contains details of all the new books issued by Penguins as they are published. From time to time it is supplemented by *Penguins in Print*, which is a complete list of all available books published by Penguins. (There are well over four thousand of these.)

A specimen copy of *Penguinews* will be sent to you free on request. For a year's issues (including the complete lists) please send 50p if you live in the United Kingdom, or 75p if you live elsewhere. Just write to Dept EP, Penguin Books Ltd, Harmondsworth, Middlesex, enclosing a cheque or postal order, and your name will be added to the mailing list.

Note: *Penguinews* and *Penguins in Print* are not available in the U.S.A. or Canada

Kiss Kiss

Roald Dahl

If your taste is for the macabre, the sick, the outrageous,
the unexpected, the horrifying – Roald Dahl will give
you orgiastic delight. If not, you are going to miss one of the
most sophisticated collections of short stories in print.

Also available

Over to You
Someone Like You

Not for sale in the U.S.A. or Canada

Great British Tales of Terror

Edited by Peter Haining

From 1765 to 1840, Gothic tales held Britain and much of Europe in thrall. Readers found retreat from drab reality in ruined abbeys, moonlit castles, pathless woods and blasted heaths – peopled by knightly heroes, oppressed maidens and wicked tyrants; haunted by ghosts, spectres, vampires, animated corpses and grinning skulls.

Peter Haining introduces and provides a linking commentary for thirty of the finest British Gothic stories, charting their seventy-five-year reign of terror, mystery and suspense from Walpole to Sheridan Le Fanu. Pioneers of the macabre like Mrs Radcliffe, Maturin and 'Monk' Lewis are here. So, more surprisingly, are Shelley, Byron and Thackeray amongst many others, each providing proof that a revival of the Gothic Revival was long overdue.

Also available

Great Tales of Terror from Europe and America
Edited by Peter Haining